Mourning
Light

Also by Richard Goodkin

MONOGRAPHS:

The Symbolist Home and the Tragic Home: Mallarmé and Oedipus (1984)

Around Proust (1991)

The Tragic Middle: Racine, Aristotle, Euripides (1991)

Birth Marks: The Tragedy of Primogeniture in Pierre Corneille, Thomas Corneille, and Jean Racine (2000)

How Do I Know Thee? Theatrical and Narrative Cognition in Seventeenth-Century French Literature (2015)

EDITED VOLUMES:

Autour de Racine: Studies in Intertextuality (1989)

In Memory of Elaine Marks: Life Writing, Writing Death (2007)

FICTION:

Les Magnifiques Mensonges de Madeleine Béjart (2013)

Mourning Light

RICHARD GOODKIN

THE UNIVERSITY OF WISCONSIN PRESS

Publication of this book has been made possible, in part,
through support from the Brittingham Trust.

The University of Wisconsin Press
728 State Street, Suite 443
Madison, Wisconsin 53706
uwpress.wisc.edu

Gray's Inn House, 127 Clerkenwell Road
London EC1R 5DB, United Kingdom
eurospanbookstore.com

Printed in the United States of America
This book may be available in a digital edition.

Library of Congress Cataloging-in-Publication Data

Names: Goodkin, Richard E., author.
Title: Mourning light / Richard Goodkin.
Description: Madison, Wisconsin : The University of Wisconsin Press, [2022]
Identifiers: LCCN 2021047929 | ISBN 9780299338640 (paperback)
Subjects: LCGFT: Novels.
Classification: LCC PS3607.O56375 M68 2022 | DDC 813/.6—dc23/eng/20211029
LC record available at https://lccn.loc.gov/2021047929

Mourning Light is a work of fiction. While the story draws heavily on the
author's own experiences, no character is conceived as or intended to be a
representation of any person, living or dead.

For
PATRICK *and* CHARLIE

Death is nothing but a bridge between humans where they can meet halfway to whisper things they never dared talk about.

—MARYSE CONDÉ, *Crossing the Mangrove*

We never become really and genuinely our entire and honest selves until we are dead. People ought to start dead, and they would be honest so much earlier.

—MARK TWAIN, *Mark Twain in Eruption*

Mourning
Light

chapter 1

Before Marc Anthony Payton, the love of my life, had finished drawing his last sweet breath at 11:11 p.m. on 1 February 1991 and even though I was not sure exactly why or how, I knew it was my fault. For one thing, when I left him at 11:11 that morning, exactly twelve hours before he died, I was in my usual hurry to get to the swimming pool by opening time to be the first to dive in, and I refused to sit with him a little longer before I left as he had asked me to do. I didn't even say a proper good-bye, and moments before I returned home several hours later, he fell into the final coma from which he would never awaken. Another way I may have been responsible for bringing down this desolation on Anthony's head and my own is my choice of professional specialisation. Doctors are famous for eventually falling victim to the disease they choose to study, but how about the rest of us? I am an English professor at the University of Wisconsin–Madison with particular expertise in tragedy; what did I expect? In fact, the sabbatical leave I have received to finish my latest book officially begins today, 1 September 1993, but I've decided to start my semester off in quite another way: by writing the tale of my life with and without Anthony. It will be a labour of love but also a painful exercise; I'll try to keep it light, but I owe it both to myself and to him to come to grips with the various ways I unintentionally jinxed our too-good-to-be-true relationship, a decade-long dalliance between a classy English Adonis and a drab American serf.

If I set myself this task only today, two and a half years after Anthony's demise, it is because thirty-three days ago he sent me a sign from beyond the grave; last night, after a month-long investigation, I deciphered it. A further confirmation that the time is ripe for me to take stock of our time together is that my fortieth birthday, 2 September 1993, begins in forty-nine minutes. Yes, it's 11:11 again. Having fathomed the full import of those numbers, I vow to record the past month's terrible and wondrous discoveries, taking comfort from the thought that from now on, that simple twice daily occurrence will always remind me of where I've been in my life, and where I'm heading.

To manage my misery in the thirty months since two gloved strangers zipped Anthony's remains into a body bag, I have rented a cryogenic locker to store my heart and dutifully travelled that long lonesome highway known as "Keeping Busy," alas in vain. Any fool could discern that the breakneck routine I have perfected—working sixty hours a week and swimming, running, and cycling to the point of collapse each evening, and twice on Sundays—has not fulfilled either of my goals: experiencing once again the delights of REM sleep or escaping from the thought that I am somehow responsible for my lover's demise.

That cycle was broken a little over a month ago, on 30 July 1993, an evening when the anguish and despair that became my new normal the moment Anthony stopped breathing were suspended by an event equally steeped in the tragic and the absurd.

We all have our own third term to add to death and taxes; for me it is insomnia. Since the miraculous break from sleeplessness provided by my years with Anthony came to a close, I have rarely attempted to retire earlier than midnight. This sensible sleep skepticism has spared me not only hours of tossing and turning but also—appearing every evening on the digital clock sitting beside our double bed—the excruciating sight of 11:11.

I'm not sure I can explain about 11:11; it's probably a case where you just had to be there. Most couples have a song; Anthony and I had a number. In the first months of our relationship, when I was living in a studio apartment in New Haven, Connecticut, we began noticing that the digital alarm clock on the table next to my sleeper sofa always seemed to read 11:11 when we glanced at it in a mellow moment of afterglow. Moreover, if you turn the numerals 11:11 on their side, as happens in effect when you see them from a recumbent position with your head on a pillow, a little face appears. The blinking colon furnishes the eyes, the "1" directly above it the eyebrows. The "1" below the colon becomes a mouth, the outer numbers the top of the head and the chin.

In short order Anthony seized upon "the 11:11 face" as a euphemism for amorous pursuits, presumably in order to spare himself the discomfiture of the more conventional expressions of desire or affection that such occasions might warrant and for which I remained on the alert during the early months of our relationship—that is, until it sank in that while his general zest for life was visible from space, the legibility of his heart did not extend to his feelings about me.

The morning after his funeral, "11:11 p.m." appeared against a sterner backdrop, under the rubric "Time of Death," in the official-looking document I had just picked up from Dr. Hertz's office. As I sat in our ancient Volkswagen Beetle, my eyes transfixed by the numbers, I couldn't resist turning the paper onto its side to view the little face in the hopes that Anthony might make it wink or send some other signal that he was able to communicate from wherever he was.

He didn't. I suppose that as a lapsed Catholic and reluctant agnostic in search of something to have faith in, ever since that moment in February 1991 I have been awaiting a sign from him, a foolish hope exacerbated by the predilection for superstitiousness I inherited from my Polish peasant forebears. So I wasn't entirely surprised when, shortly before midnight on 30 July 1993, he finally sent me one.

I just didn't expect it to be transmitted through the television.

That evening, as the hour approached when I might have considered going to bed if Anthony had been present to soothe my anguish, I was feeling even more melancholy than usual. I had spent the day thinking about how to mark the two-and-a-half-year anniversary of his death coming up in two days' time. My biannual rituals to mark this sombre event have ranged from looking through old photographs of the two of us together to preparing one of his English mum's cake recipes that he'd scribbled on a scrap of paper during a transatlantic phone call. This time around I thought I might try going through Anthony's desk, which was still exactly as he'd left it.

A little before 11 p.m. I went upstairs and stepped out onto the second-storey deck that overlooks Lake Monona, one of the four lakes that grace the lovely city of Madison, Wisconsin, where Anthony and I settled in 1988, approximately eight years after he settled for me. The moon appeared swollen beyond fullness, as it sometimes does during the dog days of the Upper Midwest; its shimmering yellow reflection on the lake resembled a watery path to another world. During the last summer of Anthony's life, we sometimes used to sit close together and watch this breathtaking spectacle. Seeing it alone beneath a vast empty sky suddenly seemed unbearable, so I stepped back into the cosy confines of our bedroom, sheltered beneath the loft's slanting rafters.

I flipped off the light and was greeted in the darkness by Anthony's sky, a set of luminescent paper stars surrounding a crescent moon that he put up on the ceiling a few months before his death—"to watch over us," he said, meaning me. No sooner had I settled down on the recliner next to the French doors and turned my gaze from the little paper sky back to the real moon's reflection than something light as a feather floated onto my head.

Anthony's moon. As the largest piece of his heaven, I suppose it was the most likely to fall, too heavy for the adhesive that held it up for nearly three years.

A moment of exaltation: was this the sign I had been awaiting? It seemed too commonplace an occurrence for that, but I removed the glowing crescent from the crown of my head and nestled it in my hand. Just in case, I placed it carefully on an empty shelf where I wouldn't lose track of it.

I made my way downstairs. I was not feeling the slightest bit sleepy. It was going to be a long night.

I switched on the television, my insomniac mainstay, and as I perused the newspaper listings, I was pleased to discover that at 3 a.m. my favourite film, *Rebecca*, would be on. I've got a thing about *Rebecca*, both Daphne du Maurier's novel and the Hitchcock movie, which Anthony and I saw together at one of the Yale film societies in 1980, on the very evening we first met. Anthony read the book only after we saw the film. I, on the other hand, cut my baby teeth on that perverse tale of real and imagined love, the story of a man quite as certain of which of his two wives he has better loved, the deceased one or the living one, as his present wife is deluded about that very same question. I was in fact first fed the story by my mother, whose unaccountable obsession with it was finally slaked when life presented her with her fourth son and she came to grips with the likelihood that she would never bear a girl child by naming me—mutatis mutandis, thank goodness; Reb rather than Rebecca—for its beautiful but dastardly title character. In later years, when I questioned Mother about the peculiar choice, she replied in a dreamy voice devoid of her usual sarcasm that it was because of my jet-black hair and fair complexion—my brothers are all blonds—murmuring something about a similar contrast in colouring mentioned by du Maurier in one of the few passages that describes Rebecca. Mother and I have never been close, but I tip my hat to her for naming me for what she would eventually think of as my best feature. Though I have lived up to none of her other expectations, at thirty-nine-and-counting my hair remains thick and wavy and hasn't a trace of grey.

With such a childhood history, is it any wonder that on the day Anthony and I first crossed paths, 2 September 1980, his willingness to spend the evening with me was reminiscent of the dashing widower Maxim de Winter's inscrutable decision to keep company with du Maurier's famously anonymous and lackluster narratrix? Just as she felt herself to be a paltry substitute for Maxim's brilliant, raven-haired late wife, I could scarcely imagine what stunning specimens the dazzling Anthony Payton must have frequented before he decided—for reasons I simply could not fathom—to slum it for a while and glanced my way. Little did I know that I too would soon acquire my own private Rebecca, one as hateful to me as the first Mrs. de Winter was to the second one.

In truth there are not only similarities but also a number of notable differences between the love-hate triangle in *Rebecca* and my ten-year tête-à-tête with Anthony. He, like Maxim, was English, but unlike Anonymous, I, the grandson of uneducated Polish immigrants to the United States, am a British wannabe manqué. Anthony, like Maxim, was a boy, but unlike Anonymous and Rebecca, so am I. Anthony was not bequeathed a title or a grand estate like Manderley, largely owing to the humble origins of Gerald Payton, his Irish father, although thanks to his mother, née Lady Julia Reynolds, he did inherit an accent as posh as Maxim's. As for myself, I was born with brains but sans pedigree, my tedious mid-Atlantic diction and affectation of spelling "civilisation" and "colour" and the like in the British manner poorly masking my own much humbler origins on the South Side of Chicago.

Desperate to find a way to pass the hours that separated me from 3 a.m., when *Rebecca* would begin, I did a bit of channel surfing that yielded nothing palatable, so I made the improbable decision to thumb my nose at insomniac fate by turning out the lights, lying down on the sofa, and pretending I might simply doze off without giving it a second thought, as I have heard people do. It was a shame to miss *Rebecca*, but setting up the VCR to record television programmes was Anthony's job, one I hadn't even attempted to master.

Perhaps it was time to give it a go.

After grappling with the instruction manual for an embarrassingly long stretch, I finally saw the programming grid leap onto the screen, but the VCR remote was oblivious to my further jabbings. With so many years of lying fallow, the blasted thing was probably low on power. I retreated to the kitchen to search for batteries.

The instant I reentered the sitting room and saw the screen, I let out a rapturous cry. In my absence the VCR had programmed itself, but rather than "Saturday, 7/31/93, 3:00 a.m.," it read "Friday, 11/11/33, 11:11 p.m."

I allow five seconds to pass, then ten, to test out whether I am experiencing a psychotic break or have stepped into a dream world. The numbers and letters remain on the screen. Did my random jabbings before I went to change the batteries register as this series of numerals in a final surge of reserved power? Even if they did, which I doubt, the coincidence is inexplicable, the remote in that case functioning as a kind of Ouija board. As minutes pass, jubilation subsides into bewilderment. This is not the sort of distinct message that occurs in books and films featuring communication with the departed. The eleven-elevens clearly point to Anthony as the sender, but what is he trying to tell me? And why thirty-three rather than forty-four, or sixty-six, or one of the other two-digit multiples of eleven?

Friday, 11/11/33, 11:11 p.m. Perhaps the date hints at an overlooked event in Anthony's family history, one that could finally explain why a British heartthrob would waste ten years of his life on an offspring of the Polish lumpen proletariat. For lack of a better alternative, I consult the perpetual calendar of the World Almanac: 11 November 1933, nearly sixty years ago, was not a Friday but a Saturday, a fresh paradox. I pour myself a shot of bourbon, slump onto the couch, and close my eyes.

What occurred on that autumn day in the heart of the Great Depression? Was it some calamity responsible for the loss of Julia Reynolds's family fortune, beginning the downward spiral of their lofty position that led to Julia's socially catastrophic union with Gerald Payton and, eventually, Anthony's imponderable coupling with me? Or was 11 November 1933, the fifteenth anniversary of the end of World War I, the day Gerald's father, Patrick Payton, went on the first of the countless benders that several decades later were destined to ruin Gerald's adolescence, thus casting on the family's future a shadow of doom that culminated in Anthony's misguided choice of a partner?

I sigh heavily, open my eyes. The unrelenting bleakness of the time since Anthony's death and the futility of my getting-over-it charade have worn me down in more ways than one. As I think back on the years we shared a bed and an address—if not an equal measure of love for each other—I marvel at my naïveté in believing I should come to understand the man any better in death than I did in life.

What do these numbers mean? What might Anthony be trying to tell me?

chapter 2

The Paul Lozier Pool on the University of Wisconsin campus, named after a philanthropic deceased alumnus who would have been horrified to learn that the building constructed thanks to his bequest would go by the homely abbreviation of the PLOP, is my one regular distraction from looking after Anthony during the last months of his life. Driving to the PLOP is not an option, since our ancient little Beetle must remain available in case Anthony's parents, who have rented out their London flat and taken a small studio apartment in our neighbourhood to help look after their son in the throes of end-stage AIDS, unexpectedly have to bring him to hospital. Actually, I am glad to take my bicycle. If pedaled at a good clip it is almost as fast as the VW, and it helps cleanse my lungs of our house's sickroom atmosphere.

That Anthony does not want to let me go on the morning of 1 February 1991 is unusual. It's not as if he is ever left on his own; Gerald and Julia always arrive a good half hour before I depart. They give him lunch and sit with him until I return around two, then take their afternoon constitutional until teatime.

But as I am about to head off on this last day of Anthony's life, he must sense the end is near. Without a word of explanation, he asks me if I can postpone my departure for a little while. Poorly understanding what he is trying to tell me, I make light of his request with a breezy rejoinder about being back in no time, climb onto my bike, and am off.

It is a frigid midwinter's day. Our house, situated on the banks of Lake Monona on Madison's Near East Side, is yards away from a bike path that hugs the shoreline, winding its way towards the State Capitol and, a mile or so further along, the university.

Pedaling, pedaling, pedaling. My previous record from home to the PLOP is eight minutes and twelve seconds, and my current goal, which I have been closing in on for about three months, is to break eight minutes.

In some obscure corner of my mind, the terrible good-bye scene with Anthony replays in eerie silence. I can see his face, pleading with me to stay as he never has before, but his words are censored. I briefly close my eyes, half hoping I will crash into something hard to shake the image from my head. Peering once again through the eye slits of my face mask, I try in vain to imagine myself a guiltless soul, some armoured knight, perhaps, tilting in defence of a worthy cause; then, giving up the masquerade, I shift up into seventh gear and pump for my life.

Excrement. A stoplight.

"Lovely day, isn't it?"

Waiting to cross John Nolen Drive stands another cyclist clapping his gloveless hands together against the cold. I realise from his position that he has not bothered to press the button to change the light from red to green, an oversight that will pointlessly delay my return to Anthony and likely kibosh my aspirations to set a new record to the PLOP. As I impatiently roll myself over to punch the button myself, I mutter under my breath, "Pesky Swedes." The cyclist's assessment of the weather and disinclination to hasten his journey by pressing the button suffice for me to conclude that he is one of the region's laid-back, cheerful Scandinavians. The aptly named Dane County, in which Madison is located, was settled by the forebears of these amiable individuals with all the time in the world, Thinsulate for skin, and an inexplicable fondness for lutefisk, a delicacy reminiscent of flash-frozen blocks of industrial waste.

No discernible reaction from the Swede to my nasty comment; either he hasn't heard me beneath my face mask or he refuses to let my prickly mood deflate his bubble of good cheer. In a sour voice I toss off: "You took the words right out of my mouth. Beautiful day. I hope it lasts."

"It might last and it might not," he replies, absorbing my irony as unflappably as the front wall of a squash court deadens a smartly hit ball. "You just have to make the most of it while it does."

The words conjure up an image of a hospital examination room: a moment's reflection identifies them as an unwitting quotation of Dr. Hertz's assessment of Anthony's improved condition the previous summer. At that time, against all odds, an experimental drug had saved his life threatened by Kaposi's sarcoma, the latest and gravest of a string of AIDS-related symptoms. As I think back to the relief of that magical reprieve now drawing to a close, sodium-laden droplets cling to my chilled cheeks.

We Slavs, cursed by the double scourge of melancholy and harsh winters, have evolved high cheekbones for precisely this purpose.

The light turns green. I suck back a sob and try to mask my grief with a final rejoinder—"Enjoy your sunbathing!"—before speeding across John Nolen.

Having lost a good forty-five seconds at the light, I must find a way to make up the deficit. If there's no traffic, I'll maneuver the turn onto Bedford Street without slowing down. As I crane my neck to check for cars, I find myself careening to the ground. A long, scary skid leaves me about two feet clear of a passing minivan. The driver, a middle-aged woman, graciously stops and rolls down her window.

"Are you OK?"

"Yeah, terrific. Never better."

My disquieting smile, undoubtedly reminiscent of a serial killer parading as a harmless man on the street, discourages further discussion. The lady throws me a sympathetic look, then continues on her way.

"Bloody hell!" I rail once she is out of earshot. "I do not believe this. This did not just happen."

I know it has happened, but the various stages of Anthony's illness have developed my talent for last-ditch revisionism. My trouser legs are torn, my left ankle pulsating with pain.

"Are you all right? Did you hurt yourself?"

The friendly cyclist I've just mocked towers over me. He must be a Lutheran of the cheek-turning sort; had the situation been reversed, I, a lapsed Catholic, would have construed his mishap as a punishment from God and ridden past his crumpled form in triumph.

"I'll live," I croak, embarrassed at how shaky my voice is. Drawing on my small store of false bravado, I attempt a snicker, but all that comes out of my throat is a raspy sound reminiscent of Anthony trying to breathe when his blood oxygen dips below seventy-five.

As I remain seated on the ground and wait for the agonising pain in my foot to subside, I scrutinise the annoying cyclist through my face mask. I can't estimate his height with much accuracy from my seated position, but he is a veritable giant, perhaps a few inches short of seven feet. He wears a navy-blue windbreaker, tight black Levi's, and black, high-topped Adidas. His ungloved hands are blood red, the knuckles massive, the fingers the length of an infant's forearms. Judging from his smooth but lustreless complexion, I peg him at about thirty-five, but the ash-blond curls sausaging out from underneath his stocking cap make him resemble a seventeen-year-old prematurely going to seed. On second glance his friendly countenance, which I'd chalked up to midwestern good cheer, is unconvincing, a facsimile of happiness or a memory of paradise lost.

"May I help you up?" His smile of encouragement seems more heartfelt. He extends arms as long as clotheslines. "There's a good boy"—this as though I were a spill-prone toddler.

The pain in my foot has subsided to a throb. A mighty tug propels me into the air and we are suddenly face to face, or rather face to chest, given the height difference. And for an absurd moment, with our arms outstretched and our bodies close, it seems to me we're about to assume closed position and waltz back towards the bike path. I'm winded from the adrenaline of the fall rather than my exertions; in my hyperventilation I catch a soupçon of English Leather aftershave. It is Anthony's favourite, chosen less, he once informed me, for the scent than because the name made for an expedient icebreaker at bars, but it has been ages since either of us has given a thought to such niceties. I inhale more deeply as if in the presence of the old Anthony, the Anthony who would have been strong enough to help me up after a spill. I wrench my right hand free of the cyclist's grasp, pull off my face mask, and use it to dab discreetly at my eyes. He looks me full in the face, his own eyes widening into a masklike expression. I flash on Munch's *The Scream*; such may be the countenance of Nordic commiseration as well as angst, or perhaps it hadn't registered on my would-be rescuer that I was the same person who was rude at the stoplight and he's having second thoughts about helping me. Too late now.

"Did you hurt your leg?" he continues in a detached tone, observing my limp.

"Yes, just the left one. The right one's fine. I was on my way to the pool. The PLOP is only a few blocks away, and I can walk it."

"Isn't your bike ridable?"

A perfunctory inspection yields no signs of damage.

"Probably," I mutter. "But walking it for a while will help my ankle to loosen up."

I am about to set off when the Swede looks at his watch and clears his throat rather formally, as if he were preparing to take out a bottle of aquavit and two glasses and wished to verify that the toast he was about to propose was well phrased. "I live just down the street. If you like, you can come up to my place and throw ice on it."

I feel my right eyebrow rise involuntarily. Anthony and I have not been intimate for months, preoccupied by less agreeable concerns. Still, distressing life circumstances don't always prevent one from feeling a twinge, and it occurs to me that this man is easy on the eyes. Not that there is the slightest reason to believe that his intent is anything other than charitable.

"No thanks," I say with faux graciousness. "But I do appreciate the offer."

His place is sparsely furnished and bears appealingly little resemblance to an intensive-care unit. He forges ahead into the dining area and shoves something into a cupboard—a basket of dirty laundry? This leaves me free to admire the flawless wide-planked oak floors and the high ceilings, a sine qua non for this bloke with the wingspread of a small private jet. A futon with an indigo cover of homely weave sits with its back to a row of windows overlooking the Lake Monona shoreline. The rustic decor is completed by a weather-beaten wooden trunk that serves as a coffee table and features an improbably huge rusted lock. I wonder what hidden treasures might be stored within.

I limp over to the windows and survey the lakescape. Because of the shape of the shoreline I am unable to perceive even the general location of our house in the distance, as if Anthony has already departed for some inaccessible parallel universe.

"The bathroom's through here," says my host. "I've set first-aid supplies on the sink. Let me see if I can scare up some ice for your ankle."

The scrapes on my hands and legs are minor. These days dealing with blood has become commonplace: I regularly bring small tubes of Anthony's to the hospital to have the white blood cell count taken. The latest results, received yesterday afternoon, are worrisome, suggesting a serious infection. Yet again I block out the obvious reason why Dr. Hertz, aware of the extent and speed of Anthony's decline, has not sounded the alarm as he has so many times before.

I hobble back to the living room. The Swede has fetched a plastic bag filled with ice.

"Did you find everything you needed?"

"Yes, thank you, but the bloody ankle hurts like hell."

"Oh? Is it still bleeding?"

"No, bloody in the English sense."

This elicits a brief quizzical look, then a gesture of understanding. I prop my leg on the maximum-security coffee trunk. He slaps the bag of ice against it.

"Ouch! Watch it!"

"Sorry. Is that better?" Another wallop.

Mother Teresa needn't fear competition. As he reaches over for a third round I fend him off by easing the icebag against the swelling myself.

He looks embarrassed. An uneasy silence.

"By the way, I'm Eric. Eric Sundergaard. AA."

My working-class sense of humour suddenly gets the better of me, as it sometimes does when I've been under stress for too long. I am generally able to maintain control over this rowdy voice, but it occasionally overpowers my veneer of cultivation and refinement. It is so contagious that even Anthony, despite being a paragon of good taste, took to imitating it almost immediately after we first met.

"How brave you are to confide in me so quickly. Sorry to hear you have a drinking problem." I shake my head in commiseration.

A pause as Eric takes this in. He blushes.

"Not that AA. Sundergaard with a double *a*."

I manage a more genteel nod and am preparing to introduce myself when Eric blurts out:

"Are you still going swimming? Maybe you should head home." He takes out a hanky and blows his nose. "It might be worse than you realise," he concludes, belatedly gesturing in the direction of my foot.

Eric's comment is more perceptive than he knows: my foot injury is not the only reason I should go home. I consider doing so, but can't face being deprived of my one daily break from the nightmare of Anthony's illness: athletic activities are the only reliable way I have ever discovered to ease my chronic melancholy and crippling self-doubt, a good swim the one and only remedy for my present despondency. I vow to sit with Anthony all afternoon and evening to make it up to him for leaving so hastily this morning.

"Thanks for the advice," I murmur. "I'll take it under advisement."

"You do that." Eric stands and heads for the loo. "Don't go away, I'll be right back."

I should await his return, thank him for his kindness and excuse myself. Instead I come shakily to my feet, set the icebag atop a large potted fern, and limp out of his apartment. I don't have it in me to say good-bye, why I don't know. After all, I hardly know the man.

chapter 3

I don't see Eric Sundergaard, AA, again until the morning of 31 July 1993, a matter of hours after I receive Anthony's 11:11 message. Having stayed up till dawn trying to make sense of the numbers, gazing at the television screen as if it were a portal to the otherworld, I awaken around 10 a.m. to the sound of gulls and the delicious smell of a southeasterly breeze blowing in over the water. My eyes still shut, I imagine for a moment what it would be like to find Anthony snoozing away on a summer's morning, hugging a pillow like a little boy, as he always did. The events of the previous evening pop into my head. Deciphering Anthony's message seems a better reason to get up than my usual frenzied routine, though I have no idea where to begin.

My mother always says the best way to find something is to stop looking for it, an absurd piece of advice I've never had any more inclination to follow than her other gems of Polish folk wisdom. I decide that frittering away the morning with an aimless stroll around the farmer's market on Capitol Square would be an easy and satisfying way to finally prove her wrong.

I haven't been to the market, which takes place every Saturday morning in summer, since Anthony died. When he was still well enough, we often returned home from this quintessentially Madison event with rucksacks filled with tomatoes, cherries, and greens, our impression of inhabiting an overgrown cow town reinforced by chance encounters with friends and acquaintances of every stripe.

On this day it seems more crowded than I remember, probably because my claustrophobia has worsened since Anthony's death. My eyes are darting from side to side to prospect for an escape route when an unexpected clearing opens up. And suddenly there is Eric Sundergaard, crouching over a farm-stand display of broccoli in two distinct piles, "whole" and "destemmed."

He looks even taller than I remembered, perhaps because his khaki shorts display his legs, which resemble shapely utility poles. He is wearing a tank top with a *Y* printed on the front, matching blue-and-white Adidas, and auto-racing-style sunglasses. His longish hair, now sunbleached a honeyish colour with platinum streaks, spills out in untidy waves from beneath a Milwaukee Brewers baseball cap. Squatting without a hint of strain, he looks athletic in a disaffected way, the loose-limbed arrogance of his stance simultaneously flaunting his impressive musculature and suggesting a highminded disdain for the childishness of competitive sports.

I have totally forgotten about my impolite exit from Eric's flat on the day of Anthony's death. That entire scene, like most of the events of those last months, has been placed into the cold-storage section of my brain, the one exception being Anthony's face when I left him the morning of his death, an image that has not ceased to haunt me.

"Excuse me," I venture, not really knowing why I am approaching Eric or what I plan to say. "You probably don't remember me, but we met a few years ago when I fell off my bike and you helped me. Aren't you Eric?"

Having had enough of sniffing at the broccoli like a peckish giraffe, Eric, oblivious to my question, is now perusing the two piles with the intensity one would expect from a plant geneticist assessing the results of a daring hybridisation experiment. When he realises he is being addressed, he looks at me sideways and says:

"Oh, are you . . . ? Did you say something?"

"Yes, we met quite a while back, you probably don't remember. You let me clean up at your place." He stands up straight; I feel my head tilting back to meet his gaze. His face goes into the deep freeze. Too late I recall my rude departure on that earlier occasion.

He sneezes convulsively, then says, his handkerchief still covering his nose and mouth: "Oh, you." He turns his back to me, his body wracked with coughing.

"Are you all right?" I ask weakly.

"Hay fever." He blows his nose, takes a few seconds to recover. He is still slightly out of breath when he speaks.

"How's the foot? Not that I . . ." He turns the colour of pomegranates.

"Fine. The ankle was better after I went swimming." My turn to blush—why in the world would he remember that I had been about to go swimming? To cover my embarrassment, I moronically shake my left leg.

His scowl congeals. I thrash around for a graceful way out of the mortifying situation. "I didn't mean to interrupt your shopping. I just thought I'd say hi. That was a bad day for me. You were very kind."

"Hmm."

A long silence. Eric's eyes harden. "Why did you skip out like that?"

I lower my gaze and stare into the middle of his tank top, fixating on the Y. Does he frequent the YMCA, or is the letter there to rub in his damnable question?

"I . . . Um . . . It's kind of complicated. There was actually a reason I did that."

Most Wisconsinites are so polite and diffident that by intoning this last sentence with feeling, you can get away with anything from knocking over a little old lady in the crosswalk when your car skids on the snow to shooting a bank teller who is slow in emptying his cash drawer. To my dismay, Eric does not respond with the usual "No problem" but looks even more incensed.

"What kind of reason? If you had to leave, why didn't you just say so?"

"My . . . A friend of mine . . . I told you, it was a bad day. I was in a hurry. I'm sorry."

"You didn't have time to say you had to leave?"

"I said I'm sorry—what more do you want? I can't explain it right now. It's a long story."

He removes his sunglasses and inspects his watch, as if about to record an event in a ship's log.

"As a matter of fact," he says slowly, "I happen to have some time to kill this evening. Maybe you could spare enough of yours to tell me your long story over dinner?"

The last thing I expect. Out of cold storage comes the memory that on the day of our first meeting it occurred to me that Eric was quite a dish.

The image of Anthony's pleading face reappears, his eyes warning of treacherous waters ahead. I promise myself that dinner with Eric will be nothing more than a stage of my investigation into the meaning of Anthony's message. What else have I got to go on?

"I guess I owe you that much," I reply. "I'll make dinner."

Our eyes meet; Eric's seem noncommittal but somewhat intrigued by my more personal counter-invitation. Talking about Anthony's death isn't going to be easy—better it should be at the house. I reach into my wallet, take out a slip of paper, write down my name and address and 7:30, and hand it to Eric.

To my amusement, at that very moment one of my colleagues from the English Department strolls past, sees me exchanging an ambiguous glance with Eric and handing him what must have all the appearance of a billet-doux, and throws me a quizzical look. I can just imagine the little wheels in his brain revving up in speculation as to why I am arranging an assignation with this giant specimen of a man. The truth is that since living through the agony of Anthony's illness and the years following his death, I have ceased placing much stock in what people might say about me, but after more than two years of conspicuous solitude, I imagine that I am thought of in the university community as something of a hermit. I smile and wave to my colleague, wondering whether rumours might soon start to fly, as is typical in even a sizeable college town like Madison, large enough for people not to bump into friends or acquaintances for years but small enough to stumble upon them twice in a single week—and also, on occasion, to become unwitting and uninvited witnesses to their activities.

I return to the situation at hand. Eric glances at my information. "See you tonight," he says, not bothering to look up. "If it's all the same to you," he adds with peculiar emphasis, "I won't bother to *dress.*" He saunters away.

As I circle the Square in search of ingredients for dinner, it occurs to me that if what I have just agreed to is not a date, it might have been wise to share that information with Eric.

In spite of Eric's parting remark, when I open the door at eight, he is wearing cuffed tan linen trousers, a white shirt, and a brown woven tie that, hitting him at mid-torso, looks like a child's garment. His hair, less defiant now that it is capless, is as carefully groomed as its thickness and texture allow. He mutters an apology for his lateness and hands me a bottle of 1988 Mouton-Rothschild, which leaves me nonplussed. In terms of what Anthony used to call PQ or poshness quotient, it is several notches above what I have planned for dinner, a pasta salad made with dreary store-bought pesto.

Eric disappears into the loo to wash his hands. I mix myself a tall seven-and-seven. Once Anthony and I discovered the 11:11 face, I added that cocktail to my repertoire in the hopes it would help neutralise the power of attraction I seem to exert over any indecisive bad karma floating about the Milky Way.

When Eric emerges from the bathroom, I give him a beer and suggest we have our drinks on the upstairs deck, with its wide-angle view overlooking Lake Monona. The lake laps against the seawall at the far end of the yard and fills nearly one's entire visual field as it extends straight ahead to the town of Monona, a mile away as the fish swims, and several miles to the left and right. When the water is warm enough to swim in or cold enough to stroll on, you need venture out only a hundred yards before you glimpse the State Capitol situated at the highest point of the isthmus on which the city of Madison, a sixty-five-square-mile zone of whimsy surrounded by thousands of much squarer miles of midwestern good sense, has sprung up.

As I shut the screen door to the deck behind me and offer Eric a chair, I rehearse one of the disingenuous disclaimers I keep on hand in response to visitors' accolades about the view.

He sucks in a long, slow draft of Sprecher's, a local brew.

"Are those mallards or coots?"

I have lived in Wisconsin long enough to have learned the urgency of the local population's desire to distinguish coots from mallards. I fetch my binoculars and hand them to Eric. At least his nonreaction has the advantage of allowing me to put off talking about Anthony. But not for long.

"They're coots," says Eric, scanning the horizon. He turns towards me, the binoculars still pressed against his eyes. I hope the part of me he is seeing magnified tenfold is one that looks better enlarged. "So what's the deal with the way you acted that day?"

I take a seat on the other deck chair. The wind has shifted to the west and whitecaps cover the lake, propelling or slowing the few remaining sailboats as they make their way home before sunset while a handful of motorboats cut across each other's wakes, gaily riding the crests.

Gazing at the water, I tell Eric about the day Anthony died. I inform him that my lover had AIDS, that his mother and father had come from England to help me care for him, and that he died the evening of the day Eric and I first met. I add that I am HIV-negative, something I generally kept to myself in the months following Anthony's death so as to avoid sounding sanctimonious but eventually accepted would remain a question in everyone's mind if I said nothing. I end by explaining that in my lover's last hour of conscious life, he asked his parents repeatedly when I would be home, but that I walked through the door less than a minute after he went into his final coma.

When I lift my eyes, Eric's features are huddled together as if for protection from a northwest wind unexpectedly rising up on a balmy October afternoon.

I suggest we go downstairs and have dinner. To my surprise Eric responds:

"How about the rest of the story?"

"What do you mean?"

"Just what I said. The rest of the story."

I struggle to maintain my composure.

"You don't think I had a good excuse to get home as quickly as I could?"

"But did you go home?"

Of all the reactions to my tale of sorrow I might have foreseen, this is not one.

"No, not exactly. Yes, as a matter of fact. I just stopped at the pool first and . . ." My words trail off. Suddenly my South Side Chicago voice pipes up to defend me. "Who the hell do you think you are, the district attorney for Dane County?"

Eric says nothing but looks a trifle sheepish. A light bulb goes off in my head. I have strange intuitions from time to time.

"You really are the district attorney for Dane County, aren't you?"

"Not exactly. I'm an assistant DA."

I start to laugh. Between heaves I gasp, "I can't believe . . . my luck. . . . Just the man . . . I was looking for. . . . Save me a phone call." As my laughter dies out, I hold my hands out to Eric, palms down. "Arrest me. I did it. He was dying, and I went swimming. He was trying to tell me when I left him that morning, but I didn't understand." As the floodgates lift, I pull back my hands and bury my face in them.

I don't look up for a long while. By the time I do, the sky is getting dark.

"I'm sorry I upset you," says Eric, his voice hoarse.

"You're not the guilty one. You're just asking the questions."

I excuse myself to go wash my face. When I return, we sit in embarrassed silence for a few moments. Eric's features break into a crooked smile.

"You ever swum across the lake?" he asks in a bright voice. He is obviously trying to cheer me up.

"Too many boats," I say glumly. "Might get sliced in half."

Out of nowhere, Eric's voice morphs into an imitation of Groucho Marx reminiscent of one of my crazed spiels, either at a party after a couple of drinks or to make people laugh against their will in inappropriate situations, when they have just taken a steaming mouthful of fettucine Alfredo or are listening to a lecture about Doctors Without Borders' work with lepers.

"Just what I'm driving at!" he blurts out. "That way you could swim to both shores at the same time and wave to yourself from the other side!"

Indignation rises within me at hearing this man I've pigeonholed as a sombre Swede displaying idiotic humour to rival my own. I am preparing a sharp reply when he resumes his Nordic voice and accent.

"Sooooo." Wisconsinites, even those not connected with the law, pronounce this word as if they were coolly advising you to initiate legal action. "You've never swum across the lake. Would you like to do it now?"

⁕

When an idea goes beyond the charted limits of madness, one cannot turn it down; there is simply no choice. We change into bathing costumes; one of Anthony's suits from his beefier days fits Eric. As we walk past the living room he stops short, his upper body wavering. "Is that him?"

The photograph Eric is referring to, which hangs in the sitting room, was taken just before Anthony became seriously ill. After all this time it still evokes for me the frosty day in November 1989 when, at his suggestion and despite my misgivings, we walked over to a local photographer's studio to have a portrait taken while we still could.

"You're not too tired?" I asked. "Why don't you have a cup of tea? You just got home." Actually, Anthony was looking haler than he had for months, whether because this first blast of wintry air had put a touch of colour into his chalky complexion or because he'd just heard that his revised dissertation, *Early Marketing Practices in Elizabethan England*, had been accepted by Oxford University Press. Tenure was looking good, the publishing part of the "publish-or-perish" truism about junior faculty settled; not perishing would be the greater challenge.

"Don't be such a worry wart," he rejoined with a grin, his smile the only part of his face to have survived the months of illness completely unchanged. "We'll go out for a bite, shall we? Dancing, perhaps?" He gave me a bear hug.

I took in his aroma, a mixture of musk and cloves edged with English Leather. I forced myself to pull away.

"Sure you're feeling up to it?"

"Quite shah." Anthony's accent tended to become even posher than usual if he was on edge. His facial expression, impenetrable when it diverged from his usual moods of good cheer and expansiveness, shifted. "I know you've got loads of pictures, but . . ."

We had witnessed many such mini-dramas within our circle of gay friends, and I had long wondered when it would fall to us to play one ourselves. I waited for Anthony to go on, but after a brief lull, his voice assumed its usual buoyancy.

"If it'll make you happy," he went on, "I'll have a spot of Earl Grey and put my feet up before dinner. All right then?" The final rhetorical question, expressed in regal tones, indicated that my audience had come to an end, the elephant in the room safely restored to invisibility.

We did what Anthony suggested. We smiled for the nice man with the camera, had a lavish meal at the White Rabbit, our favourite restaurant, and danced at the New Bar, the trendiest dance floor in town, till bar time. And in the weeks leading up to the Christmas holidays, as Anthony's health made a beeline for Antarctica, the portrait increasingly seemed to have captured the final reasonably ordinary moments of the good life we had shared.

Eric and I stare wordlessly at the photograph. There it is, that face with a charm as difficult to capture as it is to forget. Anthony's straight prominent nose suggests a kind of earnestness undercut, to devastating effect, by the come-hither smile of Gerald Payton, his Irish father. From his English mother Anthony inherited his fair colouring and aristocratic features; he was spared her overcast disposition. On the picture his straw-coloured hair is more orderly than it was in real life, for it tended to fall into his eyes, and he heightened the canine sweetness of the resulting look by habitually shaking his locks clear of his line of sight rather than running a hand through them. By some uncanny coincidence his eyes were of an identical shade of aquamarine as my own, but when I stared into them, illuminated by the reading light on our nightstand, they were the portal to a world of inner peace inaccessible to my own tormented spirit.

Eric fiddles with the goggles I've lent him, stretching the band as far as it will go and snapping them on. He turns in my direction and grins strangely. "He wasn't bad looking," he tosses off. He ties the string on Anthony's suit and proceeds towards the back door. It is a humid evening and his goggles have steamed up. He stumbles and curses as he crosses the threshold.

I have never swum outdoors at night. The lake looks dark.

"How will we see where we're going?" I venture.

"There's nothing to see." The acoustics of the water give Eric's voice an unsettling undertone. "I'm not a very straight swimmer, but I'll try not to slam into you."

chapter 4

The evening Anthony and I met, 2 September 1980—coincidentally my twenty-seventh birthday—I had spent the day taking copious and, as it turned out, utterly pointless notes for my first classes at Yale as a brand-new assistant professor of English the following day. I was to teach one course on Shakespeare and a section of a large English lit survey. I was too keyed up to eat breakfast or lunch, but around five thirty I grabbed a sandwich and decided a swim was in order.

I had moved to New Haven in June and spent the summer finishing my dissertation. I sent it off to my thesis advisor at Harvard in mid-August. That left me a fortnight before classes began in order to convince myself I had not been offered the position at Yale because of the sudden death or incapacitation of all of the other candidates, which I had prayed for a few months earlier.

The downstairs pool was deserted. A twenty-five-yarder situated in a kind of pit beneath the running track, it was known as the Exhibition Pool, but the surreal geography of the place suggested something more along the lines of an Exhibitionist Pool designed to display the swimmers' strokes, for better or for worse, to colleagues and students circling on the track above. Over the summer I had also made occasional use of the Voyeurs' Track and wondered what my own stroke looked like from on high. I was about to find out.

It was the first day of classes, although I didn't happen to have any on Tuesdays. As I was soon to discover, Anthony, a first-year graduate student in history, had decided that a leisurely jog would be a good way to unwind from the heart-thumping introductory meeting of his first seminar, "Public Spaces and Private Lives in the Reign of Queen Victoria." Although it would not be accurate to say we actually met in this weird setting—that event took place a few minutes later—the first space we occupied at the

26

same time captured the essence of our respective lives up to that point. Anthony gracefully circled the track as effortlessly as he had gone through the cycles of his youth: a pleasant childhood in North London, a trendier-than-thou secondary education at Hampstead Comprehensive, and a first in history at Oxford, all achieved without breaking a sweat. I, on the other hand, an overachiever with a back designed to let accomplishments roll off without a trace and a psyche in which the slightest failing permanently lodged, expended every ounce of strength to send my body bucketing towards a concrete wall only to flip and, a begoggled Sisyphus, restart the futile process all over again. If Anthony was likely unaware of how rare the ease with which he pranced through life was, I had learned the hard way that a creature lacking any natural sense of self-worth is limited to temporary fixes like swimming, running, and bicycling, the only things I do that always make me feel better about myself.

I finished my laps and headed upstairs to the men's locker room. The sauna was deserted: on the hectic first day of classes, most people had better things to do than hang out in a wooden box two or three degrees above the ambient temperature. The peace and quiet would allow for uninterrupted fretting about how I was going to face my students the following day.

After several minutes a young man took a seat directly across from me. I registered only that he was sublimely handsome and seemed likely to be a person of the self-besotted variety I was familiar with from my Harvard years, probably a preppy who would respond to a casual hello with an arctic stare. I was thus taken aback when he himself broke the silence.

"I beg your pardon, but do you happen to know how late this place is open?"

Not only was he attractive and friendly, he was obviously British, his posh accent a particular enticement for an upwardly mobile Anglophile snob such as myself.

"Seven thirty." I didn't want to discourage him with a brief American-sounding reply, so I went on. "Or at least . . . yes, half past seven, I think. I haven't actually been to the sauna before today." This was technically true as long as one placed a comma after "before": I hadn't visited the sauna for two or three days.

A pause. I was about to resume my worrying session when the young man cleared his throat and said, "You're quite a decent swimmer." Taken aback by the non sequitur, I threw him a look. "I was jogging on the track just now," he explained. "You've got a good stroke."

A blush of pleasure spread upwards from my neck. I wiped my brow and said, "Starting to get warm in here, isn't it?"

"Mmm. Perhaps they've decided to heat the sauna for a few minutes as a little treat."

"It really is pathetic. Are you English?"

"That's following a train of thought."

"No, that's not . . . I love England. When I'm there I never want to leave."

"That makes one of us."

"But you are English, right?"

"Yes," he said with a sigh, as if caught out over a past misdeed. "Or at least, Mummy is. Dad is, too, technically, but . . . it's rather a long story." He grinned, hinting he might consider elaborating if I could muster the courage to ask him.

I could not.

"My name is Anthony Payton," he went on. "Payton with an *a*, not like *Peyton Place*."

I wondered how he happened to become familiar with the world of American soap operas. I leaned forwards and clumsily extended my right hand, nearly tumbling off the wooden risers in the process.

"Reb Matkowski," I said briskly, hoping he wouldn't poke fun at my surname as perfect strangers sometimes do, usually focussing their jibes on the long-term risks of consuming beef.

"Charmed, I'm sure." The courtly, unironic response took me by surprise. "My name is actually Marc Anthony, but for obvious reasons I go by Anthony."

"Your parents called you Marc Anthony?"

His smile was enchanting. "They're eccentric, all right," he replied, "but rather sweet. Mummy's favourite Shakespeare plays are *Antony and Cleopatra* and *Julius Caesar*. Marc Antony is in both. I sometimes wonder if that's where she got her name, too."

"Cleopatra?"

He let out a quick bark of a laugh. "No, no. 'Cleopatra' would not suit. Anyhow, wrong play. Julia. Are you a postgraduate student?"

"Assistant professor of English," I mumbled, hoping he wouldn't quite make out the first word: junior faculty at a place like Yale were at the bottom of the food chain. "Shakespeare, as a matter of fact," I added primly.

He nodded. A long silence. I thrashed about for a witty remark to prolong the conversation.

"Funny that you were named for Marc Antony," I finally said. "I was named for a character in literature, too. You wouldn't know it, though—it's not a person called Reb." The line sounded pathetic even to my own ears. Some invisible force had taken control of my voice, its timbre high and quick.

"Shall I guess?" asked Anthony gamely. He cast his eyes towards the ceiling. "Robin Hood?"

"Not bad, but no."

"Rob Roy?"

"Actually, it's a woman."

"How intriguing. A woman, perchance, with black wavy hair?" I blinked. Was he taking the piss out of me? "Rapunzel?" he went on. The word, which had acquired several extra *n*'s, sounded to my ears like a caress, but that could only be wishful thinking.

I shook my head. My throat was dry and constricted.

"Rebecca." I had difficulty getting the word out.

Anthony's brows knit. "Rebecca? You mean from the Old Testament?"

"No, Daphne du Maurier. You know, the mystery novel. *Rebecca*. Hitchcock made it into a film."

"Sorry, 'fraid I don't know it."

"Best Film of 1940. Joan Fontaine and Laurence Olivier. And Judith Anderson as Danny."

"They had an actress playing a man back in 1940?"

"Not a man, Mrs. Danvers. The mad housekeeper." It came to me that that very day I had seen a poster advertising a showing at one of the college film societies. "As a matter of fact," I went on, keeping my voice casual, "it's on tonight at eight at Morse College."

A long pause. I couldn't really spare the time to see a film, but it suddenly occurred to me that I had the right to procrastinate on my birthday. I was still screwing up my courage to ask Anthony out when he stood abruptly and gathered his things. My heart sank. At the door of the sauna he turned back and said, "Chop, chop! If it starts at eight we haven't got a moment to lose."

As the familiar dialogue of *Rebecca* echoed through the Morse College Common Room that evening and the glorious faces of Joan Fontaine and Laurence Olivier floated across the screen, I lost myself, as always, in my identification with the anonymous main character, a young Englishwoman of humble means inexplicably courted and wed by Maxim de Winter, an aristocrat who has recently lost his wife, Rebecca; the new bride's mistaken belief that Maxim could never love another as he had adored his late wife—whom he had in fact detested—colours their entire relationship. I saw this hapless young woman, as I saw myself, as utterly lacking in the sort of breeding manifested most palpably by the unfailing good cheer and stolid calm of the British gentry. If she would never fit into the set gravitating around Maxim's grand estate, Manderley, it was because her anxiety about being in the world and tendency to hang back only drew attention to her awkwardness, her shrinking manner ironically keeping her in a sickly, unpleasant limelight. Introversion was a consecrated tradition of the British upper classes; broadcasting one's introversion was not. It mattered little that I, by contrast to Maxim's tremulous young wife, utilised competitiveness, pomposity, and humour to mask my sense of inferiority; we were essentially the same. Now that, by some quirk of fate I could not fathom, I found Maxim de Winter's living and breathing avatar sitting beside me whenever I diverted my eyes from the brilliant image of Olivier's flawless features, the two men merged into a fantasy of all I desired but could never obtain or be.

Manderley, eventually doomed by Mrs. Danvers, Rebecca's demented lady's maid, in order to prevent Maxim from making a new life there with his bride, was still going up in flames when Anthony headed for the exit in a way that made me think he had hated the film. We walked briskly to Naples Pizzeria on Wall Street, took a table as far as possible from a group of hyperactive undergraduates, and ordered a large pepperoni, which we fairly assaulted as soon as it arrived.

"What did you think of *Rebecca*?" I asked once the feeding frenzy had abated.

"Brilliant." I inspected Anthony's face but couldn't tell if he was being sarcastic or not.

"How do you picture Rebecca?" I asked. "If there were a flashback, who would play her?"

"Hadn't thought, to be honest. Vivien Leigh?" He dabbed at his chin with a napkin. "Perhaps if you'd been around they'd have offered it to you for your screen début." Again I wondered why he was pulling my leg. He reached for a piece of garlic bread and nibbled at it thoughtfully. "Tell you one thing, though, I didn't much care for Manderley."

"Why?"

He sighed. "Hard to explain, but I can't stand that sort of thing. It's one reason I left England."

"Is your family . . . Did it remind you of your childhood?"

"Mmm, quite so. Manderley might have been modelled on our country estate in Dorset."

I stared, taken in by his deadpan, which he shattered with a laugh.

"C'mon, Reb. Did you honestly believe I grew up in a place like Manderley? Staff of fifty, tea in front of the fah, that sort of thing? Mummy telling some ghastly duchess, 'I'm sayo glad you popped in to see us at Miserly today, but you simply maast come down to Sheepfuck, our place in Devon. It's sayo much grander than Miserly, simply glodious in the samma and we've plenty of rum if you'd like to stop for a day or two. Paps you can come with the Douche and all the little Douchebags."

We both howled. The waitress gave us a look.

"I didn't mean to imply your family were like that," I said once we had regained our composure. "No offense intended."

"None taken," Anthony replied, waving a hand absentmindedly.

"What are they actually like? Not to pry or anything," I added, reminding myself that Europeans often find Americans they have just met indiscreet.

"Quite ordinary, really. As a matter of fact Mummy's family were rather posh at one time but the money ran out ages ago. Dad's people hailed from County Cork. He grew up in Liverpool."

"Have you got any brothers or sisters?"

"Just the one, Miranda. She lives in New York, actually."

"How did she wind up in the States?"

"A postgraduate degree at Columbia. She decided to stay. She's a psychotherapist."

"And you?"

"Pardon?"

"How did you end up here? Why do grad school in America?"

Anthony scanned the room, caught our waitress's eye, and made a hand gesture to ask for the check. She brought it over straightaway, still perusing us with disapproval.

"Well," he said, turning back towards me, "no time to go into all that just now." He glanced down at his watch, gobbled down the last wedge of pizza, and went for the bill, which I snatched away. He nodded with amusement, like a royal being treated to fish and chips by his footman.

Back on the street we fell into the uneasy silence of two people who have just met and shared an evening but don't yet know if they're headed in the same direction, literally or figuratively. Anthony opened and closed his mouth several times. He stared intently at the pavement and I was sure he was preparing a polite send-off that would discourage future contact. Instead he said,

"Would you mind if I stopped by?"

"That was quick."

Anthony rolled off the sofa bed and rubbed his eyes. Planting his feet on the parquet floor, he stretched his perfectly proportioned naked frame. After a few moments he sat back down on the bed and shook his head vigorously from side to side, as if to clear away the cobwebs. "And very nice, as well," he added as an afterthought. He screwed up his face, as if practicing a role. "Was it good for you?"—this in a raunchy American voice halfway between Mae West and Al Pacino.

"Quite."

"English 'quite' or American 'quite'?"

"What?"

"I'm surprised an Anglophile like you doesn't know this." He assumed a professorial demeanour. "English 101: in the UK, 'quite' means 'sort of, but not very.' If you said at a dinner party in Britain, 'the food is quite good,' you'd be insulting the hostess. Whereas in America, it means 'really.'"

I flushed retrospectively for all of the times I must have misused the term during my various stays in England. At least I had a fresh explanation for why most Brits I had attempted to befriend had had other ideas, a tradition Anthony would most likely carry on.

He drew his knees up to his chest and clasped his hands round them like a nude scout at a campfire. "Typical American hyperbole, this 'quite' business. Everything always has to be 'absolutely unbelievable' or 'incredibly fantastic.'" This time the American accent was steadier. "Why can't things here ever just be fine, as they are in Britain?"

He cocked his head. Several strands of hair fell terrierlike into his eyes.

"Are you waiting for a scratch?" I asked shyly. "I've never had a pet before."

He barked in reply.

I swung my legs over the side of the bed, leaned forwards, and placed my left hand on his golden crown. He let out several more woofs and then in a human voice asked, "What time is it?"

I looked over at the clock radio. "11:11."

"Tons to do. Must be getting back."

"Yes, me too."

"Oh? Aren't you?"

I waited, hoping he would see fit to complete the sentence. I admire the Brits' use of understatement in everyday conversation but half the time I'm not really sure what they're talking about.

"This is where you live, is it not?"

I nodded. I couldn't figure out by what fluke Anthony had decided to spend the evening with me; I mused how lovely it would have been if he had asked to stay the night before dancing off on his merry way, never to be seen again. I would even have considered offering him the sofa bed and taking the floor for myself. Insomniacs are capable of being unable to sleep anywhere.

As the lift doors started to close, Anthony gave a cheery little wave.

"Please call," I managed to get out at the last second.

"Haven't I just?"

I sighed. He had taken "call" in the British sense of paying a visit, thereby fending off my request.

chapter 5

To my astonishment, Anthony and I began seeing each other two or three evenings a week. He'd ring when he was winding down from the day's work around ten to see if he might stop by; needless to say, he could. Was he merely hitching a ride with a fellow traveller until he had the means to purchase a ticket for a more comfortable form of transportation? Probably, but given our relative appeal, I was not in a position to hope for more. I was so smitten I almost convinced myself it didn't matter.

He rarely stayed for more than an hour and never spent the night. For all his easy charm a fool could sense that in matters of the heart he played his cards close to the vest. One time when he blew me a kiss at the door as he was departing I cleared my throat and enquired when I might see him again. He froze like a deer in the headlights, then recovered with a breezy exit line: "I'll check my appointment book and get back to you."

I didn't take it seriously, but the following day he phoned to set up an actual social engagement. Grad-student friends of his were planning a Halloween costume party. The theme of the party was politics, in honour of the upcoming 1980 presidential election pitting Jimmy Carter against Ronald Reagan. Cross-dressing was encouraged. Might I care to come along?

As the date approached and we discussed our options, the pool of female political figures with costume potential gravitated towards two prime ministers, Margaret Thatcher and Golda Meir. But who would play whom? Anthony was clearly in a better position to imitate the speech and intonation of Mrs. Thatcher, and although the recently deceased Israeli leader and I had less in common, we were fellow midwesterners whose forebears had come to America from what was at the time Mother Russia. I rather relished playing this consummate underdog who had two disadvantages I had been mercifully spared: a Milwaukee childhood and bad hair.

When the supplies we ordered from a novelty shop in Manhattan arrived special delivery, it was clear that Anthony had received the better end of the bargain. The Thatcher head mask had tidy, businesslike hair and looked rather fetching when paired with the apricot-coloured size 24 cocktail dress Anthony had picked up for $4.95 at a Salvation Army resale shop in New Haven. I, on the other hand, after a futile search for the sort of matronly attire Mrs Meir had favoured, devised an outfit out of a drab, greenish-brown afghan crocheted by my Aunt Magdalena, a nun my brothers and I were allowed to see only at Easter. I accessorised the ensemble with chocolate-coloured wing tips and a brown belt designed to keep my garment from becoming embarrassingly décolleté. The Meir mask quite resembled the woman herself: solid features imbued with fine qualities like intelligence and courage, but not necessarily a contender for Miss World. I felt right at home wearing her face.

Anthony insisted that we don our full costumes, masks included, before leaving my flat and emphasised the importance of not revealing our true identities at the gathering even for a moment, citing an obscure superstition concerning All Hallows' Eve rituals that held sway at Magdalen College, Oxford, where he had been a student. He added that in any event the gathering wasn't a couples' sort of affair and we should both feel free to circulate throughout the evening. These directives, delivered in the tone of voice of a flight attendant going over safety procedures, made me wonder if there was more to his words than met the ear—was he hinting that he didn't wish me to be identified as his date?—but when he pulled on his mask and I received the full effect of the strapping, flouncily dressed Mrs. Thatcher for the first time, I doubled over in hysterics and dismissed the unpleasant idea.

At Halloween, Yale students give you a glimpse of something they normally make you guess at: what they fancy themselves to be. Judging from the costumes on parade as Anthony and I passed between Branford and Davenport College and approached the heart of the campus, power and fame seemed to be the main components of the collective fantasies of 1980. A brassy pair dressed as Ronald and Nancy Reagan overtook a more genteel one decked out as President and Mrs. Carter, as if an era were slipping away before one's very eyes. The blingy costume of a disco-dancing John Travolta was apt to trigger an aluminum foil shortage throughout southern New England. And there were numerous other reminders of the raunchy, decade-long communal lapse in taste known as the 1970s. An overstuffed Elvis had too much padding for hip gyrations. More uplifting was a chalk-faced Evita who waved to her adoring crowds, her raised arms helped along by a dozen pink helium balloons attached to each wrist. A tall black man wore the bottom part of several types of plants taped to his scantily clad body. Mrs. Thatcher stared but couldn't make sense of this last accoutrement.

"Who is he meant to be? He must be freezing."

"Kunta Kinte." I had seen a similar costume the previous year at a Mardi Gras party in Back Bay.

"Who?"

"You know, *Roots*?"

"Ah yes. Just made it to the BBC last year, I believe." Above the street noise I discerned the Margaret Thatcher voice Anthony had been perfecting for over a week. "Quite a riveting tale, although not entirely plausible, according to the better class of historians."

Kunta Kinte, ambling along ahead of us in the same direction, was accompanied by an emaciated Gandhi with wisps of blond hair escaping from beneath a bald pate. Just as we were about to pass the couple, Gandhi accosted Mrs. Thatcher with an unpacifist-sounding shriek and exclaimed:

"Is that you, Anthony? I can't believe y'all had the nerve to go through with it!"

Mrs. Thatcher responded with decorum, lifting her right hand to Gandhi's lips. After a quick *baisemain*, Gandhi pressed Mrs. Thatcher's hand to his forehead as a sign of reverence. He spoke with a shaky South Asian accent undermined by Tidewater diphthongs.

"Memsa, I am honoured, truly honoured to make your acquaintance. I know that in your heart, you are a woman of peace."

We all laughed and I waited for Anthony to introduce us, but he said the street was too noisy. Perhaps he felt the same once we got to the party because he never did present me to his friends, but I later discovered that Gandhi was Laura Gladstone, also a first-year student in history, while Kunta Kinte was her boyfriend, Willis Smith, a grad student in English. They both hailed from Savannah and had met as undergraduates at the University of Georgia.

When we arrived at the party, the uproar of approval was gratifying. Rumours of Mrs. Thatcher's possible visit had brought out other well-known Brits like the Queen, Winston Churchill, and John Lennon, who, though questionable as a political figure, would become an indisputable symbol of the lost idealism of the sixties and seventies by getting himself shot about six weeks later. Lennon took it upon himself to welcome Mrs. Thatcher, who introduced the rest of us simply as "representatives of our former colonies." Everyone laughed except for Kunta Kinte, who maintained a self-possessed air. Mrs. Thatcher completed the introduction:

"Madame Meir, Mr. Kinte, and Mohandas, this is John Lennon, the lead singer of the Lennon sisters. He is presently doing specialised training in— I'm sorry, what was it? Musicology?"

"English literature." Lennon, who I later learned was a Japanese American grad student from Milwaukee named Molly, had a mezzo-soprano voice that explained his slight build and small feet.

"Quite. A lyricist, no doubt. Where's Yoko?"

Yoko Ono, seated at the far side of the room on one of those beaten-up, olive-green couches that are a staple of university ghetto decor, wore a geisha head mask complemented by a straight black wig. She was clad in a haphazard kimono pinned together from tie-dyed bedspreads. To avoid confusion, "Yoko" had been painted in lime green acrylic paint across her bosom, the flatness of which was somewhat compensated for by shoulders that were unusually broad for a Japanese woman.

John and Yoko turned out to be our hosts. The party had a Hispanic subtheme, the fare consisting of corn chips, salsa, and sangria. Gandhi wasted no time breaking his fast. He carried about his own personal bowl of chips, frequently replenished, and I lost count of how many sangrias he had downed. Mrs. Thatcher was more than keeping up, but only in terms of sangria.

As John ladled out a glass of punch for a buxom Che Guevara, Gandhi wavered along with his umpteenth refill and herded together our little group, then pressed a wobbly finger to his mouth.

"Shhhhh. Between you and me, don't y'all wonder sometimes if people really *do* it? Take John over there." We dutifully followed Gandhi's gaze. "She's so small. Know what I mean? Not just short, but such fine bones and all. Whereas Sonny . . ." This was apparently Yoko's real-life name. He was kneeling next to the sofa at the other end of the room, too absorbed in conversation with Abraham Lincoln to notice he was being perused. Gandhi paused as his eyes caught sight of Yoko's feet. "Gawd, I didn't realise he was barefoot. What clodhoppers!" Now Gandi shifted his still downcast gaze in Kunta's direction and went on dreamily, "Not that that necessarily ..."

I was dying to sneak a look at Kunta's feet but saw that his face was agitated, presumably because, as I later observed, he was at least a size 13.

Under the spell of sangria myself, I felt it advisable to use Mrs. Meir's diplomatic skills to raise the squirrely tone of the discussion. I modelled my accent on the mother of a childhood friend, a Jewish lady who had also grown up in Milwaukee. A frisson flashed up my spine as I wondered how Anthony would receive my first stand-up comedy routine.

"Anybody can do it with anybody," I began with fervour. "That's the way God meant it to be. Blonds like brunettes, Jews like goys, nobodies like somebodies. Look at Danny Kaye and Sir Laurence Olivier." This example of a socially mismatched coupling was well known in the gay community but a bit obscure for general consumption, so I fell back on my scanty knowledge of the Old Testament. "As our revered patriarch Solomon used to say, if a chihuahua should lie down with an Irish wolfhound, so be it. It is not body parts that count, it is the union of souls." Kunta nodded gravely. "On the other hand, let us pray that that wolfhound is the female." An explosion of laughter—apparently a few neighbouring guests had overheard my preposterous patter.

Now Mrs. Thatcher, as figurehead of the former British Empire, felt compelled to throw in her tuppence. She assumed the patronising tone of voice we were to hear throughout the crises of the 1980s, that of an embattled adult beset by swarms of naughty children. There was a break in the hubbub and the entire assembly suddenly seemed to be tuning in.

"One must never make assumptions about these things," began Mrs. Thatcher sententiously. "I recently had occasion to see a young man of an Olympian build similar to that of Ms. Ono, without, if you may pardon the expression, benefit of costume."

From across the room Yoko scowled and turned away. I swallowed and prepared myself for the worst: against all odds, Mrs. Thatcher's routine was shaping up to surpass my own for tastelessness.

"This young man," Mrs. Thatcher pursued, "was enamored of a great beauty of diminutive stature, and Lord only knows how, that is to say, whether ..." Out of the corner of my eye I saw John Lennon vainly motioning to Kunta to cut Mrs. T short but the runaway train gathered speed. "As to the question of whether or not these two talented young musicians to whom you have alluded, Ms. Ono and Mr. Lennon, are well suited to one another and make a good 'fit,' so to speak, I should not be overly hasty in passing judgement. Interracial couplings, like unnatural acts between persons of the same gender, may occasionally be fulfilling, but they are quite against God's intentions."

What had been a relaxed lull in the merriment tautened into silence; Mrs. Thatcher was learning the hard way that the ground rules of satire about race and sexual orientation were distinct in Britain and America. Kunta, one of the few guests not wearing a face mask, visibly winced. John Lennon put a hand to his forehead.

Kunta's retort started low, then built to a crescendo. "I hope you will allow me to disagree, Madame Prime Minister. Intimacy between a man and a woman of any race is not comparable to a man who treats another man as a woman. Two such men must be punished. Punished severely. They must be made into an example for all to abhor. If it were up to me, they would have their whoozits lopped off and duct-taped to their foreheads."

There was a brief delay, and then a meltdown blew apart in all directions. Guests shrieked or doubled over in hysterics. Kunta stood modestly in the midst of the pandemonium and sipped sangria.

By the time the room simmered down it was nearly midnight. Mrs. Thatcher, apparently famished after her little performance, scooped up all the corn chip dishes in need of replenishing and shadowed Yoko, who was carrying the empty sangria bowl, into the kitchen. During their absence John Lennon explained that the prizes would now be awarded, the winners asked to remove their masks. The panel of judges was comprised of Princess Grace, Napoleon Bonaparte, and Richard Nixon; John would play master of ceremonies. There were three categories: most unfashionable costume; biggest costume; and most transparent costume, that is, the one that revealed the most about the individual wearing it.

The first award, for most unfashionable costume, was the only one where the ruling of the judges was unanimous. The winner was Golda Meir.

The idea was that one made a short impromptu speech, fielded taunting questions from the crowd, and then pulled off one's mask. Except for that last part it was excruciatingly reminiscent of one of my classes.

When the time came for me to bare my face to the world, I sensed a ripple of curiosity in the crowd. Anthony had kept his distance all evening and hadn't really behaved as if I was his date, but some of the guests might possibly have seen us arrive together and drawn that conclusion all on their own. I remembered Anthony's instructions about not taking off my mask, but he was still MIA—what could it matter when he wasn't even in the room? As I stood there hesitating, the crowd began to clap and chant "Take it off, take it off." I felt like Little Orphan Annie at an Elks Convention. I took it off.

At that very moment the swinging kitchen door slammed open and Mrs. Thatcher and Yoko rejoined the party with their replenished supplies. Mrs. Thatcher took in the scene at a single glance, stepped smartly over to where I stood, took hold of my mask, and pulled it back over my head.

"Right you are," she said rather obscurely, shepherding me into a corner. She turned to John Lennon and said, "Move along, move along! On to the next one."

The room buzzed briefly over this odd intervention, but the guests were quickly distracted when John announced the next prize, the winner for biggest costume: Kunta Kinte. Kunta, taken aback but game, came forwards, raising his right hand in a V sign for victory. Uproarious applause, followed by a short statement from Napoleon as representative of the panel who explained that while Yoko Ono's costume was taller than Kunta Kinte's, one had to take into account width as well as length, and that the girth of Kunta Kinte's roots was completely disproportionate to his height. I expected Yoko to chime in at this point, but she had returned to the kitchen for more supplies. Kunta didn't have a mask to remove, and his acceptance speech, addressed to Napoleon, was short and sweet.

"You oughta know, big guy."

The winner of the final award, for most transparent costume, was Gandhi. When this prize was announced there was a ripple of nervous laughter from the crowd and banter I couldn't make out, but Gandhi was nowhere to be found. I turned to Mrs. Thatcher and said, "I don't get it. How is your friend like Gandhi?"

"Obvious."

"You mean she's a pacifist? Or against imperialism?"

She shook her head vehemently, her tidy hair springing to and fro. "No, no, that's not it."

"A lefty radical type? She seems too laid back for that kind of thing."

"Wrong on both counts."

I was tiring of Anthony's games. "I'll ask her myself. Do you know where she is?"

"I wouldn't do that if I were you," he said. "She's in the loo. Been chucking up for a quarter of an hour."

"Too much sangria?"

"Oh no. She usually does that after she eats."

chapter 6

As Anthony and I prepared to exit the party, he told me he'd forgotten to ask one of his colleagues a question relating to a seminar they were both taking. He looked annoyed and muttered that he would meet me in front of the building. I waited outside for half an hour, pacing back and forth. In light of Anthony's cool behaviour the evening could hardly be dubbed a success, and pounding the pavement dressed as Golda Meir was doing little to improve my mood. Finally I gave up on the idea of somehow making things right and walked home alone.

I was just dozing off when the doorbell rang. A cautious look through the peephole revealed Mrs. Thatcher's profile, immortalised in latex.

The door had barely shut before Anthony clasped me in his arms. It was so out of character that I wondered if he was still intoxicated. I pulled off his mask; a deep breath confirmed that he was. I drew back and scrutinised him in the dim light of the entryway. An expression of alarm pulsed over his features.

"What's the matter?" I asked gently.

"Nothing. Nothing's the matter."

"What happened? I waited but you never came out."

A weary shake of the golden hair. "I'm sorry, Reb. I can't really . . . I wondered if . . ." He eased himself onto a chair. "I'm knackered. Do you mind if I stay over?"

Fatigue could hardly have been what had made him stop by; his place was closer to the party than mine. Logic dictated that I should call the question, but there was something even more irresistible about the sag of his features than his usual impeccable allure.

"No problem," I replied. "You can take the bed. I'll put cushions on the floor."

"No, no, I'll—"

I hushed him with a finger. He sat motionless while I gently removed his bizarre regalia. I pulled off his shoes and socks and walked him over to the sofa bed.

"Thanks, Reb, I know I've been—"

"Shhh. You don't have to say anything."

I sat down on the bed next to him, at a loss as to how I could comfort him without knowing the reason for his distress. I rubbed his neck for a few minutes, then kneaded his temples. A single tear flowed from his left lid. Eventually he stretched out and laid his head on the pillow.

"Please forgive me. I feel dreadful. I didn't mean to—"

"Of course not," I said, pulling the covers close. I placed a chair beside the bed and stroked his hair as he drifted off. Only when I heard him snoring did it occur to me that it might have been illuminating to learn what it was he had to apologise for.

In the weeks following the Halloween party, Anthony's visits to my place continued, always without much advance notice, but he also started ringing now and again just to chat. When he announced he would be spending Thanksgiving with his sister in Manhattan, I left a lengthy pause in case an invitation was forthcoming; no such luck. He remained vague about his Christmas plans so I eventually dropped the subject. I rang him a few times on my own initiative but he was never in, so I gave up on that as well.

I had little time to fret over the matter, but now and again, as my mind drifted from a page of Shakespeare I was trying to make sense of, I wondered why Anthony was always out. Was he camping at the library, attending evening lectures, studying with friends? Or perhaps enjoying less academic pursuits with someone he would not be embarrassed to introduce at parties?

One evening during the second week of December we bumped into each other leaving Cross Campus Library. It was a blustery night and the streets were quiet. Classes were over but we both had immense quantities of work to finish up before the holidays. We walked along and chatted until our paths were about to diverge.

"Would you like to stop up for a drink?" said Anthony.

A surge of excitement—were things becoming more serious?

"OK," I replied evenly. "If you're sure."

I had never set foot in his room in the Hall of Graduate Studies; he had visited me the previous evening, which made his invitation even more unexpected. But nothing surprised me as much as my first glimpse of his living quarters. In my speculations about Anthony's digs I had pictured an architectural equivalent of "well groomed": perfectly organised files, a closet filled with neatly arranged trousers and shirts, posters commemorating lectures, exhibitions, and other cultural events at Oxford. Perhaps a formal family portrait, all the faces as distinguished as his.

The first impression I had when he turned the key and bade me enter was one of precarious verticality: mountains of paper, clothing, and books; piles everywhere, on the desk, on the bed, on the floor. He could open the door only halfway, and we carefully crossed the maze towards the only two unencumbered surfaces in the room, the chairs positioned at either end of a small writing table.

"So. Here we are." Anthony smiled grandly, as if receiving me at Manderley in an oak-panelled study with a blazing fire and a butler poised to serve sherry.

"Yes. Here we are."

At least that much was settled.

"What would you like to drink?"

"What have you got?"

"Nothing here, but there's a Coke machine down the hall. Or I could make tea or coffee." He scanned the room, picked his way over to the desk, and set to pitching papers onto the floor, eventually raising the kettle in triumph.

"Voilà. I knew it was here somewhere."

"Tea would be great."

"Super. I'll just pop out for some water."

He was about to open the door when the phone rang.

He halted, his hand clasping the doorknob, his back to me. The ringing continued.

"Don't mind me," I said pleasantly. "Go ahead, answer."

He stood immobilised in a Pompeii-like pose amidst the rubble of his room, still facing away from me, the kettle dangling from his right index finger. The phone went on, fifteen rings, sixteen. I felt as if I were counting the cars of a passing train. Twenty-one, twenty-two. Who was at the other end? I fought the impulse to pick up the phone, to implore whoever had the right to ring at such an hour not to snatch away the flimsy illusion that I might one day capture Anthony's heart.

The phone fell silent. Anthony turned back towards me. His forehead was perspiring, and he looked shaken. He said nothing but set the kettle down on a precarious pile of library books, undoing the delicate equilibrium. The tower came crashing down. Without so much as a peep, he knelt on the floor and commenced the task of constructing a stabler pile of books.

I wended my way through the maze of Anthony's room and put my hand on his shoulder. Still crouching, he took it and pressed it against his cheek. We remained motionless for a time. He kissed my hand, a more sentimental gesture than was his wont, took a deep breath, and slowly came to his feet.

"I couldn't answer that. I'm sorry to say I shall have to ask you to leave."

Something in his tone caught my attention. Was this a farewell or a good-bye?

"Rain check?" I murmured, my voice choking up.

He shook his head. "I can't do it any longer."

"Do what?" I asked, though I knew the answer.

"This." He waved a hand through the air. "What we've been about for the past three months. It was . . . unrealistic."

I had known from the start that this day would come. The phantom caller who had attempted to ring through was his true mate, my opposite: confident, assertive, unapologetic. I fought the impulse to beg Anthony for a reprieve, the concession of friendship, perhaps. Under certain circumstances are the humble not allowed to fraternise with the high and mighty? Such a request would come to naught. The first thing I gleaned from Shakespeare in ninth grade was that there are times when fate is just fate, despite our best efforts at overcoming it.

I'm not breezy by nature—with me, the slightest contretemps is high drama—but years of observing my betters have taught me how to counterfeit nonchalance. I gathered my books.

"Sorry you feel that way, Anthony. Nice knowing you."

I stood by the door. He had his back turned towards me but a hanging mirror allowed me to see his face contorted with anguish. I could barely hear his final words.

"Good-bye, Reb. Thanks for being so . . ." He didn't finish his sentence. As I tossed in bed that night listening to the shards of my heart, I felt a sickly curiosity spread over me like a creeping rash. When at last I forced myself to close my eyes, I saw the shadow of a figure whose features I could not discern and whose actual name I did not know but who was fast becoming my own private Rebecca.

chapter 7

It takes Eric and me almost two hours to swim across Lake Monona and back in the dark, including a pause on the opposite shore during which we mostly try to keep our teeth from chattering and barely exchange a word. At the house, after hot showers, the cold pasta salad I have prepared seems reasonably appetising but the dinner conversation limps along by fits and starts. Eric asks me polite questions about my childhood, and I gather a few basics about him as well. He grew up on a dairy farm near Oxford, Wisconsin, about an hour north of Madison; his parents, approaching retirement age, have sold their cows but still raise corn and soybeans. He came to Madison as an undergraduate and did most of law school here as well, having started elsewhere but dropped out after a semester and transferred back. He keeps it all vague, and aside from the coincidence of his hometown—Anthony did his bachelor's degree at the other Oxford— I cannot fathom what information remotely pertinent to Anthony's 11:11 message this softspoken colossus might yield. I am relieved that he questions me no further about Anthony.

I pour us a nightcap. The evening air has turned cool and we both remain chilled from our stint in the water; in spite of the season I suggest lighting a fire. We sit in front of the fireplace on the matching leather recliners Anthony and I bought for our tenth anniversary a few months before he died.

Eric downs his cognac, coughs, and clears his throat.

"So. What was he like?"

I catch my breath, my relief premature. I look away from the portrait of Anthony and me hanging on the wall, fearing I might break down again. I steel myself to the pain.

"He was—well, I suppose he was just about perfect."

"In what way?"

"Every way. Brilliant. Kind. Amusing."

"Lucky man."

"Yes, I suppose he was. Until he got sick."

"No, I meant you."

If he only knew, I think, but I say simply, "No argument on that one."

Eric reaches for the decanter and pours himself another glass of cognac. I have barely touched mine. He gazes into the fire.

"How did you meet?"

I shut my eyes, my mind flooded with memories of the comely young man seated across from me in the tepid sauna, glowing with health but with only a decade to live. I can recall every syllable of the odd, understated banter of that magical evening, but how can I share these relics with the random stranger seated across from me now in Anthony's place?

"At a costume party," I finally say. "It was Halloween."

Eric teases one of his curls with his left hand. "I see. Not much time for Halloween once you're living in the adult world, is there? Haven't been to one of those parties since my first year of law school. Who did Anthony go as?"

I pause, as if having to retrieve the memory. "Oh, yes. Margaret Thatcher."

"Hmm. So you fell for him in drag?"

I have overlooked that angle. It isn't true, but I have painted myself into a corner. "I don't recall, exactly. Guess I must have."

"You didn't know what he looked like the whole time he was chatting you up? Or did you hit on him?"

"No, I suppose it was mutual." Of course it never quite was, but no need to go into that. I force a smile. "How about you? Are you involved with anyone?"

"No." With his lower lip locked into place over the upper one and his blond eyebrows set, he has the engaging air of a tax criminal being questioned by the IRS.

I glance at my watch: almost midnight. I catch myself starting to nod off.

"Sorry, Eric. I don't mean to be rude, but I didn't get much sleep last night."

He stands, walks over to me, and puts a hand on my shoulder.

"I didn't say it earlier," he murmurs, "but I'm sorry about . . . it must have been very difficult for you. Please accept my sympathy for your loss."

I have received condolences from countless friends, family members, and acquaintances, but always in circumstances in which I was forewarned; with Eric I didn't see it coming. Memories flood back willy-nilly: striving to keep Anthony's illness secret, as he insisted; wondering how it would all end; after it did, never forgetting that I left him for the last time on the day he died when all he asked was for me to stay. And beneath it all, part and parcel of the barely discernible foundation of my psyche, the obscure awareness of the painful imbalance in our relationship. At warp speed I relive the daze of Anthony's funeral and its aftermath, the racing-circuit emptiness of my survivalist routine. It all clamours for release. And it is beyond my control to hold it in a moment longer.

When my crying jag has run its course, I see that Eric has taken a seat on the futon and is watching me from across the room. I make my way over and sit down beside him, I stammer an apology for my outburst and thank him for his kind words. I am utterly spent and ask him if he minds seeing himself out. He stands and smiles. I recline on the futon and close my eyes.

I awaken just as the beginnings of light are coming in from the east. Aunt Magdalena's afghan has been thrown over my legs.

I have dreamt of Anthony for the first time since his death. In the dream I am sitting next to him on the edge of our bed in the very early morning. He lies motionless and at first I think he is dead, but the phone begins to ring, and he says in the imperious tone of voice he sometimes used in the days before his illness, "Take a message. Make sure to get the name right. Hard to spell, hard to spell!" I find I have answered the phone and now Anthony is on the other end of the line, struggling to breathe. All he can do is cough and gasp, but in the dream I have been granted the power to understand these inarticulate sounds. "How could you, Reb?" they are saying. "How could you possibly let this happen to me?"

I sit up and look around, lost at sea. I can't recollect how I came to be on the futon.

"Don't be frightened." Eric, seated in one of the recliners, is gazing at me. "I didn't want to leave you alone."

He waits for me to speak. I lie back down and close my eyes.

"I haven't slept on this futon since he died. It was our bed for those last weeks. He was too weak to climb the stairs on his own and he was afraid of getting stuck upstairs if we carried him, his father and I. He was afraid he'd never make it back down."

"So the futon must be where he . . . ?"

I nod, my eyes still shut. I can see Anthony, his eyes closed, drawing his last, slow breaths. "When the nurse pronounced him dead . . ."

I fall silent. Eric says, "What did you do?"

I shake my head.

"Just tell me," he says. "Don't think about it. Say it."

He comes over, sits beside me, and takes my arm. I open my eyes.

"I felt for his pulse."

"Why?"

"I don't know. I could see he wasn't alive. His face, his colour, everything changed immediately. But it seemed impossible that his heart would have stopped from one second to the next."

"Did you feel anything?"

"What do you mean?"

"Was there a pulse?" Eric's pupils are dilated in the half-light.

"No, there wasn't."

He nods. "Then what did you do?"

"Made arrangements. I could never bring myself to ask him about it, so we looked in the phone book and called a funeral home."

"Right then?"

"The nurse said we couldn't wait. For health reasons, I suppose. Anyway, it would have been worse in the morning."

"So he died at night?"

I nod. TIME OF DEATH: 11:11 P.M. I muse at my naïveté in believing those numbers could go on evoking the happiness of love when ours was one that was never truly shared.

"What happened when they came to take him?"

"The doorbell rang. There were two men. So ordinary in appearance, as if they had stopped by to pick up old furniture we were donating. I wondered if they wore gloves with everyone or if it was because of AIDS. They said each of us could take as much time alone with him as we needed. His mother looked briefly at me, then at the floor. Her face was frozen. She shook her head wordlessly and made her way upstairs. Anthony's father, Gerald, stayed with him for a long while. I sat in the kitchen with the funeral parlour men and listened as his cries of distress filled the house.

Eventually his voice gave out and he stumbled into the kitchen, his eyes swollen shut.

"It was my turn. I went in. He was lying on the futon. I tried to imagine that he was napping, waiting for me to return from my swim. I stood in the doorway, pretending, for one final moment, that I would get a chance to relive the day and watch the skaters on the lake with him, as I had promised. I walked to the futon, leaned over, and kissed him on both sides of his forehead—it was our bedtime ritual. I whispered that I loved him more than life and asked him to tell me how I could live without him. I couldn't make myself wait more than a few seconds for a response."

Eric stands and faces the lake, his back to me, his voice barely audible.

"Did you ever figure that one out—how to go on without him?"

Is he, too, thinking of someone? I don't have it in me to question him, so I say nothing.

"Where was he buried?" asks Eric.

"He wasn't. He was cremated."

"Where are his ashes?"

"His mother has them. I never asked to see them."

"Why not?"

He waits in vain for a response. He turns to face me.

"I must get going. I promised my folks I'd spend the day in Oxford."

I stand, adjust my clothing.

"Thank you for staying with me. Can I make you some coffee? Did you get any sleep?"

"I dozed in the recliner. You take care of yourself now, you hear?"

Just before Eric exits the room he says, without turning around, "Can I see you again?"

chapter 8

In the days after I was shown the door by Anthony in early December 1980, I did my best to distract myself from our breakup. The end-of-semester crunch kept my mind occupied during the day, but at the time when he might have rung in the past, I felt the full force of his absence. I tried to ignore the alarm clock's poignant display but found my eyes drifting over to it each evening at 11:11.

I consoled myself that if our unlikely pairing had been a pipe dream from the start, at least it was not one purely of my own fabrication. For all its implausibility, my relationship with Anthony had not been a mere fantasy but had a basis in the real world. A flesh-and-blood heartthrob had been in my life for three months and to all outward appearances— if beyond all reasonable explanation—it was he who had taken the lead throughout, from start to finish. It was he who had been the one to strike up a conversation in the sauna, to suggest we see *Rebecca* together on that first evening, and to ask if he might stop by my flat after the film and dinner. It was he who was the one to visit me regularly on his own initiative, he who invited me to a Halloween party, even he, ironically, who asked me up to his room on that final cataclysmic evening. I had never demanded a thing from him or challenged him in any way, not uttering a word about his rude behaviour on the night of the Halloween party or about the fateful phone call he had received as I sat tremulously by. Perhaps most importantly of all, I had not once given him a glimpse of the extent of my adulation, knowing that it could never be reciprocated and would simply embarrass him.

When December 22 rolled around, I handed in my grades, pedaled over to East Rock Park for a long, glacial run, then curled up on my sofa bed with a glass of store-brand eggnog that I had purchased at Pegnataro's Supermarket. I had too much to do to be able to spend the holidays with my family in Chicago or celebrate with friends closer by; the next three weeks were to be devoted to preparing two new classes for the spring semester and starting the painstaking process of revising my dissertation into a book. The latter task, on the basis of my rereading of the introduction, seemed as appealing as working up memories of lame sexual encounters into a film version of the Kama Sutra.

The teetotaler eggnog wasn't doing it for me, so I dragged a kitchen chair to the high cupboard containing my small stock of alcohol and foraged about till I found a flask of bargain-basement bourbon purchased in September to celebrate having survived my first week of classes. I poured the remains of the bourbon into my eggnog and took a gulp. Like the two tasks that lay ahead for Christmas break, the combination was exponentially worse than the sum of its parts.

I was roused from a deep slumber by a ringing noise around 6 p.m. I reached for the alarm before registering that it was the phone.

"Hello."

"Anthony here."

"Whatsat?"

"Is that you, Reb? Your voice is queer. Are you all right?"

I had no idea what to say.

"Reb, are you there?"

I sat up slowly. My head pounded.

"Yes, I'm here." I took a few moments to collect my wits. "Where are you?"

Embarrassed throat-clearing at the other end of the line.

"I'm actually in the lobby. Can you buzz me up?"

The pros and cons entailed by this seemingly straightforward request were too convoluted for my woolly brain to address, so I put down the phone and leaned on the buzzer. By the time I had washed my face, combed my hair, and thrown a few odds and ends into a closet, there was a discreet knock at the door.

"Hullo, Reb."

Anthony was carrying an impressive rucksack; he edged his way in. He formed a smile with his mouth, but the rest of his face refused to follow suit, his eyes besieged, his colour sallow. He looked like the shipwrecked version of a luxury liner.

"Put that down anywhere," I said. "Take a seat. Would you like some wine?"

"Yes, please."

I poured the remains of a week-old bottle of burgundy into a wineglass and handed it to him; too bad if it tasted of vinegar. I also collected my half-consumed tumbler of bourbon and eggnog. I hadn't quite slept off my intoxication but had a feeling it would require a booster.

Anthony settled into the swivelling chair next to the picture windows, gazed over the lights of downtown New Haven bordered by the blackness of Long Island Sound in the distance, then wheeled back around to face me.

"I intended to ring," he said, "honestly I did. Please forgive me, it's not that I didn't want to speak to you."

"It's nice of you to stop by," I said noncommittally. "I thought you'd be in England or Manhattan by now."

"On my way to New York. Planning on catching the eight o'clock to Grand Central."

I nodded.

"All finished with your semester?" I asked.

He nodded. "You?"

I nodded again and drained my eggnog concoction. As it started to take effect, I turned over in my mind the tempting possibilities of this jilted lover's dream scenario, but what good would come of making a scene? The most likely explanation for Anthony's presence was that he was tying up loose ends on his way to New York so as to have a clean slate with Santa before gift-giving rolled around. I should accept his apology, if one was forthcoming, say a proper good-bye, and send him on his way.

"May I ask you something?" I said with forced decorum.

"Sure."

"What are you doing here?"

He smiled shyly and looked flustered. He spoke with a tone of voice I had never heard.

"I've come to ask you if you would spend Christmas with me and my family in New York."

All I remember of the next couple of hours is throwing some things into a bag, stumbling into a taxi in front of my building, and hightailing it onto the New York train, which we nearly missed. I must have dozed through the trip, because the next thing I recall is the bustle of Grand Central Station and a taxi ride to Greenwich Village, where Anthony's sister, with whom we were to spend Christmas, lived and had her psychotherapy practice. Dad and Mummy would arrive the following evening.

I was still feeling shell-shocked when I followed Anthony into the lobby of a large, well-appointed building on Jayne Street around 10:30 p.m. In my experience New York doormen practically fingerprint you if you want to go up to someone's flat after ten, but Anthony's voice was firm as he announced, "Anthony Payton to see Dr. Payton," and the doorman, perhaps taken down a peg by his accent, replied genteelly that he was expected.

Anthony's sister was standing in front of the lift doors when they opened at her floor. She looked close to thirty and was as striking as her brother, nearly as tall as he, her height accentuated by the long straight hair that fell to the middle of her back. It was of a deep chestnut colour that contrasted fetchingly with her light-blue eyes and fair skin. Quite the opposite of Anthony, whose earnest mien seemed more English than Irish, her face showed barely a trace of the twenty-three English chromosomes she had inherited from her mum; it wore a barely contained amusement at life's absurdities. Her stylish figure was nicely set off by black toreador pants presumably excavated from some vintage clothing store and a billowy white blouse girded by a grey canvas belt that matched expensive-looking espadrilles.

My head spinning from the quick ride in the lift, I struggled to maintain my equilibrium as the two siblings sent loud smacking noises in the direction of each other's cheeks. The lift doors were about to shut when Anthony swung about and wedged the fingers of his right hand between them with enough force to send them snapping back to attention.

"Reb, what are you waiting for? An invitation?"

To buck myself up I reminded myself that this was the timorous young man who several hours earlier had humbly asked me to spend Christmas with his family. Since Anthony was not forthcoming with an introduction, his sister said, "Oh, hello, I didn't . . . Anthony, is this that friend of yours? Rick, or Ricky, wasn't it? You were so vague on the phone last night I wasn't sure he was coming." Anthony blushed and said nothing.

I swore to myself, extended my free hand—the left one, naturally—and said shakily, "You must be Dr. Payton. I mean Anthony's sister. Are you . . . ?" Shit. What was her first name? "I'm his . . . Reb." She suppressed a giggle with the back of her hand, which made things worse. "Reb Matkowski. Not Ricky, Rebby, if you will, although no one actually—"

"I'm Miranda," she said, graciously stretching out her own left hand to take mine, "and yes, let's dispense with the formalities. You may call me Anthony's sister rather than Dr. Payton. I shall call you Rebby."

Her smile was reminiscent of her brother's, although for some reason the boy himself now looked peeved. He turned to me and said gruffly, "Come along, the hallway is no place for introductions."

In contrast to Anthony's overstuffed living space in the Hall of Graduate Studies, Miranda's flat was sparsely furnished with tasteful pricey items. She ushered us to a white leather loveseat in the sitting room. I gazed with longing at the matching sofa, wishing I could stretch out and let my head spin me peacefully into oblivion. Before I had the presence of mind to protest, tumblers of scotch had been set down on two of the handsome Wedgwood blue coasters that were positioned round the Danish teak coffee table with perfect symmetry, their hue echoed by slate-coloured flecks in the geometrically patterned grey-and-white area rug.

I calmed down a smidgin after a swallow of scotch—Miranda's expensive tastes extended to whiskey—but eventually the siblings' chatter tapered off and I sensed that the dreaded ritual of discussing the nature of my relationship to Anthony was upon me. It was a topic on which I myself could have used a debriefing.

"So, Reb. Are you a postgraduate student like my darling bro?"

"No, I teach at Yale." The statement sounded only a tiny bit less absurd to my ears now that my first semester of teaching was over. Miranda smiled but said nothing, as if encouraging me to go on. I had nothing more to say on the matter, so my South Side voice adlibbed, "Yale University in Connecticut. Have you heard of it?"

Miranda skipped a beat, then went on in her therapist's voice.

"Yes, I have," she said with a smile. "You seem quite young to be a member of the faculty."

"Don't feel so young. You just think, because my hair—"

I attempted but failed to stifle a sneeze, which broke my train of thought.

"Your hair, you were saying?"

"Yes, you know, because it's not gay. I mean not grey."

I spilled scotch on the coffee table in attempting to set my glass back down. Miranda took care of the mishap and refilled my glass. Anthony shot me a look.

"Sorry, Miranda. Reb is not quite himself this evening."

Miranda sat back down and crossed her legs.

"So, how did you two become acquainted?"

She looked at me. I looked at Anthony.

"It's quite a funny story, really," said Anthony. We met at a . . . oh, you know, one of those language tables at one of the colleges. A French table. Everyone sits round and practises their French while they're eating lunch."

I wondered why Anthony had made up this story. Nothing untoward had happened in the sauna on the day we met, but perhaps the fact that we had eventually hit the sheets that first evening made him reluctant to discuss the occasion.

"How was that a funny story?" inquired Miranda.

"Well, not funny ha-ha," said Anthony, "but you know, funny strange, sort of . . ."

"How so?" pursued his sister.

"Not strange, it was just a coincidence."

"Oh, did you know each other already? Then how did you actually meet?"

I had a feeling Miranda could see right through her brother and was waiting for his nose to start growing. She let him stammer for a moment, then said:

"God, they never stop, these Americans. Self-improvement while you eat. Perhaps they'd do better practising their English rather than their French."

I didn't find this funny but managed a guffaw.

The doorbell rang. Miranda stood and walked slowly towards the foyer.

"How peculiar. Usually the doorman rings ahead, and I'm not really expecting—"

The sound of the door opening.

"Dad! Mummy! What a lovely surprise!"

chapter 9

Before I had quite registered what was happening, there they were, Mr. and Mrs. Payton, poised in the entryway. Anthony rose to greet them, his pallor suggesting that the Ghost of Christmas Future was allowing him to preview a scene for which, in the event, he had no idea how to prepare in real life.

"Hullo, Mummy, what a nice surprise!" he got out. "I thought . . . Miranda said you were arriving tomorrow evening."

A handsome woman about the same height as Miranda strode into the room. Her face was a severe variation on Anthony's. That Julia Payton was an army nurse during the Second World War, as I later discovered, didn't surprise me, as she had retained her military bearing. I assumed her to be in her fifties, but she had the hale radishy complexion of a younger woman who spent much of her time outdoors. She wore a beige jacket-and-skirt combination purchased at the kind of high-end store where customers pay through the nose to look casual. Heelless walking shoes had been chosen to avoid accentuating her three-inch height advantage over her husband, but it was rather a wasted gesture in light of the towering pompadour into which she had arranged her lovely ash-blond hair.

Mrs. Payton gave her son a businesslike peck on the cheek.

"Darling, I know it was to be tomorrow, but the booking agent rang us yesterday with a last-minute cancellation and we thought, why not get a good night's rest before the preparations are hard upon us? I expect Miranda will be grateful for the extra pair of hands to lighten her load." Mrs. Payton was turning towards me when her husband made his entrance.

"Anthony," he exclaimed, "aren't you going to give your old dad a Christmas hoog?" He spread his arms wide, and he and Anthony engaged in the usual male back-thumping ceremony.

Mr. Payton must have been a heartbreaker in his younger days, but unlike his wife, a sturdy perennial, he was a flashy annual gone to seed. He was short, five-seven perhaps, and aside from a bit of a pot belly, remained reasonably well set up, but his smile, a dead ringer for Anthony's, couldn't quite distract from his sparse white hair, rheumy eyes, and sagging skin. His wardrobe smacked of clearance tables: out-of-style bell-bottom jeans, white tennis shoes with brown laces, and a navy-blue jumper of the type you could in 1980 still find at any number of Oxford Street stores for ten quid.

There was a clumsy silence during which the new arrivals resisted staring at me.

"Well, Anthony," said Miranda brightly after seating us all, "are you going to do the honours, or shall I?"

Anthony nodded.

"Mummy," he began slowly, "this is Reb. Reb Matkowski. Reb, my parents, Julia and Gerald Payton."

Julia Payton nodded courteously. I stood and shook Gerald Payton's hand.

More silence as everyone, excluding Anthony but including myself, wondered what exactly I was doing in their midst.

Miranda bustled into the kitchen and came back with a tray. She served Gerald a tall gin and tonic and set the bottles nearby in case he needed a refill, then poured her mother a glass of sherry.

"Reb, was it?" said Julia politely after taking a sip. "What an unusual name."

I knew Julia Payton had named Anthony after a character in Shakespeare and thought it likely that was also the case for Miranda, surely an homage to *The Tempest*, but it seemed doubtful she would approve of calling a child after an evil character of the wrong sex deceased before the story even begins.

"It's an old family name," my South Side voice chipped in without having asked my brain's permission. "It means 'fiercest of fighters' in Middle High Polish. In the fifteenth century it was reserved for the prince's honour guard. My great-great-great grandfather, who was a prominent landowner near Krakow, was called Reb."

A line appeared between Julia's brows as she attempted to process this pixilated nonsense.

"How interesting," she said evenly. "Have you come to New York to celebrate the holidays with your family?"

I waited for Anthony to speak up, but Miranda had whispered something in his ear and the two were laughing. Our eyes locked briefly, and I tried to transmit a Morse code SOS with rhythmically raised brows, but he didn't seem to be following, so I turned back to Julia.

"No, actually, Mrs. Payton, I'm originally from Chicago. I live in Connecticut now. That's where I met Anthony."

"Chicago. Aha." She smiled benevolently and addressed her husband. "We've been to the East Coast and the West Coast in America but never to the Midlands, have we, darling?" Gerald, two and a half sheets to the wind, briefly came to attention and shook his head. "Are your family still there?"

"Yes."

"How nice that you could spend a bit of time in New York on your way to visit them."

Anthony was still engaged in a giggly whispered exchange with Miranda, whether by chance or by design I couldn't say.

"As a matter of fact," I said, "I'm not on my way to Chicago. My understanding is that I am to spend the holidays here with you fine people."

A sharp intake of breath from Julia. Anthony drew himself up and said: "Sorry I didn't make myself clear earlier, Mummy, but I've invited Reb to spend Christmas with us. I hope it's all right. Miranda said there's plenty of room."

"Super," said Miranda. "I was hoping you'd be able to join us. I've put Anthony in my office, and there are two couches in there that are quite comfy for sleeping. I made them both up this morning, just in case, because last night when I spoke to you on the phone . . ."

"Been through all that and now we're here aren't we?" Anthony punched out words like a teletype machine. He shook his hair out of his eyes and continued more tranquilly. "Say, anyone else feeling peckish? We haven't had a bite to eat this evening because the timing didn't quite work out."

That was putting a bright face on the evening's upheavals. Julia Payton lifted a Wedgwood coaster from the coffee table and examined it.

"Miranda, are these the ones Auntie Barbara sent for your birthday? She mentioned them last week when she rang up to wish us bon voyage. Massive sale at Harrod's. Clever her, to have remembered those little blue flecks in the carpeting." She put the coaster back and took another sip of sherry. "Something to nibble on mightn't be a bad idea. The food on TWA is not what it was. Don't go to any trouble, Miranda. Have you got any bread and Marmite? You know how irritable Anthony gets when he's famished." She looked at her son and smiled grandly. "When the day comes that you bring along the girl you're planning to marry, that's the first piece of advice I shall give her."

The odd assertion seemed to imply a hidden agenda but as I didn't know Julia, I couldn't be sure. Anthony, who presumably was, went red in the face, his mouth set.

Gerald Payton, whom I had been watching go down by the stern, was just passing through forty-five degrees. His eyes were closed and his head drooped a few inches above the armrest.

"Honestly, Julia," he said, opening his eyes and sitting up, "what's the point of asking for bread and Marmite? Where would Miranda find Marmite in America?"

"Strange as it may seem, dear Papa," said Miranda, "I have actually got Marmite. You can find anything in America if you know where to look."

As if Miranda's last line were a preestablished cue, Anthony cleared his throat, shot a meaningful glance at me sitting beside him on the loveseat, and encircled my shoulders with his arm.

"You're quite right, Miranda," he said. "Mummy, Dad, I've only been in America for four months, but I've found something I could never have found in England. He's sitting right here."

In the past five hours I had done what I could to maintain my tattered dignity in light of the turbulent turn of events, but this was too much. I pulled away from Anthony, let out a yelp of laughter, and clapped my hands over my mouth, like a third grader who has just heard Teacher utter the word "penis" aloud. I closed my eyes, counted "one thousand one, one thousand two, one thousand three," and waited for the kaboom.

I looked up to find Julia Payton sitting motionless, white as marble, like a statue of Niobe or some other martyred mother as rendered by a gay artist with equal influences from classical sculpture and Roy Lichtenstein. Her face was a dignified veil of sorrow, but her hands had flown instinctively up to her pompadour, as if to ascertain that she could count on the consolation of thick, lovely hair in the wake of this sudden blow to her dynastic ambitions. Miranda, by contrast, was enjoying herself, which confirmed my suspicion that well before Anthony's announcement she knew exactly what was what.

Suddenly Gerald Payton, whose reaction to the little minidrama was illegible, broke the silence. He raised his glass and said:

"That's saying it like it is, my boy. Let's drink to friendship. Most important thing in a man's life."

Anthony hesitated, as if debating whether or not to point out that this toast to friendship between men was not quite on topic. I saw stars; everything was far away. As I slumped over onto the loveseat I heard Julia's voice, now stripped of even a veneer of etiquette, cry out:

"Anthony, I shall never forgive you! How can you say such a thing at Christmas?"

The last thing I heard before passing out was the sound of her flats stomping from the room.

chapter 10

When I came to, I was lying on one of the couches in Miranda's office and Anthony was removing my shoes. He helped me into my pajamas, pulled the covers back, and guided me onto the bed, stroking my hair and humming "Macushla" as a balm to the evening's events.

I reached up and put my arms around his neck. I was still drunk and took little care about it, pulling him towards me recklessly. How tired I had grown of the cat-and-mouse game we'd been playing for the past hundred days! Suddenly his arms were around me, too, his lips pressing against mine.

A knock at the door.

"Boys, are you all right in there?" Miranda's voice, "Is there anything I can bring you before I retire?"

We held our breaths, waiting for the door, which was unlocked, to swing open, but it didn't.

"It's fine, Miranda," said Anthony, his voice as placid as if he were giving an update on the weather. "See you in the morning."

"Good night, then. Try not to fret about Mummy. She just needs a day or two to get used to the idea. We'll bring her round."

Miranda's footsteps receded down the hallway.

I sprang up, locked the door, shed my pajamas, and threw myself back onto the bed next to Anthony. I lost myself in the smell of his hair, lemony with hints of sand and vanilla, my arms clasping him as if he might come to his senses and flee into the Manhattan night.

Suddenly he thrust me away and sprang from the couch.

"I can't."

"What do you mean? What are you talking about?"

"There's actually . . . something I haven't told you."

I propped myself on one elbow. My head was throbbing, my body wracked with longing.

"What?"

"I've been . . . seeing someone. I've known him . . . I already knew him when I met you."

I fell back onto the pillow.

"Yes," I said wearily, "I guessed as much. Are you still seeing him?"

"No."

"Then what . . . ?"

Anthony sat down on the other sofa.

"I know it's dreadful telling you like this. It was getting serious. He was supposed to spend Christmas with me and the family, but I was not sure that would happen. Last night I finally rang Miranda to tell her I was bringing him to New York. And then this morning . . . It was a terrible scene." He choked up briefly, regained control. "I can't go into it. It's over, but I need time. You must give me time."

Be careful what you wish for. Anthony had belatedly come running, as I had dreamed, but only because he had been cut adrift by the heartless creature he coveted but could not have. He didn't really want me; he just needed me to soothe his battered pride. Asking for time implied that his feelings might one day change, that I would grow as dear to him as the man who had just rejected him. A flash of inebriated insight told me otherwise.

Oh, he would go through the paces. He was not cut out to play the villain of the piece. He was fond of me, perhaps loved me, even, in his way. But he would never share the kind of unslakable longing I had begun to feel for him. That would be reserved for Rebecca.

What would it have been like for Anthony if his dream of an eternal union with his soulmate had come about? My head resting on a pillow, I shut my eyes. The world was revolving rapidly, helped along by the drink but propelled by my sickly obsession. I found myself in the eerie motionlessness of a storm's eye, the deceptive lull between Anthony's thunderclap of a revelation to his family and the beclouded conditions in which I was now being asked to live out our relationship in place of his lost happiness.

Against the treacherous backdrop of a fickle blue sky surrounded by a whirling cyclone, my mind's eye imagined a perfectly turned-out young man dressed in a white tuxedo, his manicured fingers clinking a champagne flute against Anthony's in a setting reminiscent of Manderley. The air was heady and fragrant, as sweet as lilacs and as salty as the sea. The two young men, attended to by a small staff, sat on sandstone chairs before an immense, intricately carved mahogany table, its white lace cloth and matching napkins bearing a family crest embroidered long ago by some aristocratic forebear of Julia Payton's. White porcelain, delicately wrought silverware, and the finest crystal had been laid in preparation of a formal dinner party, to be held out on the lawns that sloped down to the ocean, in celebration of the union of Anthony and his Rebecca.

Rebecca laughed, his teeth flashing a flawless malignant smile less out of joy than a spiteful sense of victory over me. A strand of auburn hair fell onto his brow; Anthony reached over and pushed it back, gazing at his perfect lover's deep-set chestnut-coloured eyes, his skin like burnished marble. As the guests looked on in wonderment, Anthony led him down a secret path towards the sea. And there, on a bed of soft leaves and moss sitting beneath a centenarian oak, in a secluded spot along the little harbour open only to the splendour of the sea's waves, the two were joined for all time, heart, body, and soul.

If I did not know—would never, perhaps, find out—the reason Rebecca had given for forsaking Anthony, nothing could shake my conviction that Anthony would always experience the moment when his true lover escaped from his grasp as the death knell of his most precious longing.

You must give me time, Anthony had said, and the words now took on their full ironic meaning. The time would never come when his passion for Rebecca would be extinguished, a like desire for me ignited in its place. For him the passage of time would bear no fruit beyond whatever modest enjoyment he might receive from our union of convenience. To his mind every moment he had shared with Rebecca until the very end—however it had come about—had been an occasion for their love to bloom anew. Our time together would be built upon mildewed hopes, dreams in decay.

I opened my eyes and sat up. Anthony, still seated on the other couch, was looking bereft. I helped him to undress and to get under the covers. I kissed him on both sides of his forehead, a gesture that from that day forwards became a nightly ritual. I sat by his bedside. His face was peaceful but sombre. A thousand questions pounded in my head. I thought naïvely with a sudden surge of relief that however circumscribed his feelings for me might be, we would now have all the time in the world to get to know each other more fully—if only he didn't wake up some morning, come to his senses, and quietly slip away.

A single dark query scurried by like a renegade cloud passing across the sun in the wake of a departing storm.

"Anthony, just tell me one thing. This man, do I know him?"

He turned towards the wall.

"Let's not talk about it now, Reb. Or ever. I'm absolutely dead. Sorry it wasn't much fun for you this evening. I'll make it up to you, I promise. Think about the future." His voice was trailing off into sleep.

I waited for him to give me something more, but he spoke from his dreams.

"It's over."

My heart stalled as a wave of premonitory terror passed through my body. How could I have foreseen that these would be the very words pronounced by the nurse at Anthony's deathbed, imagined the futile hissing of the oxygen, Gerald's despairing grimace, Julia's queer extinct eyes? And yet the future I envisioned as I crossed the room and settled down on the other sofa suddenly seemed tinged with foreboding. A page had been turned in our relationship, but the story about to unfold would not lead to a shining dénouement. Anthony had made a commitment, certainly, and I would respect his request not to ask for details about the Other Man. And yet I was coming into his life not at the beginning of something that would belong to us alone, but rather at the end of something we would never share.

The destiny lying before me was to play Anonymous to a Rebecca against whom, in my heart and mind, I would never cease struggling.

chapter 11

The fact that Anthony didn't exactly treat me well in the first months of our acquaintance seemed like nothing out of the ordinary. Ever since my grandmother's death on New Year's Day 1959, I had assumed that love, like red hair or green eyes, was something you were or were not born with, and that I was not one of the chosen.

I was five at the time, and as long as I could remember I had always shared a room with my grandmother, whom I called Baba and who was my best friend. Baba spoke only Polish and couldn't read or write. In spite of having lived in Chicago for most of her adult life, she had rarely ventured beyond our neighbourhood in the enclave around Ashland and 49th Street, just behind the Union Stockyards. There she lived for decades, first with her husband—my mother so matter-of-factly referred to her late father as "the SOB" that I was seven or eight before I figured out this was not the Polish word for grandfather—and then, after his death, with us. Baba still dressed much as she had on the day she first set foot on American soil, in high-necked, ankle-length dresses of her own fabrication, with small white buttons all the way down the front from chin to shin, and knee-high stockings that revealed not an inch of leg even on the hottest summer days. She rose at dawn to bake bread every morning but Sunday, when the entire family went to Mass at Saints Peter and Paul Church on Paulina and 38th Street and Baba then prepared an enormous Sunday dinner for our extended family, including a dozen or so of my first cousins. Whatever she was doing, her wire-rimmed glasses always seemed to be smudged with flour or cooking oil. Of the two dresses she owned, one was always hanging out to dry.

Aside from my father, Baba was the only person who never treated me as if I was a nuisance. Daddy, a taciturn, gentle man who had had to quit high school at sixteen to work in the stockyards, never showed a hint of bitterness at the measly pleasures life had doled out to him; he always treated my mother and my three brothers and me with kindness. Mother, on the other hand, never forgave me for being the oops with the healthy appetite that came along when she already had three sons to feed and was longing for a daughter. However rambunctious my brothers were, none of them ever pushed her buttons as I did. I spent most of my childhood in the doghouse, not understanding why.

On weekday afternoons, while Mother was out bargain hunting at the supermarket and my brothers, Jim, Jack, and Ken, were at school, Baba would sit me down and make me "coffee," which consisted of a table-spoonful of the hot black liquid from her cherished coffeepot, the only household object she brought with her from Poland, mixed with loads of milk and sugar. She would join me at the table, pour coffee for herself as well, and set down a plate of paczki or kolachki fresh from the oven. She enjoyed listening to me babble away in English, which she could fol-low reasonably well, though she couldn't pitch in more than an occasional fractured response. And yet she always made me feel that she understood my trials and tribulations and I could confide in her about anything.

Staring into her resigned, unflinching blue eyes, I would sometimes wonder who took care of her when she was a little girl. The answer to that question, I later discovered, was no one in particular. Baba was born on a farm near Krakow, orphaned as a toddler, and raised by various struggling aunts and uncles. At seventeen she was married off to a per-fect stranger, who promptly announced they were moving to America to live with a brother of his who had settled in Chicago. The harshness of Baba's own life was likely one reason she was so good at soothing my melancholy.

You would think I would have been thankful to have Baba there, but boys will be boys, and sometimes I could not help wishing I could have a room of my own. One day, when my worst bout of insomnia ever kept me up most of the night, I awoke to discover that God had mercilessly granted me my wish.

That particular night, New Year's Eve, Baba had spent hours trying to calm me down. The older boys were allowed to stay up until eleven to lis-ten to the radio account of New Year's Eve in Times Square—we couldn't afford a television—so Baba sat with me in our room with the lights on, mending socks. Soon the only sound permeating the flat was my father's snoring, which on most nights would eventually lull me to sleep, but I was more agitated than usual because Mother had announced at dinner that she was expecting a baby; the situation clearly displeased her because of our precarious circumstances. It seemed inevitable that the impending birth would make things even worse for me.

Through the night Baba sat on the edge of my bed, stroked my hair, and brought me warm milk. She took me to the bathroom and let me walk around the kitchen like a grown-up free to wander in the middle of the night. Back in our room, she rocked me on her lap and sang songs whose words I could not understand but whose well-loved airs threaded a path through the labyrinth of darkness.

When I awoke after ten, I stumbled into the kitchen, rubbing my eyes and expecting to be greeted either by Mother berating me for sleeping so late or by Baba asking me if I wanted some juice. Instead, Aunt Eva, one of Mother's sisters, was there to tell me that shortly after dawn Daddy had had to take Mother to the hospital and that Baba—she said the words with no preparation at all—had suddenly had a stroke and died.

I knew it as soon as the words were out of Aunt Eva's mouth. I killed Baba. I kept her up all that previous night, depleting her life force by my constant demands and sick anxiety. In one of her signature rants Mother had once told me, when she found Baba and me sitting in the kitchen in the middle of the night, that if I didn't start acting like a normal child and let Baba get her rest, I would be the death of her. And today the prediction had come to pass. Although I accepted my responsibility for Baba's death, I would sooner have joined her in heaven—where I was confident that she now was but doubtful that I myself would ever gain admittance—than reveal my guilty secret to my mother.

In the long run my silence was futile. Mother lost her baby, a girl, the day after Baba died, and came home from the hospital looking as if she, too, would be an easy mark if death should decide to tap her on the shoulder. I refused to go to school for a month. I knew that as soon as my back was turned someone else would die and that that, too, would be my fault. I begged Daddy, whose death I feared most, to take me to work with him, but he patted me on the head and sighed without a word. To give me a balanced view of mid-century American parenting techniques, my mother spent the entire month of January shrieking at me. What kind of foolishness was this, not going to school? I was breaking the law. The police would be there any minute and take me away. I shouldn't bother to call her from jail, because she wouldn't come get me; I could rot in a cell until I came to my senses. It was just as well I didn't go to school. What could the teacher do with someone so stupid? Baba was better off dead. If she had seen her grandson acting so shamefully it would have made her die; I was what killed her, no matter what the doctors said. Sharing a room with me drove Baba to an early grave, my mother concluded triumphantly, and living in the same house was going to do the same to her.

The cops never came, but I knew my mother was right about everything else, so I could never hate her but only myself. For hours on end I hid under my bedcovers and whimpered. I begged God to bring Baba back and take me in her place. I even tried huddling alone in Baba's bed for a few days until Ken, my next-older brother, realised I now had my own room and took over my bed, leaving me permanently in Baba's, which he said spooked him out. He figured he'd be better off in a room with negligible me than with our oldest brother, Jim, who was a force to be reckoned with. It all seemed perfectly normal. When Ken replaced Baba as my roommate, I saw it as the first installment in God's plan to punish me for the rest of my days for killing my best friend.

One Sunday in August 1966, Mother and Daddy went out for dinner. We almost never ate at restaurants because of the expense but they usually allowed themselves that luxury once during the summer months. When they left the house I was so busy trying to get my brothers to pay attention to me that I didn't say good-bye.

Daddy never came back. And the following morning, before Mother's blunt announcement of his death from a massive heart attack had even sunk in, it seemed to me that the remotest possibility of ever again being worthy of love had been taken from me forever.

Daddy was six feet tall and built like a storage shed, undoubtedly a factor in his premature passing, but to a child he just seemed ample and reassuring, his height and girth inseparable from the other things I loved about him: the cigarish smell that, like me, followed him around; his rough whiskers in the evening when I climbed onto a kitchen chair to greet him with a kiss on the cheek; the way he would rocket me up without warning and give me a ride on his shoulders; and his shy, kindly smile.

After Baba died, every Saturday afternoon, despite the never-ending protestations of my brothers, to whom he never offered an explanation, Daddy would treat me to a little adventure, just the two of us. Right after lunch we would board the 47th Street bus, change to the El at State Street, and ride up to Lincoln Park. There we would spend hours walking along the lakefront, picking out our favourite boats in Belmont Harbor, strolling through the zoo, and eating hot dogs. I would trot along to keep up with his strides, take his huge hand when we crossed the street; occasionally he would give me a shoulder ride even after I was too heavy for such frivolities. That he didn't talk much more than Baba had didn't matter; he was a man of few words.

The last substantive conversation I remember having with him took place several months before I turned thirteen. It was a glorious Saturday afternoon in June 1966. On that particular day Mother had really let me have it at the lunch table because I had accidentally knocked over a glass of orange juice and soiled her freshly washed tablecloth. Daddy tried in vain to smooth things over; I got through Mother's high-decibel review of my failings by pretending I was small enough to climb inside my shoes.

That afternoon, after a long boat-choosing session at Belmont Harbor, Daddy and I sat along the rocks that line Lake Michigan and enjoyed the stiff northeasterly breeze. We both put on our jackets, though in our neighbourhood a few miles inland it had been in the upper 80s. How I longed to spend all my days in Lincoln Park, in the temperate atmosphere of Daddy's gentleness! I was still aching inside from Mother's knockout du jour; the various adjectives she had used to describe me—clumsy, selfish, inconsiderate, and the like—ran through my brain like a dreary fugue. I had never broached the subject of Mother's vendetta against me with Daddy. I knew he was too loyal ever to say a word against her, but what did I have to lose?

"Daddy, why is she always mad at me?"

For a while there was only the sound of the waves lapping against the rocks. Daddy peered across the lake as if he were expecting the answer to come steaming in from southern Michigan.

"She's not always mad at you, Reb. She just has a temper. She gets mad at everyone."

"Even you?" On occasion I had noticed Mother shooting daggers at Daddy, but I had never heard her raise her voice to him.

A pause.

"Even me."

"But why does she yell those things at me? I didn't mean to knock over the glass."

Daddy said nothing. He chomped off the end of a fresh cigar and spit it into the lake; elegant circles arced out from where it had hit the water. As was our ritual, he handed me his lighter so that I could flip the little wheel and guide the windblown flame to his cigar. I breathed deeply of the familiar aroma of cigar smoke mixed with lighter fluid and a hint of Old Spice aftershave.

"Your mother is a wonderful woman," he went on. "She just has a temper. Don't forget, she's had a rough time of it. Much rougher than the rest of us." Nobody had ever explained to me in so many words about Mother's abusive childhood at the hands of her alcoholic father, but I had picked up enough allusions to it to have some idea of what Daddy was talking about. He took a big puff on his cigar and turned to exhale so as to avoid having the smoke blow back into our faces, then rested his eyes on the turquoise waters. "Reb, you're too young to understand this now, but you'll find out some day that when you love someone, you have to take the bad with the good. Your mother loves all of us. She has to put up with a lot from us, and we have to accept things about her, too. She just has a bit of a temper," he concluded, as if saying the words for a third time compensated for the understatement.

Daddy died less than two months later, and in spite of my past history and the high risk of recidivism for young offenders, I wasn't aware that I had killed him until my mother informed me that I had.

For weeks after Daddy's death she didn't speak to me but she had become unusually taciturn, and it took me a while to catch on that she was giving me the silent treatment. This was a disciplinary technique I feared even more than her screaming, not only because she reserved it for truly heinous crimes but also because her silences left one to one's own devices to discover what one had done to deserve annihilation. My anxiety built as the days went by and Mother said nothing. When I asked her for something, she would either do what I asked or shake her head. To any other utterances she would simply turn her back.

One beastly late-August night, when no one in the house besides Ken, who could sleep through a tsunami, was getting much rest, I heard Mother get up to go to the loo in the middle of the night. I looked over at Ken, who was about to go off to college at Southern Illinois University on a sports scholarship, and wished with all my heart that Baba were here to reclaim her bed. Mother had not invented the silent treatment until after Baba died, but I was sure Baba could have found some way to fix things with Mother. I could bear it no longer. I sprang up and intercepted her in the hallway.

I could scarcely make out her features, her eyes puffy and red from one of the weeping bouts that she was careful to hide from us but that we all overheard in the darkness.

"Why are you so mad at me?" I stammered.

Mother looked me up and down, shook her head.

"Holy Mother of Jesus," she said in a calm voice more frightening than her shouting, "what have I done to deserve a child like this?"

"Please just tell me. What did I do?"

"What's the point? It's too late to change anything." As determined as I was not to cry, I couldn't hold back my tears. "Shhh, you'll wake the others. Now go back to bed. You know what you did. Just you think about it."

I stifled a sob. "I'm sorry. I didn't mean to do it." I was used to apologising without knowing what I had done. "Please, please don't be mad at me."

"Shush, I said. Now go to bed. All I need is for you to wake everyone up on a miserable night like this." I stood my ground. She took a deep breath. "All right, you asked for it. You didn't say good-bye to Daddy. He commented on it on the way to the restaurant. He said, 'I wonder if Reb's mad at me, he didn't say good-bye.' You broke his heart. All you ever think about is yourself. Poor man worked himself to death to put food on the table, took you out every Saturday, and you couldn't be bothered to say good-bye to him the day he died!"

I crept back to my room. I'm not quite sure how I survived that night, or the next night, or the next one. All I knew was that the pain that never completely left me was only fair punishment for killing first Baba, and now Daddy, the two souls who had loved me the most.

chapter 12

I can see how Mother might have had difficulty forgiving me for killing Baba and Daddy, but why did the Fates punish me further for so many years after they were gone by not sending anyone to allay my solitude? The morning after Daddy's funeral, Mother, in deep mourning for the husband she had adored as only a hard-nosed woman can love a dreamer, set her features, put on her new black outfit, boarded a northbound bus, and got herself a job as a legal secretary in the Loop by the evening rush hour. She also worked nights and weekends typing manuscripts for University of Chicago faculty in Hyde Park, a very long five miles from where we lived. Soon Mother decided our brighter economic prospects would allow us to move to the North Shore suburb of Evanston. My brothers' high school had become quite rough, and she wanted me to attend one where the cafeteria could safely be stocked with metal cutlery. The last occasion at which I was of the same socioeconomic background as most of my familiars—an event I think back on with a certain *nostalgie de la boue*—was my eighth-grade graduation in 1967, attended only by those pupils who were neither in police custody nor carrying around in the oven members of the class of '82.

Four years later, to everyone's astonishment, including my own, I was offered a full ride at the University of Chicago, and it was there that I met my future ex-fiancée, Anne Younger. The first week of fall quarter we both found ourselves cowering in the dining hall at a table so small we had to say something; we soon discovered we shared sexy, cutting-edge interests like meteorology, rock gardens, and dead languages. We took Sanskrit together. We kept track of the annual precipitation. We sometimes spent entire dinners talking breathlessly about tornadoes. Anne, too, hailed from the stormy Midwest—the Youngers were among the founding families of St. Paul, Minnesota—but we were both funnel-cloud virgins.

We were also virgins in the more usual sense. At Evanston Township High School I attributed the quickly waning interest of the few girls I dated to my unattractiveness rather than my lack of self-confidence and began to form crushes on the kind of upper-middle-class boys I never would have laid eyes on in our old neighbourhood. Several of them were friendly but I never made much of an attempt to get close. Having sneaked in to see *Midnight Cowboy* with Ken and forced him to explain the parts I didn't understand, I knew men could have sex with each other, though I wasn't clear on the specifics—Ken didn't know or wouldn't say.

Anne and I never saw any tornadoes, but we did lose our virginity together, and the sex was great. In fact, so was everything else. She was sweet, funny, beautiful, and intelligent. In spite of her complete disinterest in social standing, her Mayflower-studded family tree included a Supreme Court justice, several well-known philanthropists, and two United States Senators. On several occasions I visited the Youngers in the Twin Cities, and when I was seen in public with them and basked in their aura of fame, I had to pinch myself to believe it was all really happening. What was I, an immigrant chattel whose grandmother had not been able to read, doing hobnobbing with American nobility?

Anne and I spent our junior year studying in London, and it was there, on a glorious October afternoon as we strolled through Hampstead Heath, that I asked her to be my wife. Being in a new place made it easier to propose than I had imagined; the fact that the Brits tended to show a certain condescension towards all Americans, regardless of their origins, mitigated the effects of the social disadvantages from which I had long suffered in my own country.

Too late I realised that what I was experiencing as an initiation into high society seemed to Anne like the crassest form of *arrivisme*. How she must have cringed at the phony British accent I assumed, traces of which, along with my idiosyncratic vocabulary and spelling, persist to this day. I became evasive about my origins, murmuring vaguely if pressed that my family was thought to be descended from Polish nobles impoverished by political turmoil; my given name, I said, was a throwback to the English branch of the family I had fabricated for myself, declaring that they had settled in the South and fought with the Confederate "Rebs" during the Civil War.

Back in Chicago for our senior year, Anne and I began to plan for our wedding, which was to take place the summer after graduation. We would both commence postgraduate study in the fall, Anne to become a civil-rights lawyer, I, a professor of English literature. I was accepted at Harvard, she at Columbia; Boston and New York were separated by a quick train ride. The pattern of heartbreak that had plagued me for so many years finally appeared to have been broken.

In anticipation of the wedding, or so I thought, Anne lost ten pounds and started to wear contact lenses in place of her bottle-thick spectacles. At graduation she got to talking to the guy next to her, a science nerd named Peter Bianco who was planning on becoming a dentist. A week later, Anne said in her usual unruffled way that she thought we should postpone our engagement, and by early July she and Peter were registering at Marshall Field's, which she and I had done in April.

In the end, the only pattern that changed was that of the china Anne and I had selected which, to add insult to injury, Peter vetoed—or so Anne reported to me in an uncharacteristic moment of archness—as recherché.

When Anne dumped me for a dentist, I decided not to get mad but to get even. My first move was to accept the advances of Steve Hernandez, an ex-boyfriend of hers whom I had met at our engagement party the previous summer. Steve had dated Anne in high school before announcing during his senior year that he was gay. After college he moved to Chicago. A week or so after Anne broke it to me that she was moving out, I called Steve and asked if I could stop by his place in Wrigleyville. Although I was not conscious of having had anything in mind besides crying bitter tears on the shoulder of someone who knew Anne well, other bodily fluids eventually entered the mix.

Steve was a handsome bloke, with striking dark-brown hair and eyes and a gym-bunny physique; I told him I had no experience and we didn't attempt anything ambitious. It was agreeable enough while it was happening and if I subsequently felt sheepish about it, it was not because he was a man but because when I informed Anne of my delicious dastardliness at a dreary Hyde Park tavern where we had one last drink in August 1975, she shrugged her shoulders and asked if she should write Steve's name next to mine on the wedding invitation she was about to mail out.

I declined the wedding invitation, appending to my RSVP a crisp five-dollar bill with a note wishing Anne and Peter that many weeks of wedded bliss. Then I packed my things, moved to Boston, and spent a full month recovering my groove by reading, not the hundreds of pages of English Renaissance literature assigned for my graduate courses at Harvard, but the complete works of Agatha Christie, my favourite popular author and one unsurpassed, in my opinion, as a soothing voice in challenging times. Thus roused from my funk by Ms. Christie's unshakable moral core in the face of human atrocity and insightful investigations into the mysterious twists and turns of the human psyche, I caught up in my classes by late October, which left me well positioned to form a new long-term plan by the end of the semester: hurtling forwards into the dangerous realm of revenge through self-improvement.

I resolved to write the most brilliant dissertation in the shortest amount of time. I would land the most prestigious job available. I'd become a jock and compete in triathlons, lose twenty-five pounds, and dazzle people with my musculature. Athletic endeavours, at which, as a born nerd, I had only recently discovered I was more than passably good, were among the few activities that gave me regular blasts of self-confidence; in light of Baba's and Daddy's early demises, pursuing such activities might have the extra benefit of raising my life expectancy above forty-five. As for matters of the heart, I had a handful of escapades in the years between Anne and Anthony, with both men and women, but nothing serious. I reassured myself that my love life would undoubtedly fall into place once I had established myself as someone worth knowing.

In the summer of 1980 I moved to New Haven. I had my doctorate in hand, a great job, and a vermin-infested flat with a view. I was only $17,000 in the red, better than most recent PhDs I knew. I had broken the elusive thirty-minute barrier in 10k races; my waist size was down to thirty-one; and my hair remained thick, jet black, and wavy. It was time to call Anne and gloat.

She had sent me a Christmas card the previous year, so I knew she and Peter were living in New York and had a two-year-old daughter, Emily. Anne sounded pleased to hear from me and we arranged to have dinner in Manhattan towards the end of August. She suggested Chinese, but I insisted on something more upscale; it would be my treat to make up for my snide wedding gift. We arranged to meet at the Café des Artistes on 67th Street near the Park.

To demonstrate my savoir vivre, I had suggested we dine fashionably late. When the maitre d' showed me to the table where Anne was already seated, she stood and gave me a brisk hug and a peck on the cheek.

"Reb. It's good to see you. You have something on your chin."

It turned out to be a small piece of chocolate coating from the ice cream bar I had wolfed down on my way to the restaurant. I flicked it away, right onto my brand-new white linen shirt. Already I had an inkling that the evening was going to be a flop.

Anne was looking great, though I couldn't say why. She inherited a taste for simplicity from her Quaker parents; the only thing distinguishing her black ankle-length sack dress from an Amish woman's was buttons. Her light-brown hair, as always in summer graced with red highlights, was pulled back in a utilitarian ponytail. She'd gone back to glasses but with nicer frames.

"So, Reb. It's been a long time. How have you been? Why didn't you answer my card?"

"I'm sorry about that. I was finishing my dissertation and looking for jobs. It was all a total blur until last month."

"What do you think of New Haven? Peter and I were up there several months ago for a play at the Long Wharf. It's pretty grotty, isn't it?"

I thought it was, too, but I certainly wasn't going to say so.

"No, it's really nice. I've got a great flat, quite high up, with a view of the Sound."

"If you smell it as well you should get a break on the rent."

I faked a laugh. "You look good, Anne. Have I changed much?"

She took a few seconds to inspect my face in her usual unflustered way. "No, not really. You look fine. Pretty fit for an old guy. A few little lines here and there, like the rest of us." She gave my cheek an affectionate pinch. "Anyone in your life? Man, woman?—animal, vegetable, mineral? I'll bet a nice man like you could get married in a heartbeat. If that's what you wanted, of course." Her brown eyes contemplated me with fond amusement, and I remembered with a pang how utterly open-minded she had been when I told her about my fling with Steve Hernandez and my bisexuality.

To cover up how sad I was feeling about losing her, I said: "Yeah, I'm quite a catch."

"Yes you are, but that's not what I meant. I'd just like to see you happy, that's all." She smiled sweetly and looked at the menu. "I haven't eaten here before. What do you think is good?"

That's the way the entire evening went. Anne was not impressed by a single thing about me. By the time eleven o'clock rolled around and we had got through dinner and two pricey bottles of bordeaux, we had fallen back on our old standby. We were talking about tornadoes.

After dessert, which was so delectable we ordered seconds, under the combined influence of alcohol and sugar I took Anne's hand.

"There's something I need to ask," I said. "Why did you dump me? Was I that much of a loser?"

She gently withdrew her hand and assumed the sympathetic smile I used to see her give to down-and-out people when she felt compassion for what they were going through.

"Of course not. You weren't a loser then and you aren't one now. You just started acting like nothing and no one were ever good enough for you. You were always so snooty and sarcastic about everything, even making fun of things that were really important to me. I got sick of it."

"Why didn't you tell me?"

"I could see that you were going through hell, but I didn't know why—I still don't. It's not easy confiding in someone who sounds bitter and abrasive so much of the time." She sighed. "You were funny and adorable when we were first together, but after a while it changed. You were constantly demanding something—admiration, some kind of pat on the back. It was starting to drive our friends away, too."

"Like who?"

"Like Janet and Doug. You made it pretty clear you thought they weren't worth your while."

"They were incredibly dull. High school sweethearts from Akron—come on, give me a break."

"God, Reb, how did a nice guy like you turn into such a piece of work? Listen to me. I'm going to say this now because somebody's got to shake you by the shoulders. You're always trying to make up for not being classy or sexy or *British*"—she enunciated the word as if it were associated with a wasting disease—"but you're the one who's a snob. I never cared about that garbage."

"Then how come you got into shape, bought contacts, and looked for greener pastures?"

"To cheer myself up. I was miserable by the end. I just couldn't find a way of telling you."

I took a fistful of twenties out of my wallet and threw them onto the table. I stood, nodded politely, and said, "Thank you for sharing." I wasn't about to wait for change.

Back in New Haven I was so preoccupied with the start of classes that I dismissed my New York outing as a pricy but inconsequential error in judgement. It was not as if my five-year plan had been designed with Anne specifically in mind. I had known all along that what I wanted to get back at was not her in particular but life in general. There would still be plenty of opportunities for that.

I met Anthony, the man of my dreams, about a week later, and when, after that tumultuous Christmas in New York, he and I officially became an item, I considered taking a hiatus from seeking revenge on the world. Obviously he and I got off to a rocky start, but once we were really together I began to wonder if my destiny, at least as viewed from the outside, was not turning out to be rather enviable. If Anthony's reserve in matters romantic contrasted with what I imagined to be his constant displays of passion for Rebecca in the past, how many people are fortunate enough to bed down each night next to preternaturally attractive partners they adore, whatever the extenuating circumstances? After all, no one but Anthony and me knew the cruel truth, which I for one was not about to disclose: that he was the man I had chosen, I the one with whom he was making do.

chapter 13

The two and a half months that separated Ronald Reagan's election in November 1980 and his inauguration in January 1981 upended the lives not only of Anthony and myself but also of his entire New Haven circle. A matter of days after the murder of the actual John Lennon in December of that year, his Halloween-party impersonator, Molly, got ditched by Yoko Ono, who soon took off for parts unknown. Gandhi and Kunta Kinte, aka Laura Gladstone and Willis Smith, called it quits just about the time Laura's weight fell below three digits and she was diagnosed with bulimia nervosa and dropped out of school. At loose ends, Willis asked Molly out to dinner one evening and the two fell pragmatically into each other's arms. Anthony, having been given his notice by Rebecca, brought in the second string, yours truly, and after making it through that stilted Christmas at Miranda's in New York, we returned to New Haven and started keeping company.

If Anne Younger was quite a catch—or would have been, had I not bobbled the ball—Anthony was a glowing meteorite grabbed white-hot on the rebound. Astounding good looks, cultivation, intelligence, and class, or what in America passes for it: wowed by his accent and manners, few of the Yanks he met thought to question him about his Irish surname or his father's family tree. His outfits were always slightly offbeat but in ways that tickled the eye: sage-coloured jeans, white oxford shirt, and camel hair sport jacket; grey pleated trousers worn with a red flannel shirt, a black vest, and beige wingtips; khaki shorts, matching cotton top, and tan moccasins. Whether Anthony's yellow hair was combed or windblown, it suited his look to a T. His voice so incongruously blended the cultivation of a "U" British accent with the conviviality of an Irish tenor that he could bewitch his listeners while reciting a weather report or tickertape stock prices. At his passage, women and men alike turned to steal a second look at this extraordinary creature. They all wanted Anthony, but he was mine. Or so everyone believed.

On my way home from the library each evening at around half past nine, I walked over to the Hall of Graduate Studies and phoned Anthony's room from the locked street door. He always sounded pleased to hear my voice and would soon bound through the gate and give me a bear hug. As we walked over to my flat a few blocks away, he was enthusiastic and attentive, matching my steps, remaining close by my side, even clapping a hand round my shoulder from time to time. His eagerness as we entered the lobby of University Towers must have led the smirking doorman to wonder what shenanigans were occurring once the lift doors had shut behind us.

No sooner would we cross the threshold of my flat than Anthony would become restless, guarded. We would undress in silence, sit side by side. As I contemplated his eyes they would become unfocussed, as if gazing at a distant seascape. While I lost myself in my passion, he acted with a sort of deliberateness, as if the matter at hand had an etiquette that kept the participants from overstepping certain unposted but agreed-upon boundaries. For me, our nightly embraces were a series of revelations about how much I could love a man. Anthony treated me with the tenderness one might show a homeless pup.

There were certain amatory activities that we had not engaged in during the three-month dry run of our relationship and from which we continued to refrain. I was unsure of the reasons but followed Anthony's lead, afraid of rocking the fragile buoyancy of a boat I feared might capsize under weighty demands. Because I had lived out the first years of my love life with a woman and the flings I'd had with men before meeting Anthony had been quick and superficial, I had few set expectations about the details of what men did with other men to express a deeper kind of love. While I have never thought that the gay categories of "top" and "bottom" are as rigid as some people seem to believe, it did occur to me that some sort of incompatibility along those lines might exist between Anthony and myself, but questioning him about the matter might encourage him to dwell upon yet another unsatisfactory aspect of what from his perspective was clearly a less-than-ideal bond. The last thing I wanted to do was to send him in search of greener pastures.

Be that as it may, we soon fell into the type of routine typical of long-term lovers, and I was content with the terms of our nocturnal pursuits.

The only aspect of their mechanics that seriously concerned me was that Anthony's reserve seemed clearly attributable to Rebecca's phantom presence between us. To my mind, and in spite of the passage of time, I, not Rebecca, remained the interloper.

On Valentine's Day 1981 a bouquet of red roses was delivered to my door first thing in the morning. I felt touched by the gesture but let down that Anthony had added nothing in his own hand but a small *A* to the card's preprinted message.

He always slept late on Saturdays, so I waited until eleven to ring him. We had not seen each other the previous evening because he had a paper overdue for his Renaissance history seminar.

"Anthony here." His voice was fuzzy; he must have been up most of the night.

"Thanks for the flowers."

"Oh, is that you, uh, uh, Reb?" he replied in a flustered tone. I wondered if he sent Valentine bouquets to too many people to have all of their given names at his fingertips.

"Nope, Loretta Lynn here to sing you a valentine." We had recently seen and loved *Coal Miner's Daughter*.

A noise of forced amusement. "Appreciate the sentiment," said Anthony, "but I'll pass. Got a bit of a migraine."

"Poor dear, shall I stop by and bring you one of my grandmother's folk remedies?"

"What's that?" asked Anthony mechanically—I pictured him looking at his watch.

"Moldy rye bread soaked in vinegar."

"Ah." A pause. "Glad you liked the flowers."

"May I return the favour? Dinner tonight?"

"Love to, but so much to do. It never ends, does it?"

"I'll treat you to the Chart House. You can't say no to that."

I had hoped that a seaside dinner would set the stage for a lovely romantic evening, but once we were seated across from one other at a candlelit table overlooking Long Island Sound, all Anthony seemed interested in discussing was the fact that in the fall he would not be able to afford to live in the Hall of Graduate Studies for a second year. He would soon have to look for a room in town or perhaps a flat to share, which he hadn't got time to do.

To my surprise he invited me to stop at his place after dinner. I had not been there since that first December visit cut short by the ringing of the telephone. A tremor of anticipation ran through me as I paid the bill. Would Valentine's Day mark the occasion when Rebecca started to lose his hold?

This time Anthony's room was in relatively good nick, books and papers hastily arrayed on shelves and the bed carelessly made, but hardly had we seated ourselves than he announced he was done in and would have a quick shower to clear his head. Was he hinting that the evening was at an end? As he began to disrobe, I said in an even-tempered tone, "Perhaps I should head back."

"No, wait."

"But if you're exhausted . . ."

"I'm all right. I shan't be a minute. Make yourself at home. If you'd like something to read, help yourself."

He slipped on a robe. I heard his steps retreating down the hall towards the communal bathroom, the shower's dull whir.

I absentmindedly glanced around the room. The only book sitting on Anthony's desk was a little blue volume placed in a prominent spot. My heart sank when I saw what it was: his address book.

Suddenly it all made sense. He had sent me flowers to assuage his conscience over the upheaval the evening would bring. He had kept his distance all throughout dinner, then lured me back to his place not for a tender interlude, but rather so that I would see this perfidious tome, staged where it could not help but attract my attention. To spare Anthony the agony of a direct confrontation, the book would somehow communicate to me, whatever Rebecca's real name was, that he remained the jewel of Anthony's heart. Among the columns of names, Rebecca would be no vestigial listing of an obsolete affection but rather the insignia of an inexhaustible infatuation. Anthony had invited me to help myself to reading materials while he exited the room to allow me time to examine his address book and understand what he was too kind to tell me—that his love for my rival, though unrequited, had prevailed, our dalliance at an end.

Of what other Valentine trysts had this date reminded him? If all of our encounters were combined, would it amount to a single night of their passion? What recollections of candlelit tête-à-têtes had been tormenting my lover while he counted the minutes in the restaurant, droning on about his housing woes to avoid any expression of sentiment, eager to slip the yoke of my touching, trying attachment? He had no desire to hurt me. This tidy blue address book, so anodyne in appearance, would be the tool to drive a final wedge between us.

I opened the book with caution, stared at the A names, and began to flip forwards. Anthony's script managed to be florid and tidy at the same time. Here and there a name, always a man, was written in careful block letters. Under C there was Simon Collier-James, at D Gordon Darcourt, and in the E section John Entwistle. F had two capitalised names, Giles Farley-Evans and Jeremy Finch. The addresses listed were in either Oxfordshire or trendy parts of London. Old flames from Anthony's undergraduate days? Yes, that was it—block letters must be the sign of a romantic attachment.

Which one was Rebecca?

To distract myself from that thought I turned to the letter M to see if and how I was listed. A surge of pleasure: Matkowski was written in block letters. But on closer inspection I discerned something sobering. Pencil marks crossed the entry out.

A mafioso reading his own name on a hit list must experience a similar feeling. This was what Anthony had been trying to tell me: he was ready to call it quits. This was why he had not written a word on the Valentine's Day card, why he had talked of nothing but impersonal matters at dinner. Back in his room, facing the excruciating task of handing me my walking papers, he had postponed it one last time with the shower ploy. At this very moment he was searching for the right words, preparing himself for the tearful scene he knew awaited him.

I was about to put the book down and leave before Anthony returned when my eye fell on the last entry under M. In that space, a rather unformed, rounded hand that resembled Anthony's usual script but had a more boyish look about it had written: RM and MAP. The lines for the address and the phone number had been left blank.

Hearing footsteps in the hallway, I set the address book carefully back in its place and tried to look nonchalant.

Anthony, rubbing his head furiously with a towel, sat down across from me. It seemed to take him an eternity to dry his hair, after which he walked over to his desk and shuffled through some papers for a few seconds. Then he turned back towards me and in a businesslike tone of voice, said:

"What say we look for a flat together for the fall?"

We began perusing the newspaper for apartments but had found nothing viable when on Income Tax Day, April 15, I bumped into Anthony between classes in Machine City, a grim congeries of vending machines in the underground passageway that linked Sterling Library with Cross Campus. To complete my tax return and prepare my classes I had pulled an all-nighter, a feat that, as ill luck would have it, is scarcely easier for insomniacs than for anyone else. I was sitting at a table sipping watery espresso when Anthony bounded up.

"Did you get any sleep?" he asked, looking equally bleary-eyed as he took a seat. I shook my head. "Poor lamb. Can't stay long—I've got a seminar report to give. But there's actually—I just bumped into Willis and . . ." He interrupted himself, reached across the table, and swept an unruly wave from my forehead. "Darling, how many times have I told you to comb your hair when you're on campus? I don't mind how you look, but if your colleagues or students—"

"OK, OK." I took out a comb and gave my hair the once-over. I was too tired and cranky to be cowed by Anthony's remonstrances. "Spare me the grooming lesson. I'm having a day."

Anthony frowned obligingly. "You are a sight."

"I know, I know. What about Willis?"

"He and Molly are moving in together. They wondered if we shouldn't all share a place."

Was living with Willis and Molly Anthony's way of not being alone with me? Would he soon suggest we all four take a huge studio apartment with the beds in the same room, spend our evenings toasting marshmallows, playing Monopoly, and singing camp songs?

"Sure, Anthony, no problem. Just as you like."

"Darling, what's wrong? If you'd rather not, tell me."

"No, no. If you prefer to look for a place just with them, or on your own . . ."

"Don't be daft." Anthony stood to go and planted a kiss on my forehead, producing a startled look on the face of the white-haired gentleman at the next table, an emeritus professor of Romance linguistics ancient enough to have learned Old French at his mother's breast. "See you tonight, darling," Anthony cried out over his shoulder. "Mad about you!"

After weeks of hunting, Willis and Molly and Anthony and I put a security deposit on the top two floors of a shabby brownstone on Bishop Street. The looks we got from the neighbours on the steamy August evening we moved in suggested that a more oddly assorted foursome had never set up house together in the history of Connecticut. Molly Matsuda, a five-foot-tall Asian American beauty, had long bleached-blond hair and was attired in cut-offs and a snug tank top that displayed plenty of cleavage. Her paramour was a handsome, six-foot-four black man with scholarly looking bespectacled hazel eyes and an afro the shape and roughly the size of Romania. As usual, the trousers he wore that day were out of fashion and a bit too short, as if he hadn't had time to shop for clothing since high school. To give the group a minimum of stability, the second couple, Anthony and myself, were of roughly the same height, eye colour, and gender.

We had so few material possessions amongst the four of us that the move took barely an hour. As we all sat in the nearly empty living room sipping lukewarm Coke, it took on a surprisingly pleasant feel, helped along by the fact that the electricity had not yet been turned on and we were seeing it by candlelight.

Around ten thirty we headed for our respective bedrooms: it was going to be beastly hot without fans but there was nothing to be done except open the windows and pray for a breeze off the Sound. Anthony and I had drawn the short straw in the bedroom lottery; our double bed left a corridor of only about two feet on either side, barely enough space to exit the tiny room without using the mattress as a trampoline.

My usual nighttime anxiety began to rise, exacerbated by the claustrophobic setup. A candle was burning on the nightstand on Anthony's side of the bed, casting ghoulish shadows in the still night air. My studio had been small but the bedroom there was the size of the whole apartment. Here the walls seemed like magnets straining to converge. I ogled them with distrust, as if they would squeeze me to a pulp as soon as I closed my eyes. I tried conjuring up a vast landscape, an endless cornfield under a cloudless Great Plains sky, but the lovely image didn't help a bit.

Anthony was nodding off. He came to and said sleepily, "Shall I kill the candle?"

"Not yet, I may have to read for quite a while. You know I never fall asleep before at least midnight."

His face morphed into a caricature of commiseration reminiscent of a jowly beagle. "Poor old Reb. What are we going to do with you?"

He mussed my hair in an irresistible way. I burrowed my head against his shoulder.

"I hope you know what you've let yourself in for," I said. "I might be up for hours. Shall I go into the kitchen to read?"

He stared intently at his fingernails as if debating the matter. Suddenly he sprang from the bed.

"Hold on—I've got it. Just the ticket."

He disappeared into the sitting room, where we had dumped most of our things, and I heard him rummaging about. He returned carrying my toolbox and an implausibly long rolled-up tube I couldn't identify by candlelight.

I sat up and rubbed my eyes. "What the hell is that?"

"Guess."

"A whale condom?"

"Wrong. It's the world."

He stood on tippy-toes, grasped the tube by its wooden rim, and let it unroll with a flourish.

It was a map of the world. Anthony had bought it for ten dollars at one of the fire sales occasionally sponsored by Sterling Library to make room for their ever-expanding treasure trove of printed wisdom. He had been storing it in a corner of his room where I had never noticed it.

"What are you planning to do with that? It's enormous."

Anthony poked his head out from behind the huge old map, grinning. I had never seen him look so much like his father. "The world is, you know?"

Seeing him half-asleep parading as a leprechaun to cheer me up at bedtime, I felt a rush of adoration I couldn't put into words, so I smiled and said, "It's upside down." He had unrolled the map from the bottom.

Still holding the map high, Anthony dutifully craned his neck to look at it. "Right you are."

He set it on the floor, fished out some nails and a hammer from the toolbox, climbed onto my side of the bed, and set to pounding it in place on the wall, oblivious to Molly's and Willis's voices calling out terms of affectionate abuse from their bedroom upstairs.

The map filled my entire side of the room, wallpaper of the world. I started to say something, but Anthony put his hand to my lips to shush me, then settled into bed.

The candle blew out in a puff of wind; I reached over him, felt around for the box of matches on the nightstand, and relit it. "Do you think this is safe? What if the candle—"

"Shhh, it's fine, darling. Don't fret. I'm here, nothing bad can happen to you now." He turned on his side. "Read as long as you like, it'll just burn out. Or why don't you try lying back, there's a brave laddie. Come on now, put your little head on the pillow. Look at the ocean—the waves will rock you to sleep." His breathing promptly took on the regularity of slumber.

At first I felt stranded, but as I breathed in Anthony's scent and stared at the vast expanse of blue in the flickering candlelight, my eyes grew heavy. That night, and for the following nine and a half years, I slept like a baby by his side.

chapter 14

From the moment Julia Payton stomped out of her daughter's sitting room upon hearing that in America one could with perseverance find not only Marmite at the supermarket but also homosexual lovers God knows where, it was clear as Waterford crystal that she was appalled by Anthony's choice of companions. I later discovered that before his dramatic announcement he had never discussed his proclivities with the family; it was as if someone they had always assumed to be a vegetarian were revealing that his preferred plat du jour was steak tartare. We somehow survived Christmas but in the years that followed, Julia took pains to avoid talking to me or even having to acknowledge my existence. After Anthony and I moved in together she delegated to Gerald the task of ringing their son so that she would be spared the sound of my voice.

Gerald and I, on the other hand, had no difficulty exchanging cordial greetings if I happened to answer the phone, and I eventually worked out that he did not fundamentally disapprove of me as Julia did. When on that fateful December 22 in New York Gerald registered that the toast he was proposing to friendship between men was not applicable to Anthony and myself, his intoxicated roar resulted not from moral indignation but rather from cognitive dissonance. Gerald had expected his son to bring home a young lady of the loftiest social standing, thus carrying to full fruition his own upward mobility by giving him grandchildren with a higher destiny than his illiterate mother would have dreamed possible. Even with a demi-litre of gin under his belt, it cannot have been pleasant for him to observe his ambitions go up in smoke, and yet once Gerald got over his shock, he was quick in his acceptance of me—or at least the idea of me, since I didn't actually see the senior Paytons again for years. He sent me yearly Christmas cards at the bottom of which he printed, in a hand so painstaking it approached calligraphy, "All the best for the New Year from your English

Dad." I never did figure out what it was about me that Gerald took to. Perhaps he found it reassuring that in spite of our distinct ways of mangling the Queen's English, we were both frustrated upstarts, proletarian brothers under the skin.

⁂

I learned much of what I came to know about the Paytons from Anthony's sister, Miranda, in the course of a weekend I spent with her in New York while Anthony was in London during the summer of 1982, after the first year he and I lived together. That Saturday evening Miranda and I went to see *Evita*, then stopped for a nightcap at a little dive off Sixth Avenue called the Golden Fleece. It was a gorgeous summer's evening, warm but with a fresh breeze off the ocean. AIDS was barely a blip on the horizon, the term not even coined until later that same year, and it seemed all of gay New York, as well as most of the straights, were taking the air and allowing their eyes to rove over the city's stunning nightscape as well as its lovely array of human flora and fauna. We sat outside and ordered a first round of drinks.

Miranda, tall and tan in a strapless denim dress and navy-blue sandals, downed her scotch in a single go. Without warning she crowed revised lyrics for the show's most famous number.

"*I screwed for you, Argentina . . .*"

We exploded in laughter, as did several people at the next table. Miranda deadpanned in a crisp BBC voice, "I admire any woman who shags for her convictions."

"But why single out poor Evita?" I countered. "Happens every day." I drained my seven-and-seven and gestured for another round of drinks. "She strutted her stuff to get out of the gutter."

The waiter, mustachioed and sporting a tank top so skimpy he might as well have been bare-chested, brought our refills. I did my best to ignore his wink.

"Kind of like Dad, right?" said Miranda. Or myself, I mused silently. My facial expression must have led her to believe I was questioning her observation because she shot me an ironic look and said, "Yes, yes, I know, I'm not saying he didn't fancy Mummy. But why?"

"Why not? She was probably charming." An image of a Walkyrie wearing pumps and a strand of pearls darted across my mind. Julia was an attractive woman, but I was fairly sure that even in her youth she was a mite too overbearing to have evoked the adjective I had suggested.

"D'you reckon?" mused Miranda. "Somehow I don't think that's why Dad chatted her up." She took a swig of her fresh scotch, leaned back in her chair, and held forth like an Oxford don. "The Reynolds descend from Edward II—fourteenth century. My maternal grandfather was a peer. The Paytons puked their way across the Irish Sea in steerage from Dublin to Liverpool about ten minutes before Dad popped out so that he would have a better life. Granny Payton could barely sign her own name."

I hadn't known how old a family the Reynolds were. And could Anthony have actually had a granny like Baba?

"I grant you they're an odd couple," I said, "but you've conveniently skipped a generation. Your peer of a grandfather didn't marry your illiterate Irish granny. Your parents are both very well educated. Why shouldn't they have been genuinely attracted to each other?"

"I s'pose they were, but I still think what really piqued Dad's interest was the name. Mummy was sweet on him all right, but a large part of it was that she was tired of being shunted off as a good match. She was pushing thirty by the time they met and was something of an old maid, at least by the standards of the day. I will give it to Dad, he has come a long way."

I had already got from Miranda that her father was once an up-and-coming architect, who in spite of his intimate knowledge of how buildings were put together, had been unable to engineer his way around his very own glass ceiling. I gathered that for the son of an illiterate immigrant to go as far as Gerald had was far more unusual in the UK than in the US.

It occurred to me that Anthony rarely talked about his parents, and I said so.

"Oh Anthony," sighed Miranda. "He wishes England had sunk into the sea as soon as his flight for America became airborne. Dad's no fool, however much he conducts himself like one at times. He was a scholarship student at a very posh public school just outside Liverpool. He turned eighteen in '42, so there was no way he could have gone to university then—did you know he was a flier for the Royal Air Force?" I sipped my cocktail and shook my head, squelching a one-liner about being surprised the RAF advertised in that way. "After the War he actually passed the entrance exam for Cambridge, but Granny was ailing and he decided to go to Liverpool University to help out."

A final round of drinks was delivered by the bartender. Over her third scotch, Miranda waxed philosophic.

"I suppose Dad's got a decent heart as well as a good head. He's really quite devoted to his children. Not so much to Mummy, but then in her own inimitable way she belittles him so. For Anthony or me he would gladly walk through fire. Don't really know why I've never given him the time of day. Perhaps it was just more expedient to model myself on Mummy." She glanced down at her watch. "God, it's late, we should be getting home." She knocked back her drink and dropped two twenties onto the table—I had paid for the theater. As we tottered up Sixth Avenue, without warning she exploded a kiss on my cheek and put her arm round my neck. "You know, Reb, that's one of the things Anthony loves about you—you're so unsnobbish. He's told me all about your family, how you came up from nothing. He's not the sort to talk much about his feelings or those of other people, but I hope you know how much it means to him to be loved purely for himself."

I knew Anthony and his sister were both wrong about my not being a snob, but it was time to test just how openminded he was about the masses—not to mention how tolerant my mother actually was about my eclectic sex life. I had told her about being bisexual just after Anthony and I moved in together; to bolster my courage I had reminded myself that in spite of her explosive fits of temper over matters of little consequence, she was tolerant on social issues. She surpassed my expectations by reacting to my announcement that Anthony and I were an item by pinching my cheek and saying, "What else is new?" Thus it was that in September 1983, to mark my thirtieth birthday, she insisted Anthony and I spend Labour Day weekend in Chicago so that she and my three brothers could help us mark the occasion with dinner at George Diamond's Steak House on South Wabash Avenue, my family's idea of a fancy restaurant.

When Mother greeted Anthony and me at the door of her flat in Evanston that evening, I was pleased to see that without being asked, she had pulled out all the stops for our little celebration. She wore a Prussian-blue evening dress of a soft, flouncy material, nicely understated, matching high heels—she is sensitive about being only five foot two—and a silver necklace with a sapphire pendant. The blue palette was flattering to her eyes and fair colouring. I felt a swell of pride at the thought that for some-one whose own mother barely owned a change of clothing, she has rather good taste. Her hair, greying but with more than a few remaining streaks of blond, was pulled back into a twisted bun. It was the first time I had seen it done that way, and a pang went through me: swanky wardrobe aside, she now resembled Baba.

Anthony passed his unsnobbishness test with flying colours, and my mother instantly took a shine to him; to this day I'm not sure exactly why. Possibly it was because she has a weakness for blonds: she still tears up when reminiscing about Larry Krapuchnik, her high school sweetheart, whom she nicknamed Goldie because of his wavy yellow locks. Then, too, though she didn't say as much, I think she appreciated Anthony's classiness almost as much as I did.

Ah, hindsight. If only during my miserable childhood I had known what was coming down the pike, I would have informed my mother when I was six years old that I would grow up to be an Ivy League bisexual with a classy British boyfriend. Maybe when I spilled a glass of milk all over the kitchen floor that would have earned me a modicum of consideration.

chapter 15

On Saturday, 7 August 1993, exactly one week after my first non-date with Eric, I find myself walking down the bike path along Lake Monona towards his flat in downtown Madison for our second one, an after-dinner drink. As I ring his doorbell, I realise I am early. He takes a long time to answer. Though he is dressed neatly in jeans and a black polo shirt, his hair is a huge fuzzy mass of yellow. He may soon be vying for the title of world's tallest blond Rastafarian.

"Sorry, I was in the bathroom." He shows me in. "Remember the place?"

"Mmm." The long futon sits in the identical spot; the wood floors remain flawless. I feel a rush of spite at the uneventfulness of the man's life over the past two years, like a flood victim desperate to pump muddy water into the high-and-dry home of his neighbour up the hill.

"What'll you have?"

"I dunno, anything."

I seat myself on the futon and scan the room. The high-security coffee trunk is open, its hinged top ajar. Inside are piles of white envelopes covered by a large rectangular object facing down. Eric says, "Hard or soft, what do you prefer?" and snaps the trunk shut. It takes me a moment to register that he is referring to the drinks on offer rather than suggesting the trunk's contents are pornographic.

"Hard," I answer, hoping my blush is not noticeable.

Eric nods and disappears around the corner, then quickly returns with a bowl of pretzels and a couple of bottles of Leinenkugel's. "Music?"

I say nothing and he pops in a CD. My ears, expecting Norwegian folk calls or, at best, Sibelius, are stunned to hear the sublime opening measures of Bach's Fourth Brandenburg Concerto, one of Anthony's favourite pieces.

I clamp my eyes shut, sucked into the time warp. When I have regained my composure, I thank Eric for listening to me talk about Anthony the other night.

"Uh-huh," he gushes, inspecting the fingernails on his left hand.

Measures and measures of silence, Bach the only modulation. It comes to me that these white walls are curiously naked. Has Eric no family, no friends, no memories? The emptiness is oddly claustrophic, as if Eric inhabited a large unfurnished prison cell. I vainly attempt to swallow a rising wave of angst with my last gulp of beer.

"Say, it's getting warm in here," I manage to get out. "Shall we go for a stroll?"

I breathe more easily as we meander down the long stretch of bicycle path between North Shore and Lakeside, sparsely used after dark. The moon has risen above the water. Traffic is light for a Saturday evening. A southerly breeze lulls the sloshing of the waves into a steady rhythm and in spite of the fact that two full summers have come and gone since Anthony's death, I feel that I am taking in the lush aromas of early August for the first time since that event. From my gut rises a savage desire to walk beside him once again, to press his hand in the benign air and lose myself in the lovely ebb and flow of British banter.

A glance to my left shocks me back into the present. I turn away and pretend to tie my shoelace. I wrack my brain for a subject of conversation that might distract me from my anguish.

"So, Eric," I say in a matter-of-fact voice, "have you been involved with many people?"

He peers at the lake, a Viking raider staring out to sea towards plunder or memories of home.

"Not many."

Why would a handsome, intelligent man in his thirties not have had many relationships unless he is a psychopath or suffers from inadequacies undiscernible to the clothed eye?

"Anything long-term?"

A pause.

"Yes."

Oh goody—another round of twenty questions.

"Someone you met in college?"

"Yes."

Seventeen to go.

"How long were you with, uh, that person?" Oops, not a yes-or-no question. If only I had had the guts to ask: was it a boy?

"A few years. Till my first year of law school."

"I seem to remember you transferred in your first year. How come?"

"Things. Just things."

"Where did you say you started?"

"I didn't. Harvard."

"Harvard? You left Harvard Law to come here?"

"Yeah, I know. Sounds like a dumb move. I had my reasons."

"That's incredible. I went to Harvard for grad school, too."

"I thought . . . I assumed you went to Yale. Don't they usually hire their own students?"

"Not always. When were you in Cambridge? I was there from '75 to '80."

He thinks for a moment, then says, "Started in 1980. I guess I just missed you."

"How old are you, anyway?"

"Thirty-four."

"Did you live right in Cambridge?"

"Yeah, just for a few months." He skips a beat. "With my girlfriend."

So he's been with a woman.

"All the law students I knew at Harvard complained about it nonstop," I say, "but they were too driven to leave. What made you buck the trend?"

"The classes . . . they were OK. It was personal. There was someone else. Broke up with my girlfriend and it fell apart. First semester of law school, it was too much."

"So you transferred to Wisconsin in the middle of the year?"

"It was too late in the year to transfer. I moved back home and helped out with the cows. It was cheaper to continue in-state, so I started up again in Madison the following fall."

"Were you still with that other person?"

"No. He found someone else."

And also with a man. I can imagine why Eric didn't make it through the first year of Harvard Law, reputed to be stressful even for those few students not involved in bisexual love triangles.

"Wow, that must have been . . . How long did it take you to get over it?"

The moon goes behind a cloud, and we walk in silence along the cause-way separating Monona Bay from the main body of the lake. Nowhere in Madison does one have a keener sense of being on an isthmus than on this narrow strip of terra firma, a lick of land just wide enough to accommo-date the road, the bicycle path, and some sleepy railroad tracks.

"Get over it?" He makes a sound between a snort and a neigh, like a wistful stallion with a sense of the absurd. An old red convertible chock-a-block with rowdy teenagers whizzes by, their shrieks of merriment low-ered a tone by the Doppler effect as the ancient vehicle passes.

"Come on. Don't you think . . ."

"I know." Eric has clearly done the drill. He continues in a monotone. "I don't mean I haven't gone out with other people. But looking back, nothing has added up to a goddamn thing. Guess I've just been putting in my time. I don't have to tell you what that's like."

I fight the urge to take Eric's hand. At my suggestion we sit on the rocks lining the shore. The spray feels good. Eric clears his throat.

"There's something . . . I hope you don't mind my asking. I never . . . the person, that guy I got involved with never introduced me to his folks. I didn't tell mine about him either, they would have . . . I just couldn't. What was it like with you and Anthony's parents?"

"We didn't exactly hit it off, but we made peace when he got sick. They moved to Madison to help me take care of him. I certainly wasn't their idea of a good match."

"What were they like?"

I reflect for a few moments.

"A strange combination. Julia's from a posh family and very proper. I suppose she has a beating heart like the rest of us, but . . . let's just say she doesn't often show it. Gerald was quite the opposite, warm and funny. A bit of a clown at times." I add snootily, "Very humble origins," as if my own were to be found in the Gotha Almanach rather than the register at Ellis Island.

"When did you meet them?"

"New York, 1980. Anthony's sister lived in Greenwich Village—still does, actually—and we all spent Christmas there. It was a few months after Anthony and I met."

"Did they know you were lovers?"

"Anthony made an announcement about it the evening we arrived."

"Out of the blue?"

"Pretty much."

Eric lets out a low whistle. "I can't imagine a scene like that." He shakes his head. "But after he told them, did it bring you . . . did you get closer?"

The moon makes a half-hearted appearance, a ring of brightness back-lighting a mesh of ragged clouds.

"We did get closer at that point," I say, choosing my words with care, "but not really because of his parents. We went back to New Haven the day after Christmas and started hanging out, mostly at my place."

"Did he move in?"

"Not then. We got an apartment together the following fall, in 1981. We lived there until 1988, when we both got jobs here. We shared the place in New Haven with a straight couple, Willis and Molly."

Eric has been collecting ammunition without my realising it and he now skips several small stones, one after another, across the water.

"You lived with a straight couple for seven years?"

"They were our best friends."

"How did they react when Anthony got sick?"

I blink at the non sequitur. "They were distraught, of course."

"Do you think they were afraid for themselves?"

"You don't get AIDS just by living with someone."

"I know, but people can be irrational."

"I suppose they can," I say. "But anyway, we had all left New Haven by the time we told them he was sick. It was in 1990, two years after we moved to Madison and they settled in California. Anthony didn't want anyone to know, but we called them up in Palo Alto when things started to get really bad. They came out to visit us in May of that year."

Eric nods. "Are they still around?"

"Willis and Molly? What do you mean?"

A final pebble belly-flops. "I don't know."

"Like, are they alive?"

"Of course not. What I meant was, did they keep up with you?"

"I told you, they were our best friends. They came to the funeral. They visited Madison the first Christmas after Anthony died so that I wouldn't be alone. I talk to them at least once or twice a month. Why do you ask?"

"I just can't imagine that people wouldn't . . . that some people, when they found out, wouldn't drop you."

"I suppose some people would, but not anyone I'd be best friends with."

We head back. A freight train makes its way onto the causeway, chugging along at five miles an hour and stopping and starting at unpredictable intervals, its mournful whistle superfluous. At North Shore Drive, on the very spot where Eric and I first met under extraordinary circumstances two and a half years ago, he suddenly turns to me and says:

"Did he go home with you?"

"What?"

We have come to a halt. "That first evening you and Anthony met at the Halloween party. Did he go home with you?"

The premise of the question is erroneous—the Halloween party is not, as I have led Eric to believe, the evening Anthony and I first met—and I am taken aback by its abruptness, but I make myself answer truthfully. "Yes, he came over."

"Did he stay?"

"That night, yes. But that was the only time in those first few months."

"Why?"

Rebecca, always Rebecca. I shift my weight back and forth, unwilling to commit myself to either an outright lie or the whole truth.

"It just wasn't like that. He was . . . not distant exactly, but detached. I could never pin him down. He would become playful to avoid talking about certain topics."

We resume walking.

"I wasn't under the impression he was the sort of person who joked around much." Eric ducks unexpectedly, then waves away a hovering hornet. "From the picture, I mean."

"You think so? With that smile?"

"Is he smiling in the picture?" Eric takes out a handkerchief and blows his nose. "What kind of things did he joke about?"

I ready myself for the rush of pain as I try to remember those first few months. They were filled with anxiety but led to years of, if not exactly blissful happiness, at least steady-state contentment. I wish I could go back and tell myself to shrink-wrap my worrying and keep it safe for when I really needed it.

"Oh, I don't know. New Haven. Graduate school. England and America, that kind of thing. He did an awesome imitation of the Ugly American, the big hulking blond guy who splits the crowds wherever he goes."

As soon as the words are out of my mouth Eric looks like someone who has just been told, upon attempting a first kiss, that he has garlic on his breath.

"I'm sorry," I stammer, "I didn't mean . . . You're the last person I would call hulking. You just happen to be tall. You aren't the type he was making fun of." Eric still looks upset. "Hey, come on. You know what the Ugly American is like. It has nothing to do with you."

Eric is not convinced.

"I just think that's nasty. I mean, do we go around making fun of the Brits? He should have been more considerate of other people's feelings."

"OK, you're right. I'm sure Anthony meant no harm, and I certainly didn't. I just have a talent for putting my foot in it."

"Guess I'm touchy because I spent my junior year studying in England. You take a lot of ribbing over there if you're an American. Especially a midwesterner or a southerner."

"Where were you in England?"

"Coventry, in the West Midlands. University of Warwick."

I hold my breath as he pronounces the last word, bracing myself to hear him sound the second w, as Americans tend to do, but thankfully he doesn't.

"Did you have a good year?"

"Outstanding."

It is strong language for a sardonic Swede. I don't want to pry, so I let it pass.

"Is Coventry a pretty town?"

"Beautiful. It got bombed during the war, and they left the walls of the cathedral standing. They built the new one right next to it."

A fine example of how Madison, for all its being a glorified cow town, can at times be surprisingly cosmopolitan. This local farm boy has travelled to a place in England I never visited with Anthony, who vetoed my idea of Coventry—I was intrigued by a photo I had seen of the two cathedrals—saying he didn't care for the town, and took me to Lincoln instead.

When we reach Broom Street, the turnoff to Eric's, it is late. I say I might as well continue on up the path towards my house. Eric says in a husky voice, "Do you have to?"

More vibes, but what do they mean? Rather than helping solve the puzzle of Anthony's message, Eric is becoming a fresh series of question marks. I can't fathom why he has dropped into my life. Maybe, at least for now, it is just as well that he drops back out of it.

"I'm afraid so. But let's do it again sometime."

We are standing right at the shore, shielded from the road by a large maple tree. Eric looks up and down the bike path to check that no one is approaching. Without warning he wraps me in his gargantuan arms and pins me against the tree. I close my eyes, expecting a kiss, but instead he puts his face next to my ear and, in a flat tone curiously at odds with the message being conveyed, whispers:

"No, let's do it now."

chapter 16

Anthony and I had spent four convivial years with Willis and Molly on Bishop Street when one blustery Friday morning in late September 1985 I made it to campus only to discover that classes had been cancelled for the day: Hurricane Gloria, having missed a left turn at Florida, was implausibly poised for a direct assault on the Connecticut shoreline. Willis and Molly were away hiking in the Berkshires for the weekend, so Anthony and I would have to weather the storm on our own. As I paid for emergency supplies on my way home, I relished the idea of hunkering down in our cosy sitting room to witness the spectacle of my very first hurricane. I hoped the experience would somewhat compensate for the fact that the tornado viewing aspirations I had shared with Anne had not panned out any more than our engagement.

It occurred to me that I might find Anthony still abed; he had decided to forgo teaching that semester to make quicker progress on his dissertation but as far as I could tell was mainly sleeping his time away. If he was arising later and later each morning, it was, he claimed, because of a lingering bug he had caught in mid-August. I thought the real problem was that, for reasons unknown to me, he was anxious and depressed. The few times I had brought up that theory, he had waved it away with a regal gesture signifying "We are not pleased."

In late 1985, had I not assumed that a psychological factor was the underlying cause of Anthony's inability to rebound from a routine infection, alarm bells would have rung. AIDS had become a staple of headlines across the country. Anthony and I knew several people who had the disease, and one of Molly and Willis's New York friends was afflicted as well. If in my mind I downplayed the risk of contamination for Anthony and myself, it was for a combination of reasons, some logical, others not. On New Year's Day 1981, shortly after returning to New Haven from Christmas with his family in New York, we had agreed our relationship would be exclusive. Later that same year the first conference about the "gay cancer" was held, and as time went on and the trickle of information about the ways the disease was transmitted developed into a stream and then a flood, I reassured myself that in all likelihood my limited encounters with men before meeting Anthony had not been risky. From time to time I did find myself thinking back to that fateful Valentine's Day when I had rifled through Anthony's address book in his room at the Hall of Graduate Studies and gathered that he had had undergraduate flings, but I managed to convince myself, without attempting in any way, shape, or form to gather supporting data to support the theory, that in the 1970s gay sex in London must have posed less of a danger than it did in New York or San Francisco. Finally, deep in my peasant's heart I clung to the superstitious notion that our vow of monogamy, proof of our bona fides, protected us retroactively against any earlier risks we might have unknowingly run.

So I was taken aback when, the evening before Hurricane Gloria struck, Willis waylaid me in the kitchen where he'd been washing dishes, I on a quest for a midnight snack.

"I've gotta go pack for our camping trip," he said, drying his hands, "but can I grab you for a sec?"

"Grab me? Sure. Whatcha got in mind, big boy?" I lifted and lowered my eyebrows à la Groucho Marx. It had been a very long week and, exhausted and unprepared for my Friday classes, I welcomed a moment of comic relief.

"Big boy yourself," Willis answered indulgently, patting my cheek. "Nothing as pleasant as that, I'm afraid." He shut the kitchen door so as not to be overheard by Anthony and Molly, who were both reading in the sitting room. "Listen," he said in a more solemn tone, "there's something I've been meaning to talk to you about."

"You have my attention."

"Don't you think it's time Anthony saw a doctor? It's been over a month since he got the flu or whatever it is, and he's not recuperating like he ought to."

That on several occasions I had successfully repressed a similar thought gave me ammunition to use on Willis now.

"What would be the point?" I snapped. "There's nothing the doctor can do if it's a virus. And he's improving. It just takes time."

"But they could at least check to make sure it is a virus," Willis rejoined. "What if it's something that would respond to antibiotics?"

"Maybe." I trotted out another counterargument I had used to convince myself. "Anthony gets bad reactions to penicillin."

"Hey, this is 1985. They've developed plenty of other antibiotics. I still think it's worth doing some tests."

We exchanged a glance.

"What are you driving at?" I said shortly. "Is this about AIDS?"

"I don't know," said Willis, "you tell me. Have you thought about AIDS? I'm just saying Anthony should see a doctor, maybe get tested."

Willis, whose father is a Baptist minister in Savannah, can be a trifle self-righteous at times, though his heart is always in the right place. What he was saying was in no way out of line, but it didn't fit the tale of AIDS immunity for Anthony and myself that I had carefully woven and become accustomed to taking out of mothballs whenever I needed to pull the wool over my eyes.

"I appreciate your concern," I said, choosing my words, "but it's not like he's seriously ill or getting worse." Willis looked dubious but said nothing. "We've been safe for years. He doesn't have any of the obvious symptoms. Anybody could take a while to bounce back from the flu, don't you think? He's probably just stressed out over his dissertation."

"Let's hope so," said Willis without conviction. "I still think it would be worth getting checked out, just to be on the safe side." His features relaxed. He clapped me on the shoulder and gave me a quick bear hug. "OK, we're good. Just be sure the two of you are taking care of yourselves, or else you're going to get a piece of my mind, you hear?"

The following morning, the day of the hurricane, I walked back to our flat as quickly as I could, struggling with my package of supplies against the approaching storm. The front door squeaked open: silence. When I entered our room, I found Anthony lying on his side clutching his pillow, his left foot poking out from underneath the covers. I sat down on the bed. The wind had reached gale force and was whipping through the gigantic oak that stood in the front yard, which our bedroom overlooked. Anthony's map was slapping against the wall to a regular beat like slow applause.

I tickled his foot.

"Whoozat?" He sprang out of bed, discombobulated. When he had composed himself, he sat back down on the bed, having apparently taken no notice of the rising wind. In a grumpy voice he said, "Reb, can't you act normal for just five minutes?"

"I doubt it, but I'll take it under advisement." Not a shadow of a smile from His Royal Highness. "Sorry, Anthony. I didn't mean to give you a start. Shall I make some espresso?"

His Majesty rubbed his eyes. "Yes, please. Sorry I snapped. I was having a dream."

About whom? I dismissed the thought as best I could. Celebrating our fifth anniversary a few weeks earlier had sent my Rebecca obsession into hibernation.

From the kitchen window I noticed that the spindly little poplar in the backyard was swaying in the gale. I shut the window, the storm window, and the blinds, feeble protection, I realised, if we took a direct strike but better than nothing. The height of the storm was forecast to hit New Haven within an hour or two.

It wasn't until Anthony had had his first sips of espresso that he seemed to emerge from his semi-coma. He noticed the time and thought to ask what I was doing home so early on a Friday.

"They've called off classes because of the hurricane."

He reached for an English muffin and made a scoffing noise.

"You Yanks, always going on about the weather. Last night on the news you'd have thought the weatherman was discussing Armageddon. The weather's a thousand times worse in Britain than it is here and nothing ever gets cancelled."

"The weather may be gloomier in Great Britain, but it's much less extreme." Anthony had forgotten he was addressing a weather nerd. I assumed my meteorologist's voice and paraphrased the *World Almanac*. "The United Kingdom enjoys a mild maritime climate, which prevails over the entire country."

"QED. Maritime means there's wind."

"Perhaps if you're right on the coast, but not if you're inland, which is where most of your population centers are."

Anthony finished chewing and went on in a more thoughtful voice.

"That's a tidy theory, but all I can say is that I have spent time in the very middle of England and seen howling winds there as well."

"Coventry?" I asked, to display my bottomless knowledge of useless trivia, especially where weather or geography are concerned.

"More or less. The actual centre of England is Meriden, a town nearby. I went cycling around there with a friend and we were lucky not to be blown off the road."

"You appear to have survived the ordeal," I said drily. I reached for a muffin and buttered it liberally. "I thought you didn't like Coventry—that's what you said when I suggested we visit."

Anthony wrinkled his nose.

"I said I didn't care for it, not that I'd never been." He stood and peered out the window. "Not much of a storm if you ask me. Garden-variety Burberry weather."

"If Your Lordship is willing to don his mackintosh, we'll go outside and see for ourselves."

By the time Anthony was dressed and we had made our way downstairs, lawn furniture and planters were proceeding northwards, fleeing Long Island Sound at a steady clip. A few sizeable branches were down and smaller trees looked like limbo dancers.

I rushed out to retrieve our trash cans.

"Are you mad?" Anthony exclaimed with a hint of panic in his voice.

I secured the bins in our shed and bounded up the steps.

"No harm done," I said, surprised to find him upset.

We holed up in the sitting room in front of the television. The howl of the wind gradually escalated to a steady roar. Before long the electricity cut out, the screen ironically going blank during an update on the storm's position. The lights gasped and succumbed, and the fridge went silent. I picked up the phone to call in the outage but it too was dead.

I turned on the transistor radio and set up the hurricane lantern I'd just purchased. The eye of the storm was passing over Long Island and had set its sights on Bridgeport, twenty miles down the coast.

Anthony curled up on the recently purchased futon on which five years and some months later he was destined to breathe his last. He stared listlessly at a book, making occasional notations on a pad of paper in the dim light of the lantern. The world had rotated ninety degrees, the onslaught of rain horizontal. By some cosmic fluke or perturbance of the earth's magnetic field, my watch battery had just run out.

As the hurricane gained strength, Anthony stopped all pretense of reading and fixated on the spectacle of the storm. A strand of hair had fallen into his eyes, and when I reached over to brush it back, his forehead felt hot.

"Your fever's rising," I said. "Maybe you should take an aspirin."

An inarticulate noise of negation.

"Shall I make another batch of espresso?"

"How? The power's out."

"The electricity's out, but the gas should still be OK. I won't be a minute." I headed towards the kitchen.

"Don't light the gas. It might spark and explode."

"Why would it spark if the electricity is off? I'll have to light it with a match."

The entire house suddenly shook, and we were engulfed by a great burst of noise.

The shaking stopped. The roar subsided to a high drone.

I rose, assuming Anthony would follow so that we could inspect the damage. At the sitting room doorway, I turned to discover he was riveted to the futon.

"Don't worry," I said, once again taken aback by how frightened he appeared. "It's probably just a tree limb."

"Stay here!"

I had never seen him like this, his face a mask of terror, his breathing quick and shallow as if he were just emerging from a body of water and gasping for air. I was not the designated consoler in our relationship. I didn't know what to say.

"I'm sure it's just a broken window," I got out. "The storm will pass through soon. We'll put that piece of plywood across it—you know, the one from the storage room. I'll go and fetch it, shall I?"

"No, please don't go." Anthony's mouth was contorted, his eyes queer. "Don't leave me here."

I sat beside him and took his two hands in mine. I gazed at his face, surpassingly handsome even in fear. I kissed his cheek and, recalling how often he had comforted my own anguish, plumbed my memory so that I could use his words of reassurance for his own benefit. We sat listening to the roaring wind for a long while. Anthony's breathing calmed to a slower rhythm, his apprehension subsiding into anxiety.

After about half an hour the wind gradually began to diminish. We were in the eye; I knew it wouldn't last long. I stroked Anthony's hair and said I'd be right back.

He looked frightened again but let me go. I checked the windows in the sitting room, the kitchen, and Willis and Molly's room; they were all intact. But when I opened the door to our bedroom, I found the window shattered, shards of glass littering the floor. A large branch from the oak tree had been sent careening into the room and rested atop our mattress. One of its extremities had scraped across Anthony's map of the world, severing the New World from the Old and leaving the Atlantic Ocean in tatters.

The cleanup took the better part of a week. The following Wednesday evening, as I rounded the corner from Orange Street onto Bishop, I saw Molly and Willis in the distance standing on the sidewalk. A huge gap marked the spot where our oak had stood.

Willis's arm encircled Molly, a pose that their sixteen inch height differential made faintly comical, but as I approached the house, their grim expressions formed a more sombre tableau. Molly pulled away from Willis and gave me a hug.

"Reb, can you believe this? They just cut down the oak tree. Without even letting us know. They could have at least tried to save it. We should write a letter to the city or something."

Willis shook his head.

"What's the point? It won't bring the tree back."

Anthony had seemed more energetic that morning and had been planning to spend the afternoon in the library, but when the three of us got upstairs he was slumped on the sofa, staring listlessly at the television screen. Without making eye contact he mumbled, "Is that you?"

"No," I said, "it's Prince Charles, Princess Di, and Genghis Khan."

He reached for the remote and turned up the sound.

"How did the writing go today?" I shouted.

Anthony responded with a snort barely discernible above Dan Rather's Texas drawl announcing that Rock Hudson, one of the first celebrities to have acknowledged having AIDS, had succumbed to the disease. After a quick biography of the actor, the newscaster went on to explain that as the HIV test, which had only recently become available, came into more widespread use, many people, some with no symptoms at all, would be in for a shock.

None of us uttered a word. It was my turn to make dinner, so I busied myself in the kitchen. When I called the others to the table, Anthony was a no-show.

"He's gone to bed," said Molly with a shrug. "He said he wasn't hungry. Looked like he just lost his best friend, but here you are, so I guess it's something else," she added with forced joviality.

After supper I crept up to our room. I opened the door as quietly as I could. I thought from Anthony's breathing that he wasn't asleep. I whispered his name. No answer.

"Are you sleeping?"

"Obviously."

"Would you like me to bring you a plate? You should eat something."

"Not hungry. Might grab a bite later."

"Can I talk to you?"

He moaned. "Told you, asleep."

I sat down next to him. "What's bothering you?"

"Nothing. Just the bloody dissertation—sick of it. Don't know if I'll ever finish the bleeding thing."

"Why wouldn't you?"

"Running out of steam. I can hardly bear another day of thinking about it."

"Are you sure that's all?"

"Yes. What else should it be?"

Anthony rolled over to face in my direction. It looked to me as though he'd been crying.

"What is it?" I said. "Please tell me, what's bothering you?"

"I'm just feeling low."

He was the only one of us working mainly from home; he was obviously spending too much time on his own, feeling lonely and at loose ends. Questioning him further about his sagging spirits would only make matters worse. We had not been intimate for nearly a week. I stretched out on the bed beside him and held him close. Suddenly he pulled away and swung his feet onto the floor.

"Anthony, what is it? What's wrong?"

"Nothing. I'm sorry." He gathered up his pillow and covers and, without explanation, bedded down on the death futon.

On my own, I spent a sleepless night. Without Anthony by my side I couldn't seem to settle down, and even his map, which had been clumsily repaired with masking tape but had a jagged fault line running down the middle, offered little comfort.

chapter 17

When Eric wraps me in his arms behind a maple tree on the bike path in Madison and suggests that we go on from there, I don't know how to reply. There is no point in denying that I am attracted to him and touched by his tale of loneliness, but I can't seem to make heads or tails of his peculiar blend of squeaky-clean uprightness and simmering resentment.

I pull away from the embrace, catch my breath, and run a hand through my hair. "Can we walk?"

"I take it that's leading up to a no."

"I don't know what it's leading up to. Just give me a second here."

We cross John Nolen Drive and proceed up Broom Street in silence. Soon we are in front of Eric's building. "Time's up," he says in a tone devoid of humour.

My patience is wearing thin.

"I'm sorry, but I can't give you an answer at this very moment. I need some time to think it over."

"What is there to think about? You want to or you don't want to."

"It's more complicated than that."

"No, it isn't. Are you or aren't you attracted to me?" The recorded voice of a public-opinion surveyor asking you to press 1 for yes and 2 for no.

"I . . . you're . . . Yes, I am. But there are other things to consider."

"What other things? I'm not asking you to go steady, if that's what you're thinking."

I look him up and down, equally annoyed by his presumptuousness and amused by the old-fashioned term.

"I didn't think you were." I take a few moments to consider my reply. "It's mostly that I haven't been with anyone since I lost Anthony."

"So what? Me neither."

I shoot him a puzzled look.

"I mean it's been a while for me as well. Anyway, what's the difference? It's your decision. Yes or no."

"Why does it have to be decided right now?" I counter. "I hardly know you."

"So what? You went home with Anthony the first night you met him. That's what you told me, right?"

"Excuse me?"

"I just mean that you did it in the past, so it's not out of the question. This is our second date."

"Who said it was a date?"

"What would you call it?"

"We had a drink and went for a walk, that's what I'd call it." My voice rises a notch. "You know something? You're way out of line here. You didn't know Anthony and you don't know me. So don't go telling me what I did with him and what I should do with you."

"If that's how you want it, man," says Eric in a monotone. "OK by me." He turns to enter his building.

I can't leave it like this.

"Come on, Eric, you're not being fair. First you give me an ultimatum, then you go off to sulk when I can't give you an answer in five seconds." I pause. "It's not that I'm not flattered, it's just that . . ."

He folds his arms across his chest and waits.

"Look, can't we start over?" I go on. "I'm not making any promises, but I would like to see you again." Pause. "For a date."

"When?"

"This is going to be a really busy week for me," I lie. I need time to get used to the idea. "How about next Friday night after dinner, around nine? We can sit on my deck and have a beer."

"Friday the 13th? Great. Sounds real promising."

"OK, Saturday."

"No, Friday the 13th is perfect. It's just perfect."

The lie I have told Eric about being busy in the coming week turns out not to be one. My two encounters with him having yielded no useful information about the 11:11 message, I decide that the single item most likely to help me make sense of it is Anthony's address book, the small volume I flipped through in his room at the Hall of Graduate Studies just before he asked me to live with him. I searched for the little book right after he died, to inform those of his friends I didn't know of his passing, thereby also alerting the block-letter individuals in the book—one of whom I assumed to be Rebecca—of the importance of being tested in case Anthony had not contacted them himself after he received his positive result, something we never discussed. But in the dark and dreadful days of February and March 1991 I had more pressing matters to attend to and quickly gave up my search.

In light of Anthony's message, finding the address book takes on fresh urgency. His old friends and former lovers would dismiss me as delusional if I told them the full story of 11:11, but surely I could find a discreet way to inquire as to whether the date 11 November 1933 had been meaningful to the boy in some way, perhaps the birthday of an important person in his life. In the late 1970s, a man born on that day would have been in his forties, a plausible candidate for one of Anthony's undergraduate flings, perhaps even Rebecca. I had always pictured my archrival as a fresh-faced ephebe, but there was no reason to exclude the possibility that he had been a man of a certain age.

I begin my search by turning Anthony's massive oak desk inside out. It has remained exactly as it was, and I force myself to go through his notebooks, the papers he wrote in graduate school, and the voluminous research materials from his dissertation, which I cannot bring myself to discard but which have now been given a semblance of order. My hunt gradually broadens to the entire house, including the basement and the garage. I rummage through reams of documents, clothing, calendars, merchandise, and the like, dispose of or give away boxes of miscellaneous belongings. Some of the medical equipment from the time of Anthony's illness turns up in odd locations I cannot account for; strangely enough, the store of morphine Dr. Hertz entrusted to us a fortnight before Anthony's death, and of which we administered very little, is not among the supplies.

By the end of the week, I am pleased to have tackled so many tasks that required my attention. I have reorganised all of my old teaching materials from my years at Yale, filed official documents and receipts relating to the house, and even pruned my wardrobe for the first time since Anthony's death. But in all those hours of rifling through the chaos my life has become, not once do I run across Anthony's address book.

Like the man himself, it has apparently dematerialised.

On Friday, 13 August, Eric rings my doorbell at nine on the dot. He looks utterly alluring in tight shorts and a tank top. A cold front has passed through and turned a lovely afternoon into a chilly, damp evening, so we sit at opposite ends of the rattan sofa on the screened-in porch and listen to the rain. There has been so much of it across the Midwest this spring and summer that the lake has flooded my boathouse, and it is difficult to block out the pounding of its wide double doors being sucked back and forth by the high waters to the rhythm of a fluttering heart. The breeze off the lake is gusty and the leaves of my Norwegian maple tickle the roof of my house with a rustling sound that sends pleasant shivers up and down my spine. I wonder if before the evening is up, similar sensations will be caused by this scantily clad Swedish spruce.

We sip our beer, each waiting for the other to break the ice. Finally I say: "I've told you about Anthony. Tell me about your boyfriend. The one who never introduced you to his family."

"Yeah, what about him?"

"Describe him."

"He was . . . I never met anyone like him."

"What was unusual about him?"

Eric leans his head back against the wall and stretches out his legs, which practically touch the opposite wall of the porch.

"Everything. He was really . . . intelligent. I suppose you would say, some people might say he was brilliant." Pause. "Lots of friends. More than I'll ever have." A longer pause. "But in other ways he wasn't . . . Not like you'd expect from someone so . . ." His voice softens. "He was . . . what do you call that? I'm blanking out." He slaps at his arm, presumably a mosquito. "Vulnerable. That's it. He was vulnerable." He sounds pleased at having unearthed such an original term for a person in a love relationship. "Someone that attractive, you'd think they would be a show-off, boasting, typical male kind of crap. I hate that. But not . . . he wasn't. Not cocky. None of the usual guy things."

It's been clear from the start that Eric is no extrovert, but I wonder if he has ever spoken about his lover with a living soul before this evening.

"What did he look like?"

"Hard to describe. Pretty tall, but not like me. Eyes the colour of yours. Good build."

"Where did you meet?"

"Oh, at a pub . . . a pub . . . *ah-choo!* Excuse me. Have you got a tissue?" I reach for the box and hand him one. He blows his nose. "We met at a public library," he continues.

I chuckle to myself, conjuring up the wholesome scene: their eyes locked above the pages of the *Christian Science Monitor*, then they strolled over to Pop's drugstore to share a root beer float.

"How long were you together?"

"Two and a half years. Like I said, I had a girlfriend. It was . . . no one knew about him."

"Did he ever ask you to break up with your girlfriend?"

Silence, then: "No."

"Why did you?"

"I thought it was time. Things weren't going all that well with her by then. I never told her about him. I took a chance and I was wrong, OK? Like I said, he met someone else."

"I'm sorry, I didn't mean to pry. Was there anyone you could talk to about it when it happened?"

"No."

"Why not?"

"City boys, you don't get it. You should try talking about stuff like this in the country. I didn't know anyone who would understand."

"How can you be sure if you didn't try?"

He sniffs, blows his nose again.

I feel a flood of compassion; Eric not only went through hell, he went through it alone. I can't imagine how I would have survived the months after Anthony's death without the daily phone calls from Willis and Molly, who arranged it so that one of them rang me every single evening, or faced that first Christmas without their visit. How would I have made it through the funeral if I hadn't felt my ex-fiancée Anne's arm gripping my shoulder throughout the service, as if to remind me Anthony was not the only person I had ever loved?

"Eric, I didn't say anything last week, but when I was talking about the friends we lived with, you sounded like you could hardly believe two straight people stayed so close to us through it all."

Eric winces.

"I'm sure your friends were great—no, perfect," he replies in a voice edged with sarcasm. "But I can guarantee that in my circumstances Willis and Millie would not have been much help even if I had confided in them."

"Molly. Why is that? Can't you imagine having straight friends who stick by you?"

"I can imagine a lot of things. It doesn't make them true." Eric stands and walks to the door overlooking the lake. He continues in a more earnest tone. "I appreciate your concern, really I do. I know it's important to talk about things. But sometimes you don't know where to begin." He drains his beer mug, sets it down on a sill. "My whole life, since he left—I know it's crazy, but it's true. It's been a waste. Even the good things, without him . . ."

I stand close to Eric, say his name. He shakes his head and continues, still facing away.

"When he . . . when my boyfriend left me, there was no one . . . And really, come to think of it, there was nothing to say."

"There's always something to say."

"Not this time. He found someone he liked better than me, that's all. I've never stopped loving him. I'll never forget him."

"I'm not suggesting you forget him. I'm talking about moving on."

"Where would that get me?"

"I'm still trying to figure that one out for myself."

"In that case, why don't you butt out?" he says, his voice rising a pitch. I have overstepped some boundary.

"I'm sorry, I was just trying to help."

"Have I asked for your help? Do I seem like someone who needs help?"

No and yes, I think, but I say nothing.

The rain has stopped. I make the rounds of the porch, opening the windows, and the rush of cool air feels like a balm, whether of my own wounds or of Eric's I am not sure. Turning back to him I notice for the first time that his eyes are opaque, greyish flecks overspreading the irises like storm clouds in a blue sky.

"Eric, I'm sorry you've been through hard times. We both have. I wasn't telling you what to do. All I was trying to say was that you don't have to forget him to get close to other people."

"You say that like it's easy."

"Maybe it is, if the time is right."

"It doesn't seem so easy for you. When I tried to get closer, you ran away."

"Fair enough. But try to understand, Anthony and I were together for ten years. You and your boyfriend had two. That's a long time, but not quite the same thing."

Eric ponders this for a moment. "It's true, the time I was with him went by so fast. Maybe that happens when you're perfectly happy. But once it was over it felt like it had been my whole life."

"You say you were perfectly happy—how about him? He must have been happy at the beginning. What changed?"

Without warning Eric's face takes on a mask of rage.

"Are you ever going to stop talking about him?"

He kisses me savagely on the lips and runs from the room. I am too stunned to follow. Fifteen seconds later I hear the sound of tires screeching up the hill.

chapter 18

Anthony's prolonged bout with the flu and general discouragement eventually passed, driving back into hiding the health concerns Willis had expressed the evening before Hurricane Gloria hit. By mid-October 1985 Lord Payton was once again on top of the world. He travelled to London for Christmas and spent several months in England during the summers of 1986 and 1987 to complete his dissertation research. By the fall of 1987 it was clear he would submit his thesis by the following spring. It was time to seek gainful employment. There were no openings Anthony could apply for in the History Department at Yale, so in the fall of 1987 the two of us perused the job listings in our respective fields in quest of that most elusive of goals for an academic couple, two jobs within commuting distance. In the early spring of 1988 we hit the jackpot: we were both offered positions at the University of Wisconsin–Madison, Anthony's on a tenure track, mine with tenure.

To my surprise Anthony demurred about the decision to move to Madison. He commented that he had had friends who had lived there and not found the place to their liking, which astonished me given the utopian descriptions of the place that Molly, who did her undergraduate degree at Wisconsin, had often furnished. The only cloud that retrospectively darkened her sunny image of Madison was the subsequent breakup of her relationship with the infamous Yoko Ono from the Halloween party where we all met during our first semester in New Haven. She had met Yoko as an undergraduate in Madison and would occasionally allude to him—only when Willis did not happen to be present, and especially while under the influence—intimating that she had been utterly devastated by their parting in December 1980, shortly before Anthony and I became an item.

The checklist we drew up of the pros and cons of moving to Madison clearly had more pros than cons, and reason eventually prevailed. When we informed Willis and Molly of our decision, Molly nearly damaged her vocal chords with her shrieks of delight. She took the opportunity to rhapsodise yet again about the beauty and conviviality of the city and its great university. In a further stroke of good fortune, Anthony and I managed to find an affordable fixer-upper on Lake Monona that could be made cosy and livable with taste and elbow grease, his strong suit and my own, respectively. As I packed my things and prepared to move back to the Midwest of my upbringing, I wondered if Destiny had confused my file with someone else's. I couldn't remember a time of greater serenity.

By 2 September 1988, my thirty-fifth birthday and our eighth anniversary, Anthony and I had been living in our new Madison home for a month. Our respective departments, history and English, were going out of their way to be welcoming. We enjoyed discovering the city, but once we were settled in the house and the excitement of the move had passed, Anthony seemed on edge. Anyone might feel jitters when facing the uncertainties of a first job, I told myself, and by the eve of our anniversary he was again in higher spirits. We marked the occasion with a romantic ride down State Street in a carriage powered by a flower-bedecked, poker-faced draft horse and piloted by a matching ponytailed driver with a conspiratorial now-I've-seen-it-all grin.

On the day itself I went to the airport to pick up Willis and Molly, who were flying in from California, where they had taken twenty-four-carat tenure-track positions at Stanford. Anthony mumbled something about having business to attend to, which I suspected was related to my birthday present.

Molly and Willis emerged from the jetway to excited banter and the merriment of a reunion of old friends in pleasant new circumstances. As we rode home from the airport, I was pleased to find Willis so buoyant, his natural reserve leavened by the exhilaration of his accomplishments, but Molly, who had been no less successful, was not quite herself. It was true that ever since the job-interviewing season had begun the previous year she had been toning down her bad-girl image: after a long stint as a blond she had gone natural, and her hair, which she had been accustomed to wearing nearly down to her waist, was now coiffed in a tidy power do. Her hourglass figure, in earlier days emphasised by racy outfits, was downplayed by the kind of broad-shouldered jackets, plain tops, and no-nonsense skirts that professional women across America adopted in the 1980s as an emblem of their intention of working their way up to the glass ceiling—which I was convinced Molly would be in the vanguard of shattering—in comfort. Back at the house Willis and Molly admired our view and greeted Anthony, who was once again in a reserved mood but pleased to see our dearest friends. We had booked a table for 7 p.m. at the White Rabbit, an upscale restaurant we had recently discovered.

As the four of us were being led through the bar towards the main room of the restaurant, Willis gestured to our group to approach and said quietly, "Nice place. What'd you say it's called, the White Rabbit? How come they're letting Molly and me in?"

"Or me, for that matter," my South Side voice chimed in as Anthony scanned the other diners to check if we were making a scene. "Did you see that sign next to the cash register? Polish Peasant Night, Kielbasa and Borscht, Tuesdays only!"

Anthony and Molly smiled politely but didn't join in the hilarity. We were shown to our table by a maître d' who, in typical Madison fashion, looked more amused than indignant at our horsing around.

Willis, normally a teetotaler, ordered a martini, which he sipped at a sedate pace. Molly asked for a double scotch, straight, and chugged it as if it were a beer. After her second drink came, she took another gulp and gestured to Anthony and me to approach as closely as possible. I could tell from the look on her face that she was in the process of conjuring up her inner wild child.

"Psst. You over there, you two white boys." Her curling index finger was coy. "If the waiter tells us to leave, this bro and I will wait for you outside." I prayed the mixed-race couple at the next table couldn't hear Molly's stage whisper, which was as discreet as cats mating in your backyard. "You two look like real nice boys," she went on. "Wonder Bread in a package. If I had a pat of marge, I'd spread it all over you and pop you both into my mouth. Two big bites." She smacked her lips, painted a tasteful dark red as opposed to one of her old fruity colours, apricot, lime, or pink grapefruit.

Anthony and I broke into hysterics. Willis retained the kind of paper-thin faux dignity he assumes when he's preparing to dismount from his high horse.

"Mind your tongue, Mademoiselle," he said—and Molly promptly stuck it out. "Might I remind you," he added with gravitas, channelling Jesse Jackson, who had recently run for president, "that we are members of the faculty at a distinguished private institution, which my confidentiality agreement, unfortunately, does not allow me to identify?"

We all roared. We did our best to act grown-up when the waiter brought over the bottle of Veuve Clicquot Anthony had ordered. As is my custom when I have the giggles and need to compose myself, I thought of Daddy. Aside from wishing he were here to say happy birthday, I realised with a jolt that he was barely a decade older than thirty-five when he died.

Anthony raised his champagne glass, and we followed suit.

"Two toasts to Reb. First with champagne. May your next thirty-five years be full of bubbles."

My memory of Daddy had worked only too well. "Thanks for the sentiment, Anthony, but I have as much of a chance of making it through another thirty-five years as . . . Oh, never mind." No reason to inflict my genetic woes on the others.

To my surprise Anthony's voice, rather than teasing or reproachful, became pleading. "Please don't say that, darling. Not tonight. You must live another thirty-five years." He downed his champagne and was instantly overcome by a coughing spell.

"Are you all right, Sir A?" Molly stood and clapped him on the back.

Anthony gasped and sputtered for ten long seconds before finally catching his breath.

"Fine, fine," he panted. "Went down . . . wrong way. No extra charge for the show," he added weakly. Molly, visibly shaken, returned to her seat.

Anthony raised his water glass. "Now our second toast, with water, since Reb spends half of his life in it." This was an allusion to my swimming, about which Anthony often teased me. "May you one day see your reflection in the water through my eyes."

An embarrassed silence; none of us was accustomed to such unguarded sentiment from him. I squeezed his hand. He flushed, called for the waiter, and ordered a basket of bread.

It was after midnight when we arrived home. We got Willis and Molly settled into the downstairs guest room, which needed repainting and was furnished with only the bare essentials but still seemed luxurious in contrast to the New Haven digs we had all shared.

As I was preparing for bed I heard noises from downstairs and found Molly perched on a kitchen stool, rummaging around in a high cupboard. She let out a short scream when I called out her name.

"Holy Moses, Reb, you could warn a person before you creep up behind her," she said, climbing down in disarray.

"Sorry, sweetie pie. Something I can get for you?"

"I just wondered if you had some decaf lying around. It helps me sleep. Sorry—it was rude of me not to ask."

"Decaf? You've come to the right place." I went to the appropriate cabinet and produced a jar of Sanka. "Is instant OK? Since when do you have trouble sleeping?"

"Instant is perfect." Molly filled the kettle and plugged it in. "As far as sleeping goes, good question. I suppose since life caught up with me."

"Life?"

A wistful smile. "The usual grown-up stuff—no longer being a student, pressure at work. Just this and that. Say, do you have any cream?" I took a container out of the fridge and plunked it onto the counter. "Thanks, hon." She thought for a few seconds. "Sorry if I was a bit of a dishrag this evening. I didn't want to say anything, especially in front of Willis, but being back in Madison—it's as lovely as ever, but it's been churning up some painful memories."

"Yoko?"

She nodded, tears rolling down her cheeks. This wasn't the first time I had seen Molly weep over her breakup with Yoko so many years earlier. I gave her a quick hug.

"Maybe you should call him and have it out if it still hurts after so many years. He's probably living thousands of miles away, in Australia or Thailand or something, but you could track down his number, don't you think?"

Molly's tear-stained eyes hardened.

"I probably could," she said abruptly. "Oops, there's the kettle."

She strode across the room and unplugged it.

"Sorry if I made things worse with my suggestion," I said sheepishly. "I wish I could do something to help. Well, time for beddy-bye. I hope you get some sleep."

I tried to peck her on the cheek but she pulled away. "Too tired for good-night kisses," she said. "Don't worry about me. I have my Sanka to keep me company."

I took a quick shower and towelled off. Anthony was already in bed, read-ing. It had been a scorchingly hot summer, but as a birthday present to me a rush of cool Canadian air had been special-delivered that afternoon, and a stiff easterly breeze off the lake lent our bedroom a pleasant autumnal cosiness. As I pulled on my pajamas, I was flooded with gratitude at the great good fortune that was mine. The carpe diem of Renaissance sonnets was rubbish. Middle age promised to be a million times better than youth.

I settled in on my side of the bed and let the pillow coddle my head, pleased at the thought that my insomnia had subsided to such a degree that I no longer needed to read to relax. As Anthony had reassured me years ago, on that first night in our newly shared dwelling on Bishop Street, with him looking after me, nothing could go wrong.

I glanced over towards his side of the bed. He was sitting upright in bed, still as a statue, weeping. Something in me must have known, not the nature of what was about to transpire, but its enormity. I took leave of my body, observed the scene from afar. What did this tableau remind me of? A mater dolorosa, a sculpture of the grieving Virgin Mary, that I had seen in Rome the previous summer. But which sculpture, I mused dully. Who was the artist? In what church?

Anthony rose and walked to the French doors overlooking the lake. He faced away from me but I could hear his voice distinctly.

"There's something I must tell you. I've been contacted by someone I hadn't heard from for a long time, years. He was once . . . we used to be together."

He fell silent.

Rebecca.

It would sound impressive to write that I had been clever enough to know all along that Rebecca would one day resurface, but that's not the way it was. On the contrary, I had finally come to believe that like a cancer suc-cessfully treated, he never would.

A deadening spread through my veins. So this was what Anthony's mysterious appointment that afternoon had been. He had not gone to pick up my birthday present. He had spent those hours in the arms of the man who had never ceased to inhabit his secret dreams. He had whiled away the afternoon discovering that a passion of that vintage, delicious and heady when it tastes of the vine, is irresistible in the power of its maturity.

Anthony knew that the celebration we had just shared was my send-off; that explained his moodiness. Probably he had reconnected with Rebecca only after the plans for the weekend had been put into place. Rebecca had been the one to contact him; Anthony had hesitated, then given in. Of course they must see one another again. They were meant for each other. How could our union of mutual affection but pedestrian passion overcome their memories of abiding ecstasy?

Anthony finally had a stable position in life. He had completed his education, found gainful employment, and could look ahead to a future filled with success and recognition. It was time to reassess what the coming years would bring. Now that he could finally stand on his own two feet, did he really want to spend the rest of his life standing next to me?

Perhaps for the moment he was actually feeling too guilty to stand on those two feet of his, because he had slumped to the floor. I walked over and yanked him up. Let him give it to me straight—no blindfold for the firing squad of this condemned man.

"So you've been in touch with him all this time? Is that what you're trying to tell me?"

"Of course not. I hadn't spoken to him in eight years. What makes you think that?"

"How did he get your number unless he knew you were in Madison?"

"He rang the History Department at Yale and found out I had taken a job here. I was in my office on campus when he reached me."

"I see."

I couldn't bear the thought that Anthony might be lying, had perhaps been in touch with Rebecca and even seen him from time to time in the years we had been together. It was more than I could contemplate; I just wanted it to be over.

"Anthony, don't worry about sparing my feelings. I think I know what you're going to say. Say it quickly, so that I can make my plans."

He blinked compulsively, his features overtaken by panic.

"Make your plans? What do you mean?"

"We'll have to sell the house. I don't think either one of us can manage the mortgage payments on an academic salary. Too bad we didn't wait to buy."

"What are you talking about? You're not going to . . . Darling, please don't." He clutched me, trembling. "I'm so sorry, I know it's dreadful for you. I pray that you'll be spared. I can't face it without you."

"What do you mean? Your friend, your boyfriend . . ."

Anthony pulled away and sat abruptly on the bed.

"I thought you understood. He told me to get an HIV test. I picked up the results this afternoon. Positive."

✳

That night I sat on the edge of the bed as Baba used to and watched over Anthony's restless sleep, murmuring, whenever he stirred, that everything would be all right. Just after dawn he became more peaceful. He rolled onto his back and smiled in his sleep. I gazed at his face, immersed in a dream, once again at peace with the world. It was the only Anthony face I'd ever been able to make sense of. His eyes fluttered open briefly without his fully awakening as sometimes happens in the midst of a dream. In the late-summer morning light streaming into our room, their deep turquoise colour was reminiscent of the English Channel on the breezy June afternoon we had once spent together on the beach at Bournemouth, with the heavens cycling through sun, clouds, showers, and rainbows, an English summer's day when no condition lasts more than a moment but each has its magic.

I thought of all the things I hadn't asked about. Assuming that Anthony had been infected while at Oxford more than eight years ago, what was his prognosis? Had the doctor mentioned treatment? I would have to be tested as well but there was nothing to discuss on that score; we would simply have to await the results. The one thing Anthony had made clear was that as long as his health remained stable, his own HIV status was not to be revealed to a soul, not even Willis and Molly.

One final matter I had not brought up. Who was Rebecca? How long had they been together? Assuming they had met in England, how had Rebecca remained in Anthony's life during his first months in New Haven? Perhaps that fateful telephone call in Anthony's room had been a trunk call across the Atlantic—that seemed the most likely explanation. Now Rebecca had told Anthony to be tested, so there was a good chance he had transmitted the virus to Anthony. Logically speaking, other scenarios were possible, but what my mind could only surmise, my heart knew: Rebecca must be to blame. I had never so thoroughly despised another human being.

I glanced down at my lover with the dawning awareness that our days together were probably numbered. My thoughts shifted to the matter at hand. Anthony's passion and my hatred for Rebecca were no longer of any importance. From this day forward, I must use every ounce of energy to attend to my lover.

He stirred again and opened his eyes. His expression was grave. I stroked his hair, kissed him on both sides of his forehead.

"Darling, please don't worry," I said. "I'll look after you, I promise."

His features softened and I smiled as he fell into a peaceful slumber. If he had never truly needed me before, he needed me now. And I would not let him down.

chapter 19

Things continued on an even keel for a little over a year. Anthony was put on AZT and his health remained stable. My HIV test turned up negative. But in November 1989, shortly after his book was accepted for publication, he began suffering from a persistent cough and noticeable weight loss, posing a problem for the Christmas holidays. He had planned to fly home but risked being stranded in London if his condition worsened or he was refused reentry into the United States; HIV screening for all visa applicants had recently been put into place. The obvious solution was to invite Gerald and Julia, still completely in the dark about their son's condition, to Madison for the holidays. They accepted without asking a single question, either too clueless for AIDS to be on their radar or too wary to invite an explanation. To round out the party, Miranda, who had recently married a fellow psychotherapist named Ed Rosen, would join us on Christmas Day.

Having had nine years to accustom herself to the idea, Julia took in stride the notion that I was to be the cohost of our Arctic-style holiday extravaganza; I was the one who dreaded pregnant pauses at the Christmas table while Anthony coughed his lungs out. At least anodyne conversation about the weather would provide suitable distraction for a group of Brits, as it had thus far been an unspeakably frigid winter.

With wind chills approaching absolute zero the afternoon I picked up Gerald and Julia at Dane County Regional Airport, Anthony stayed home and rested so that he might give the best possible first impression. I spotted Julia striding down the jetway, decked out for a disembarkment off the Queen Mary: pearl-grey suit with matching hat, shoes, and purse. Attired in cuffed black wool trousers, black-and-white houndstooth sports jacket, and a new Burberry, Gerald, who had clearly ascended several rungs of the sartorial ladder since we last met, struggled with a couple of oversized carry-ons.

Julia and I shook hands briskly, like army buddies at their first reunion since being demobbed.

"Well, Reb," she said. "Thank you for coming to fetch us. It's nice to see you again."

"Good to see you both. I hope you've brought warm coats—it's brutal out there."

"Never fear. We've come prepared for the worst."

Not likely. To my surprise I felt a rush of compassion.

"Where's my boy?" asked Gerald after I had relieved him of his carry-ons.

"He's home marking exams," I said. Julia looked taken aback at this flimsy excuse for not meeting their plane, so I added, "He wanted to come, but it's very slow going, and grades are due today."

"Always was a perfectionist," said Gerald. "Right, Julia?"

The Snow Queen smiled indulgently. We had reached baggage claim and I gratefully set down the carry-ons, which weighed a ton.

"What's in there?" I panted. "Barbells?"

"That's telling it like it is," said Gerald with a laugh. "Thought I'd break my bluhdy back!"

"Gerald, keep your voice down—this isn't a pub." Julia turned to me. "Sorry, Reb—they didn't seem all that bad at Gatwick." Julia could probably bench-press twice her weight. "It's our wedding present to Miranda: Granny's linen tablecloth, twelve handmade lace place settings, and her good silver. All Victorian and in perfect nick," she concluded with a hint of regret, as if speaking of an organ she had been pressured into donating.

Back at the house Anthony, masking his nervousness, greeted his mother with an air-kiss.

"Hullo, Mummy," he said. "How was your journey?"

"Crammed to the gills but quite routine," said Julia. She peered at her son. "Looking a trifle peaky, are we? With this American climate I don't wonder." She made her way into the sitting room, its windows overlooking the frozen lake. "Gracious, what a lovely view you've got!"

Gerald held his boy at arm's length and looked him up and down. "What's wrong, son?"

"It's nothing, Dad. A touch of bronchitis. Just getting over it."

"Bronchitis doesn't make you look like that."

"A fortnight's holiday and I'll be right as rain."

Gerald shivered as he reluctantly shed his Burberry and handed it to me to hang up. "Not mooch rain in these parts just now, I reckon," he quipped. You'll have to be right as snow!"

The Great 1989 Christmas Debacle began with brussels sprouts.

Anthony feared raising suspicions if I was assigned to make Christmas dinner without his assistance, so Julia was appointed head chef. She decided on a feast of roast goose, creamed spinach, vegetable-rice tart, and Christmas rum cake. Miranda would add her signature dish of roasted brussels sprouts. Julia insisted that we set the table with Miranda's silver, tablecloth, and napkins to impress her daughter with her wedding gift as soon as she arrived.

When Miranda walked into the dining room, she oohed and aahed at the array of Victorian splendour. Julia's explanation that it was her wedding present set Miranda to squealing like a schoolgirl.

As we sat down for Christmas dinner, I mused that the faces around the table might not remain festive for long; Anthony was still mulling over if and when he would reveal the truth. At the head of the table sat Julia, luminous in a high-collared white wool dress with a lavender cameo pinned below the throat. Approaching seventy, she might have been in the early stages of middle age. Her cheerful mien was largely due to her children's good fortune, which to her mind redounded to her credit, finally compensating for the loss of standing brought about by her morganatic union with Gerald so many years earlier. Seated at the foot was her husband, sixty-five; although also in high spirits, he appeared twenty years her senior. He had recently retired to tipple on his own time, his one prayer for the years remaining to him being that his children—the only aspect of his life he deemed a true success—might come to need him again as they once had. Much sooner than he expected, that prayer would be granted. Miranda looked not a day older than when I first met her nine years earlier, at that bizarre Christmas celebration in Manhattan. Her mahogany-coloured hair was now worn short, and when she tilted her head at a certain angle her fringe fell into her face, the happy-sheepdog look a poignant reminder of Anthony as he once was. Anthony too had a smile on his face, but his appeared to have been affixed with packing tape. He said little throughout the meal, whether because of his dark mood or for fear of provoking a coughing spell I could not say.

"Miranda darling," said Julia as the main course drew to a close, "these brussels sprouts are a *trahmph*—it's hard to believe they're reheated. Did you add anything special? I've never tasted ones quite so delicious."

Miranda pinkened. "Nothing at all, Mummy. Just salt and butter and a pinch of mint. Would you care for more?"

"I'd love to, but I must leave room for pudding. Anthony, have another helping of Miranda's lovely sprouts. They're good for you. You're still looking a mite under the weather."

"No thanks, Mummy. Couldn't eat another bite. I'm not sure I can manage pudding. Would anyone mind if I had mine later?"

"Splendid idea, my boy," chimed in Gerald, "splendid. Unless you two charming ladies take exception, I should also like to abstain. Only temporarily, of course. I assume the other gentleman present has no objections." He ceremoniously bowed his head in my direction, whether seriously or tongue-in-cheek I couldn't tell.

Miranda said, "I wouldn't say no, either, to a bit of a pause before we attack your Christmas cake, Mummy. You've done all the work. I'll take over from here. Come on, boys into the sitting room. Anthony, would you like some coffee or something? Not quite ourselves today, I see," this in her best Nurse Ratched voice. "Sure you're feeling all right?" She did not bother to await an answer but stood and busied herself with gathering dishes and her newly inherited silverware. Julia, too, came to her feet to speed things along.

Anthony, still seated, said, "Yes, Miranda. I would love some coffee."

"Super. We'll all have some. Reb, what kind of coffeemaker have you got? Can you pop into the kitchen and set it up?"

I rose and was at the kitchen door when I heard Anthony say:

"And actually, I'm not sure I'm feeling all right."

Miranda had started sorting plates, putting the big ones in one pile and the small ones in another. She was taking great care not to spill anything onto her white tablecloth and did not look up from her task. I felt like an office worker glancing out of the window of a skyscraper and observing two cars about to collide many floors below.

Julia, collecting wineglasses, said, "What a pity Anthony isn't himself on Christmas. Anthony, do you think you might ring your doctor tomorrow and see if he can squeeze you in for a quick look-see? I'm sure he'd be obliging. Oh no, tomorrow's Boxing Day. I expect the surgeries are all shut."

"This is America, Mummy. They haven't got Boxing Day. But I don't need to see a doctor. I appreciate your concern, but I've already seen one. Several, as a matter of fact."

Julia held the wineglass she had just grasped aloft, like a stalled car at the top of a Ferris wheel swinging in midair while unseen passengers board many feet below.

"You have? Whatever for?"

"Actually, I've been . . . I'm having some problems. Rather serious ones, I'm afraid. I hadn't mentioned it because I didn't want to ruin . . . I'm sorry to bring it up like this, I had no intention . . ."

"Problems? What problems?" Gerald was sobering up quickly. "Did they find out what it was?"

Anthony nodded.

"It's nothing serious," Miranda pitched in, still basking in the aura of her wedding present. "He's just overworked. Isn't that what you told me, Reb?"

I said nothing. That is what I told her, but it wasn't the truth. Anthony too fell silent.

Julia remained standing, her eyes affixed to his image. In a smooth motion she tipped her glass as if deliberately, staining the snowy lace with purple liquid as a libation to the gods to ward off the news she knew in her heart she was bound to receive.

Miranda slumped into her chair. To maintain the family equilibrium, Gerald rose to his feet. He held up a hand to fend off the footsteps of the enemy that he had heard approaching but that was just coming into view.

Anthony said nothing, so I said it for him.

"Anthony has AIDS."

Almost immediately it all fell apart. Gerald and Julia offered to prolong their stay but Anthony vetoed the idea, so they returned to London as planned on 2 January 1990, the day after their son's thirty-first birthday. He saw the doctor that week and tests revealed that Kaposi's sarcoma, a form of cancer associated with AIDS, was spreading through his lungs. He went on weekly doses of chemotherapy and started spiking fevers of 104; we paid regular visits to the emergency room of University Hospital until finally he had to be admitted. Substitutes had to be found for his classes, so he had no choice but to go on sick leave and "inform" his colleagues of a truth they had long since pieced together.

His parents rang daily. When his voice became too weak for him to speak to them, they asked me to broach the subject of their moving to Madison.

"There's something we need to discuss," I said to Anthony one snowy Monday evening. What is euphemistically called the spring semester had begun and I had to finish preparing my classes for the next day.

"What is it?"

I fought the urge to clutch him to my breast as in some fairy tale and carry him off to a safe haven in the woods.

"It's your parents. I spoke to them again this afternoon. They really want to come. They'd like to look after you."

"But you're looking after me," he said in a ratchetty whisper. "We don't need them."

"We will soon. When you come home, who's going to stay with you during the day while I'm on campus?"

"I shan't need anyone. I'll be fine on my own. I'll get better. I'll go back to teaching."

"Of course you will," I said, "but it may take a while. And in the meantime "

"We'll hire a nurse. Why should they uproot themselves to dole out aspirins?"

"We could look into a nurse, but Julia says she can easily do whatever you need at home." The doctors had made it clear to me that Anthony's care would involve far more than aspirins. I smiled and wiped his brow; we'd cross that bridge when we came to it.

"Reb, please don't let them come. You saw how Mummy was at Christmas after I'd broken the news to them. She'll never forgive me for getting this bloody thing. I can't bear the way she looked at me."

"How did she look at you?"

"As if I'd committed some kind of crime."

"What makes you believe that?" I countered. "She looked upset. They all did."

"You don't know her. She didn't say a word but I can tell she blames me. She'll never bring up the question of how I was infected—she'll do anything to avoid talking about sex. My God, she still hasn't told Auntie Barbara and Uncle Nigel that you and I are anything more than housemates."

"Do you really think they're that gullible?"

"I'm not saying they believe her. I'm just saying that's how she is."

"So you're telling me that the reason she's upset is not that you're ill, but that she doesn't want anyone to know what it is you have?"

He reached for a Kleenex and blew his nose. I could barely make out his words. "Let's just say she wouldn't feel the same if I had a brain tumour."

He was probably right; all the more reason to prove him wrong.

"Then why is she so anxious to come here with Gerald? That'll take some explaining to Auntie Barbara and Uncle Nigel." Julia had insisted that the extended family must not be told the true nature of Anthony's illness.

"I know she's sincere about wanting to look after me. I just think it's beyond her power not to pass judgement."

I was on the verge of conceding when my mind's eye recalled the image of Gerald about to board the plane. While Julia had the haggard look of a lieutenant leading her forces into battle, all Gerald had to take back home was his terror of losing the person he loved most. He clasped his son in his arms and pressed his own head tight against Anthony's ear, so that Anthony couldn't escape his embrace or see his features twisted into a mask of weeping that differed from a child's only in that it did not culminate in a belated shriek of grief but maintained its soundlessness to the very end.

"Most people would be grateful if their family went halfway around the world to look after them," I said. "Don't you think you owe it to them to let them come?"

Anthony looked down at his lap. His hair fell into his eyes; another few rounds of chemo and it would not be so thick. I took my comb out of my pocket and parted it the way he liked it. I thrashed about for the clincher.

"Just imagine having me cooking for you every day."

He wrinkled his nose. A fortnight later Gerald and Julia moved into a little flat just down the street from our house.

In spite of my checkered past with Anthony's mother, I was grateful for his parents' assistance. All too soon I realised that, whatever improvements in his condition he might enjoy from day to day, it was possible that he could die without warning at any time. I tried to convince myself that the time of his death would be a matter of fate or divine will, beyond my control or anyone else's; if I had to be away from the house, as long as his parents were by his side I should not dwell on what might happen in my absence. Whether or not that was a judicious assessment of the situation I would soon have the rest of my life to reflect upon.

chapter 20

After his parents moved to Madison, Anthony was able to continue chemo-therapy on an outpatient basis and his health rebounded. He put on a few pounds, stopped coughing, bought a wig, and carried on as if, on the turn of a dime, our lives had magically reverted to normalcy: as if the lat-est trend was for elderly parents to move three and a half thousand miles from home practically overnight, untenured academics regularly spent their summers receiving guests from the country that their research required them to visit but that they'd unaccountably resolved to boycott, and hand-some young men barely over thirty routinely resembled the "before" pic-tures of an advert for rejuvenating plastic surgery.

Once Julia ran out of excuses to explain why she and Gerald were liv-ing in Madison, she discovered that some of life's thorniest problems can be solved by simply telling the truth and nothing but the truth but not the whole truth. In the event, she said that Anthony was afflicted with a rare form of cancer, the details of which neither she nor Gerald was quali-fied to discuss. Hopefully the implausible tale helped her to sleep at night because it certainly fooled no one else.

Her announcement set in motion a stream of visits from Anthony's loved ones in the spring and summer of 1990. Childhood friends, old Oxford mates, and Gerald's brother Nick and his wife all occupied our guest room at various times. Julia's sister and brother-in-law, Barbara and Nigel Castle, shaved four days off of their annual pilgrimage to Antibes to fly over for a long weekend visit; they took us to L'Étoile, Madison's finest restaurant, and lavished praise on Margaret Thatcher, evoking Anthony's Halloween costume in what had been, in retrospect, happier days. But of all the visits that year, the two that stand out most in my mind are those of Willis and Molly in mid-May and of Miranda in July for Inde-pendence Day.

Anthony agreed that we could no longer postpone informing Willis and Molly of his illness after his hospital stay in the early spring of 1990. They reacted exactly as I had expected—dead silence, then muted weeping on the other end of the line. They barely held it together long enough to get down the basic facts: Anthony had been quite ill but was now home from the hospital, I was HIV-negative, and we hoped they would come and visit us at the end of the semester.

On the Saturday afternoon of their visit, a splendid day in May, Anthony was well enough to take a day trip to the Wisconsin Dells to view the spectacular gorges along the Wisconsin River, so a Boys' Day outing was arranged with Willis driving the two of them up in a rental car. Molly and I, who had volunteered to make dinner that evening, decided on a quick picnic lunch at the University of Wisconsin Arboretum to admire the spectacular lilac collection at the height of its blossoming.

We did the grand tour, in rapture at the fuchsia, lavender, pink, and white blossoms that looked like miniature Impressionist paintings suspended against the sky, then settled down in a perfumed hollow to lunch on local delicacies of brats, cheese curds, and Spotted Cow beer, with a bag of Danish kringles for dessert.

We ate and drank in silence, lost in our thoughts. Molly nibbled at her food and gazed at the boughs heavy with flowers. Finally she set her paper plate down on the grass and turned to me.

"Reb, there's something I need to discuss with you. It's not an easy topic and I've told almost nobody, but you and Anthony are our best friends, and I've just got to do it. Willis also agreed it was time. Are you all right with that?"

My heart sank. Could things possibly get worse?

"Is that a rhetorical question? Do I have a choice?"

"I know the timing's not ideal," Molly said. "It isn't for us, either." She stood and stretched her legs, pressed her nose against a large purple lilac cluster, and took a deep breath before sitting back down beside me.

"Here goes. Willis and I have been having some problems."

I let it sink in.

"I can't believe my ears," I said. "You've always been our model couple. Please don't tell me you're splitting up."

"No, I don't think so. It all began a couple of years ago. We got counselling then, and we're getting more now. It's helped quite a bit. We're planning a second honeymoon to Japan over the summer. Start again with a clean slate, as they say. Although you never really do," she added with a frown.

"That's a relief." I searched for the right words. "Thanks for telling me. Is this something you want to talk about, or are you just letting me know?"

"Talk about, I guess. Not that I really want to, but I think it's a good idea." Molly reached into her handbag and brandished a packet of tissues. "I guess we could both use some of these." We laughed. "Actually," she continued, "our recent round of problems was set off when Anthony told us his news. It brought back an excruciating period of my life."

"What?"

"The breakup with Yoko. Or I should say Sonny."

"Was that his real name?"

"His nickname."

"Because he shared your sunny disposition?" I said to interject a bit of levity.

"No, that's not why. You were never properly introduced to him at the Halloween party, but that's not the reason." Molly sighed. "As a matter of fact, my shrink told me I should stop referring to him jokingly as Yoko, as if he and I were still back in 1980 and living together. She said it was also preventing me from seeing him as he really was as opposed to some kind of fantasy."

"I don't see the connection. How did Anthony's news bring back memories of your ex-boyfriend?"

"I'm getting to that. A few days before your thirty-fifth birthday party, right after you and Anthony moved to Madison and we moved to Palo Alto, I got a phone call. It was Sonny."

"I didn't realise you two had kept in touch."

"We hadn't. I hadn't heard from him once since 1980. It came out of nowhere. I'm still not sure how he got my number."

I was having difficulty following the thread of Molly's story. "So Sonny finally came to his senses and realised he was still in love with you, is that it? What's that got to do with Anthony's news?"

"He didn't call to say he was still in love with me. He called to say he was HIV-positive. He said I should get tested."

I let a few seconds pass, absorbing the shock.

"Jesus, Molly. But you are both negative, you and Willis, right?"

"Yes, that much was true. What we didn't tell you was the reason we got tested. I said it was part of our intake physicals at Stanford, but it was actually because of Sonny. On the flight back to San Francisco after our visit to you I told Willis about his call, and we arranged to be tested as soon as we got back."

The news, first bad, then good, percolated through my brain.

"OK," I ventured at last, "so Sonny said you and Willis should get tested. You did, and you were both negative. I still don't see how—"

"I'm getting there." A silence. "Sorry, but it's really hard to talk about." Molly dabbed at her eyes with a tissue. "That call from Sonny really shook me up. He was my first love. I was totally smitten from the day we met freshman year in Madison. It was a gorgeous sunny day at the Union Terrace. I was in front of him in the beer line and we struck up a conversation. We bantered about what a funny couple we would make, with me being short and him tall. He asked me to a movie that evening and we never looked back.

"We were together for over four years. I was sure we would spend our lives together. Even when he was on a study abroad program we travelled in Europe at Christmas— we couldn't be apart for a whole year. I was starting to think about the names of the children we would have when he told me out of the blue that he wanted to break up. I still remember the date. December 10, 1980—the end of life as I knew it."

Molly paused and made a wry face to deflate the hyperbole. I leaned over and gave her hand a squeeze.

"It was more than I could bear," she went on. "I fell apart. He decided to drop out of school but wanted to finish the semester and couldn't move for a few weeks, so during that whole time I basically hunkered down in the living room and stared at the walls. Went to classes when I could and managed to salvage the semester, I honestly don't know how."

"You must have been relieved when he moved out."

"I wasn't. It was like losing him all over again."

Molly wept quietly. After a few minutes, she continued her story.

"You know, Reb, if it hadn't been for Willis I don't know what would have become of me. He called me one evening when I was lower than low. He got me to laugh, a minor miracle, and asked me out. He saved me. It's been different with him than it was with Sonny, but I've come to love him deeply. What I hadn't told him, because I didn't want to hurt him, was that

I'd never gotten over losing Sonny. It was like he was in my head without my permission. I did my best to squelch it, and finally managed not to think about Sonny too much. Things were on a pretty even keel—and then in 1988 he called to drop the bombshell.

"Hearing his voice on the phone brought it all back. Willis and I started having problems in the bedroom. I kept telling him I was just tired and stressed about my dissertation and the job hunt, but eventually I had to spill the beans. We worked through it at the time—the jobs at Stanford really helped, because it seemed easier being in a new place, at least for a while. But there must still have been a wound festering under there somewhere, because when I heard about Anthony a couple of months ago . . ." Her voice trailed off, then went up a notch when she resumed speaking. "Please don't think that the first thing I thought of when Sir A told us he had AIDS was the way Sonny broke my heart. My heart did break again when I heard Anthony's news, but it was for him, for both of you, and also for Willis and me because we love you both so much. It was just later that I started having flashbacks to Sonny's phone call, and then to the years of our relationship, especially the breakup. I knew I had to level with Willis, though I dreaded it. I've always been so afraid of hurting him. Like I said, the therapy has done a world of good and Willis has been an angel. He always is."

"So I've noticed."

I kissed Molly and gave her a hug. She collected herself, looking weary but relieved.

"Say, I guess it's true that crying builds up an appetite," she said, reaching for a kringle. She glanced at her watch and, chewing discreetly, added, "We should be getting back to do the food shopping. We've got to make something really good tonight—Anthony's mother has sure earned her evening off."

We gathered our things and walked arm-in-arm to the car.

"By the way," I said once we were pulling out onto Seminole Highway, "did Sonny mention how he might have gotten infected? Was he bisexual or something?"

"Not that I know of. I asked him, but he refused to say. I also asked him if he knew who had infected him, and he said he couldn't discuss it."

"What was his family name?"

A doe dashed across the road and into the Arboretum not two yards in front of the car. I slammed on the brakes and missed her by inches.

"Thank God you didn't hit the poor thing," said Molly. "I hope she'll be safe in the park." We rode on in silence. "That scared the pajamas off me. What were you asking me about?"

"Nothing," I replied. It occurred to me that it would be kinder to Molly, who was, after all, on a mission of mercy to cheer up an ailing friend, to spare her further reminders of the man who'd broken her heart.

Miranda's Independence Day visit was dramatic in its own way. She left behind in New York her husband, whose daughter from his first marriage was summering with them, but carried onto the plane their unborn child, due some time in December. Prior to her arrival she had informed neither her parents nor Anthony of the blessed event.

When plump Miranda emerged from the arrivals area at the airport and embraced thin Anthony, I had the absurd impression that the purpose of her visit was to deliver pounds to her brother. Julia pecked at her daughter's cheek, then stood back to observe her. "Goodness, isn't it the husband that's meant to put on weight after the honeymoon?"

Miranda turned her attention towards Anthony. She did not bother to fake a smile as she took in his drawn face and baggy clothes.

"Could be worse. I thought you'd be skinnier."

Anthony, who had guessed his sister was with child, replied, "I thought you would be, too. When is it due? Shall I count it out on my fingers or is it all on the up and up?"

Julia's face froze; she began fretting about whether her future grandchild had been conceived out of wedlock a split second before fully registering that her daughter was pregnant.

Miranda was pleased to see a glimmer of the old Anthony. "Nothing that interesting, I'm afraid. She's not due till December, which gives us rather a large window of respectability." Julia's face relaxed. "We started trying straightaway," Miranda boomed in merriment, "but it takes a few months after you go off the—"

"Yes, yes, all right—your father's the one who's hard of hearing," chided Julia before turning to pleasanter matters. "Well, I expect congratulations are in order." She gave Miranda's arm a squeeze. "Have you checked any bags?"

Back at the house we all sat on the deck sipping iced tea. There was a moment of silence when Miranda announced that the child would be named Antonia.

Anthony said nothing and I could tell he was fighting off tears. Julia brushed a leaf from her linen skirt and spoke as if she had just decided to bring up an idea she had been contemplating for weeks.

"Anthony darling, are you in the mood for a bit of a fête? Perhaps I could throw something together for the Independence Day holiday on Wednesday. You could invite some of your colleagues. They'll be pleased to see how well you're looking."

The dozen or so guests arrived about an hour before sunset, the evening's main event being the annual fireworks put on by the town of Monona, situated directly across the lake. After dinner, as the sky turned indigo, we sat on deck chairs or sprawled on the lawn that slopes down to the lake and even today puts me in mind of a miniature Lake District version of Manderley. It was a breezy evening, one of those heavenly respites from July heat that make life in the Upper Midwest worth living. When the sky was almost black, the first booms could be heard from across the lake, and fireballs of various shapes and colours hurtled into the heavens. My favourite ones reminded me of Willis's afro.

Anthony was lying on the grass with his head cradled in my lap, but when the fireworks began he sat up, drawing his knees to his chest, and in the dim light I could picture the naked scout sitting on the bed in my little studio that very first night in New Haven. His mouth remained slightly open, like a child's, as if this modest display were the grandest he had ever seen. "It's absolutely super," he said, planting a kiss on my forehead and squeezing my hand. "What a perfect evening."

I did my best to forget the future, to lose myself, as Anthony had, in the charm of the moment. I rumpled his hair, almost managing to block out that it was a wig. Miranda, sitting sedately in a lawn chair, had given herself over to the enchantment of the hour as well. She crowed in delight at each liftoff, as if seeing it through the eyes of little Antonia.

The night Miranda left for New York, just after Anthony and I got into bed and turned out the light, he said, "Reb, do you think I'll live long enough to meet Antonia?"

I enveloped him completely in my arms. "Of course you will. Miranda promised they'd come out as soon as she's born."

"What if I never see Miranda again? She shouldn't travel until after the baby is born. What if things get really bad?"

"That won't happen. Trust me." I could just make out Anthony's profile in the darkness. He was looking up at his little sky, which he had recently put up on the slanted ceiling above our bed. "Please say you believe me."

He lowered his eyes and met my gaze.

"Yes, you're right. I'm being silly. I do believe you."

I didn't believe I was right any more than Anthony did; we were both right about that. He was unable to go back to teaching in the fall and by Christmas 1990 his chemotherapy treatments, too much for his weakened immune system to handle, had to be put on hold, allowing the KS free reign. The dreaded cough made its reappearance, along with shortness of breath, oxygen tanks, and hours spent at the hospital for tests and procedures that yielded all sorts of invaluable information the doctors could not do a thing about.

Three days before Christmas, ten years to the day after she and I first espied each other across Miranda's sitting room, Julia asked me to drive her to the supermarket to do the grocery shopping for the holiday meal. She was planning on making all of Anthony's favourites even though he could no longer force down more than a few mouthfuls at a single sitting. Miranda had reiterated her promise to come to Madison as soon as Antonia was born and could travel but the baby was overdue. As far as I could tell, this projected visit was the only thing keeping Anthony going.

Julia and I rode to the supermarket in silence. In the past months I had felt a grudging appreciation for the devotion with which she looked after her son, and she too had made the odd comment suggesting I wasn't the bad egg she had once taken me for. As she watched me flush Anthony's catheter, administer his inhalations, or check his blood oxygen, her face was a mask of benevolence. And yet something about the tension of her features suggested she would never become fully accustomed to seeing a thirty-something man with black hair tending to a slightly younger male counterpart who would be her direct heir if, as appeared unlikely, he survived her.

On the rare occasions we had been thrown together on our own, Julia and I had found few topics of conversation other than food preparation, Shakespeare, and the differences between the English and the American climates. Now, with Anthony in the final stages of his illness, we both knew that we were beyond chitchat. I could tell from her solemn tone of voice as we turned into the supermarket's parking lot that she was not about to share her thoughts about Madison's and London's relative chances for a white Christmas.

"Reb, there's something I should like to speak to you about. I know this is a peculiar time, but it's difficult back at the house."

The lot was jammed with holiday shoppers, and I pulled into a spot on the periphery, then glanced over towards my right. Julia's head was slumped forwards. When she resumed speaking, the awkward position of her neck weakened her voice. For the first time she sounded like the elderly lady she was.

"Reb, we both know Anthony is going to die soon. There will be difficult decisions to make. I hope you don't mind my talking to you, but Gerald is in no state to address these issues."

My mind, groggy with grief, could not grasp the British pronunciation of the last word, which to my ears sounded something like "is youse." But when my ear was able to decipher the word, I knew right away what issues Julia was talking about. How and where Anthony should die. Whether he should be hospitalised, put on a respirator, kept at home. A nurse's questions: what kind of narcotics, how much, how soon? I could imagine a time when Julia and I would speak freely in an empty room, no longer in fear Anthony might overhear, about all of those other issues that adhere to death from the posterior side. I played Julia's last sentence over in my head. Gerald is in no state to address these issues. Gerald is in no state to address these, is youse? Gerald is in no state to address, is you? Gerald is in a state of undress, are you?

"Yes, I suppose you're right," I said. "About Gerald, I mean." Gerald had been quite brave, all things considered. As he watched his son's life ebbing away, it must have been a torment to limit his drinking to the evenings, when Julia and I could attend to Anthony without Gerald's assistance. Nevertheless, some of his mornings-after made me fear he would predecease his son. Perhaps he would be better off. "About Anthony, though . . ." I went on, then hesitated. If Julia had said the sentence about his imminent demise in her usual detached voice, it would have made me cringe. But she, too, was in a state of undress. "I don't know," I continued. "I can't let myself give up. Don't you think that if he sees us give up, he will too?"

Julia's sobs sounded surprisingly natural. When she was able to speak, her voice was no longer the one I was accustomed to. "My dear boy, of course I do. Don't you understand? We must help him to do just that."

chapter 21

Several times in the weeks after Eric locks lips with me before fleeing from my house I pick up the phone to give him a call. But even if he didn't immediately hang up on me—a very big if—would I demand an explanation for his rude departure or ask him who taught him how to kiss like that?

If only I happened to bump into him somewhere, perhaps I could size things up in a neutral setting—Madison is a great town for planning chance encounters. So on the morning of Saturday, 28 August, I get to the farmer's market by eight thirty and stroll around the Square for a good two hours, trying to convince myself I'm not scouting for anyone or anything in particular. I happen upon several former students, a neighbour, and the director of the funeral home where Anthony was taken, but no Eric. In frustration I decide to ride my bike up to Devil's Lake and go for a long swim. I am enchanted, as always, by the Alpine setting of clear water ringed by high bluffs, but as I swim, eventually my thoughts turn back to Anthony's 11:11 message. I have to admit that four weeks after receiving it, I have no idea what my next move should be.

I return home well after sunset, exhilarated and soothed by my workout, as always, but utterly spent. As if drawn by a magnet, I walk into the sitting room and lie down on the futon, in the very spot and position Anthony was in when he left this world.

In his absence the place's sameness suddenly seems an act of violence: the identical furniture and decor, probably even some of the same dust particles on the blinds—I'm not much of a housekeeper. And yet no Anthony, the only part of this room that has ever mattered. I wonder how it is possible that an environment transformed by loss can fail to differentiate itself in some perceptible manner from the way it was in the past.

I close my eyes and conjure up Anthony's face but also hear his voice, unbeckoned. *Darling, please don't go, not yet. Sit beside me, just a little longer.*

He would never make a scene, but far worse than a scene is his face imploring me to stay, the defenceless features now highlighted against the blackness of my closed eyelids. Will I be plagued by this image until the day I die?

A sudden twinge in my lumbar region. From the sublime to the ridiculous: this futon is becoming lumpy. It, at least, is different than it was when Anthony breathed his last. Futons are for young people, not soon-to-be-forty-year-olds like me. Is it giving me a foretaste of the comfortless fate ahead of me if I bed down in the next decade of my life alone, without Anthony or another by my side? Perhaps it is not I who have changed but the futon that has calcified. Even if you do nothing and go nowhere, is it not the way of the world to change out from under you, like an area code?

I stand and slip my hands between the futon and its frame to flip it, as one is supposed to do at regular intervals but as I have not done since we settled in this house five years ago. And what emerges is what had to emerge.

Anthony's address book.

The last place I would have thought of looking, and yet the most logical. Anthony spent many long hours on the futon during those final weeks. He must have slipped his address book under the mattress so that it would be within easy reach.

The book is open to S. It has been sat and lain upon for so long in this position that it seems varnished open to that page. I look at the first entry: Willis Smith and Molly Matsuda, their address in Palo Alto, and their phone number. This too seems reasonable: our dearest friends must have been the last people Anthony phoned after I left him on that final day.

Already the address book has told me something I didn't know about the events of the day Anthony died. The only other entry on the S page, this one carefully printed in capital letters, also gives me a similar type of information I did not previously possess: ERIC (SONNY) SUNDERGAARD.

I ring Eric's doorbell twice, three times. I've forgotten my watch, but it must be after ten; I wonder if he is out of town. Finally I hear footsteps approaching. When he opens the door I barely resist the impulse to punch him.

"May I come in?" I say instead.

Eric is clearly nonplussed but steps aside and ushers me into the hallway with a sweeping gesture.

"Please take a seat," he says with exaggerated politeness. "What can I do for you?"

I remain standing, on my guard. "Why didn't you tell me you knew Anthony and Molly?"

The blood drains from his face.

"How did you find out?" A robot's voice.

"Anthony's address book. I had been looking for it for a long time and I just found it. I hope you'll forgive me if I don't call you Sonny."

The robot nods. "Do you mind if we sit?"

We do so. Eric says nothing for a long time.

"I know I should have been up front with you," he finally says. "I owe you an explanation. But it's difficult to know where to begin."

He extends his right arm, as long as a crane on a construction site, towards the coffee-table trunk. He lifts the lid. And what he pulls out of the trunk and hands over to me is a miracle: Anthony. The Anthony who was never mine.

I look down at the photo. On it are two young men standing close together side by side, their arms discreetly touching. They are set against the unmistakable backdrop of Coventry Cathedral, the new edifice built hard against the old, ruined one. The figure on the left is instantly recognisable as a much younger Eric. His youth, now a thing of the past, is perceptible in an expression of ecstasy of which not the slightest vestige remains today. The illumination is that of English spring, white with hardly a hint of yellow, the thin cool light of northern climes, of Eric's ancestors as well as Anthony's. The latter, standing on the right, also wears a countenance I have never seen, its features fresh and inchoate, the sea-green eyes radiant, unguarded. I met Anthony when he was twenty-one, a young man, fully formed and well protected. Here he is still a boy, a creature of careless health and nonchalant beauty. He is basking in true love, love beyond reason and beyond explanation, without beginning and without end.

When I look up, tears are hanging from Eric's lashes, but his face remains composed.

"I was Anthony's lover," he says, "long before you were."

Eric is Rebecca. He lied to me about Harvard—actually he started law school at Yale in 1980 and dropped out at the end of his first semester, when things fell apart with Molly and then Anthony. He now stares at the ground to avoid my gaze as the truth spills willy-nilly from his lips.

He admits that the main reason he questioned me about Anthony as if he didn't know him was that he had always wanted to find out exactly what went on between Anthony and me before and after the two of them split up. He was filled in on some of the basics when he phoned Anthony about HIV testing in August 1988 but couldn't resist taking advantage of a naïve narrator like myself to get a more detailed version of the story.

I listen intently but say nothing until Eric, though clearly not finished, lapses into silence, wipes his face with a handkerchief, excuses himself, and makes his way towards the loo.

"But how did you and Anthony meet?" I ask abruptly, fearing that he might be too upset to continue the story if he takes a break.

"I'll tell you when I get back."

At random I pick up pictures in great clumps from the open treasure chest, precious doubloons from a sunken galleon. Dozens, hundreds of snapshots have lain here pell-mell for well over a decade. Anthony and Eric in Oxford, in London, in Venice, in Paris. Eric's expression is suggestive of an earthly Valhalla. I can contemplate Anthony's features—this face of a man who never looked at me with the adoration I see here on display— only fleetingly before I admit defeat and avert my eyes.

Eric returns and sets down two tall glasses of whiskey. After several swigs I feel the first reassuring hints of numbness in my legs. He takes a seat in the rocker across from me. This time he looks directly at me as he is about to speak but I involuntarily shield my eyes with one hand to shelter myself from the pain of receiving the second installment of his tale.

"We met in England," he begins. "June of 1978. In September of that year I was going to start the Wisconsin junior-year-abroad programme in Coventry. I decided to spend the summer before in Oxford taking a Shake-speare course for foreigners to get used to the place—it was my first time abroad.

"We met at a pub. I had never been with a man, and it was . . . Let's just say it went quickly. All that summer we were inseparable. Once classes started in the fall we went back and forth between Oxford and Coventry every weekend. We travelled together whenever we could. Molly came over from Madison for Christmas and she and I spent the holidays in Spain and Portugal, but Anthony and I went to Paris in the spring. It was magic."

It was magic. The words slice through my chest but don't surprise me. That's how I've always known it was between Anthony and Rebecca.

"Then it was June of 1979, and I had to fly back to the States to work on my folks' farm for the summer. Anthony said maybe we should accept reality and call it a day, but I begged him to come to America for grad school once he finished his degree. I longed for us to have a chance to really be together. I called him on the phone every week that whole year—it cost me so much I had to take out a loan."

But it was worth it, I think, drawing a twisted pleasure from this variation on a story I have told myself so many times I almost enjoy the fresh permutations.

"I did finally convince him," Eric goes on. "We both applied to Yale. I didn't tell Molly about him, so she applied, too. That's how we all ended up in New Haven. It was a terrible idea." He grimaces. "I still loved Molly, but I wasn't in love with her anymore. I should have left her sooner, but Anthony was so elusive, so hard to pin down. I didn't know which way to turn. I was afraid that if I waited too long he'd get impatient, but if I left her too soon he'd feel crowded.

"In the end the timing probably didn't matter all that much. He eventually realised it wasn't working for him, the two of us together. I told him that if there was any chance he might reconsider, I would wait for him for as long as it took even though he had made it clear that his mind was made up. You do these stupid things when you're crazy in love. I would have done anything for him."

Eric's final observation diverges from my script. I look him straight in the eye.

"What do you mean? You just said it wasn't working for him. But you were the one who ended it."

Eric does a double take.

"I did not. I never would have done that. He dumped me."

I stride over to him; he stands. Given our relative sizes, he could take me out in a heartbeat, but I cannot listen to another word of his gibberish.

"Tell me the truth or I swear to God I'll kill you!"

I flail at him blindly but he easily holds me at arm's length. Eventually I wear myself out trying to land a punch. He guides me to the futon and lets me fall, sobbing.

When I look up, the trunk has been shut, a closed casket. Eric is back in the rocker, cradling an eight-by-ten photograph of Anthony standing at a spot I find vaguely familiar but can't quite place. In the picture it is a sunny day but the trees are bare; Anthony is clad in his winter coat. Before him stands a pay phone next to an iron gate.

It is the street door of the Hall of Graduate Studies in New Haven.

Eric casts tender eyes on the picture and recites the rest of his tale to it, as if bidding Anthony a final adieu.

"This was taken in December of 1980. We were supposed to spend Christmas in New York with his sister and his parents. I was going to meet his family for the first time. I was on cloud nine. It felt like after two and a half years he was finally making a commitment. I broke up with Molly. Our first couple of years together were great, but once I met him . . . She cried and cried and I felt terrible—I hated hurting her like that. I couldn't move out of our apartment right away and in the meantime I could see she was going through hell, but I couldn't bring myself to tell her the whole story about Anthony and me. I didn't know how she'd react, and it occurred to me that it might just make things all the harder for her to bear. I figured I would tell her the truth in due time, once Anthony and I let out our secret and she was over the split. But it didn't work out that way."

Eric reaches for his whiskey glass and takes a long, slow sip before continuing.

"The day Anthony and I were supposed to leave for New York, he stopped by my room. He had already told me about you in early October but had claimed it was nothing serious. At the Halloween party I figured out you two had arrived together and Anthony and I argued about it in the kitchen. After that I just stopped asking—I was too afraid of what he might say. Then, that day in December when he and I were supposedly leaving for New York, he came to my room in the afternoon, just a few hours before we were supposed to catch the train. He hemmed and hawed before lowering the boom: things between us couldn't continue. He had decided he couldn't give you up. It was over."

I say nothing but shake my head in disbelief. Still clutching his photo, Eric rises and sits next to me, waves of pain flowing from his fjord-coloured eyes.

"You must believe me, Reb. I never got over losing him. Don't you see how pointless it is for us both to think we were losers? How can I convince you?"

"You can't. After all the lies you've told me, how can you expect me to trust that what you're saying is the truth?"

I stand up to leave. Eric clamps his hands onto my shoulders, forces me back down.

"Look at this picture of Anthony," he says, his voice no longer pleading but desperate. The photo is sitting in his lap; he holds it up for me to inspect. "It was taken in December of 1980, the day Anthony invited me to spend Christmas with his family. The happiest day of my life."

I take a fleeting look, the most I can endure.

"Yeah, what about it?"

"No, not like that," Eric snaps. "Really look at it, take your time. Here, hold it yourself." He thrusts the photo into my lap.

I pick it up hesitantly. I peruse Anthony's face. All I register is the fact that it is not for me that this man I adore is smiling; nothing but my own baseline unlovability.

My fury rises.

"Thanks for rubbing it in," I cry. "All this proves is that Anthony was head-over-heels in love with someone else while he and I were having a pathetic little fling. At the time I didn't know who the other person was, but believe me, I'd already figured out that I wasn't top dog."

Eric takes the photo from me and glances at it, all he needs to do because he has memorised its every pixel. He hands it back and speaks now in a calm voice, without anger.

"Look at his eyes. Look at Anthony's eyes. What do you see?"

What is there to see? A man blissful to be smiling for the person he adores. That is what I expect to meet my gaze, but when I look more closely, it is as if by some trick of light Anthony has suddenly aged a decade. His face is that of a man grown prematurely old in a youth's body. In spite of his smile his eyes are shadowed, clouded by feelings he's unwilling to express. His features are unsettled, duplicitous. This is not the face of a man contemplating the one he loves. It is the face of a man playing the role of a man in love.

"OK, so the two of you had your ups and downs," I concede gracelessly, unwilling to give in. "What couple doesn't? That doesn't prove a goddamn thing. Maybe he could sense that you were getting impatient and were thinking about leaving him, which I'm certain was the case in spite of the fairy tale you've concocted."

Eric sits down beside me. He takes a deep breath and I think he is about to admit that his story is nothing but a fresh lie, fabricated for my benefit or to get him off the hook.

"If you don't believe me, then let me relay to you exactly what Anthony said to me that day in my room. He was terribly upset; he didn't want to hurt me. I know he loved me in his way, even though I was not the center of his world as he was of mine, and as you were of his. He cried almost as much as I did. But I could tell from his voice that he was speaking the truth.

"He said that he fell in love with you the evening you first met. He was afraid that if you found out he was seeing someone else, he would lose you. Guess I can't make you believe what you refuse to accept because you're so damned eager to knock yourself down. But that's exactly how it was."

Strange as it may seem, I just can't give it up; it is no small matter to let go of my neat story about Prince Charming and the chimney sweep. Is it not my very essence to be the flunky who patched up the prince's broken heart when the one he truly desired got away? This troubling tale, one I have never cared for, resembles a pair of faultily ground eyeglasses I was given as a child. I became so accustomed to them that when I had to exchange them for a pair that allowed me to see more clearly, I did so with a measure of regret.

"I'm not saying I believe you," I reply, "but supposing you're telling the truth, why did Anthony never bother to share those little tidbits with me?"

"He was probably afraid of letting you see how much he needed you."

"Why? What was there to be afraid of?"

"He thought it might scare you off."

"But Anthony wasn't like that," I protest, unable to process this version of an alternate universe I have apparently inhabited unawares for over a decade of my life. "He wasn't the fearful type, always second-guessing himself like me. He was strong." Suddenly Anthony's terrified face at the time of Hurricane Gloria flashes across my mind. I am no longer sure of anything but make a feeble final attempt to stave off the truth. "Come on, Eric, you knew him too. He wasn't someone who was easily cowed."

Eric reflects for a few seconds.

"I suppose that's true, but confident people also have their fears. And when he talked about you, it was pretty clear that the one thing he most feared was that you would leave him."

chapter 22

Eric offers to drive me home, but I have my bicycle; I am hoping the night air will clear my reeling head. I leave his place so completely in a daze that it doesn't occur to me to enquire about his health. Back at the house I am overwhelmed by what he has revealed. It must be midnight by now, a new day, but how can I offer myself shelter in this place where, as I now understand, my lover needed me so desperately, not only on the day he died but from the very start?

To deny myself the comforts of home I decide to spend the night camping out on the plastic recliner that resides on the second-storey deck. I sleep little, watch the stars wheel slowly about overhead. Once again, as it was on the night I received Anthony's message, the moon is waxing and nearly full, its light ancient and enervated. The sky is just beginning to pale in the east when I go inside and make espresso.

I no sooner take my first sip than I recognise the symptoms of a panic attack; a racing pulse, hyperventilation, and the feeling of a stifling mantle being thrown over my head. This is claustrophobia of a different sort. The house is not a tunnel or a closet. What I am trapped in is the present, what keeps me from asking Anthony's forgiveness not space but time. If he were alive, I would travel to the ends of the earth to find him. I would sit quietly beside him, just the two of us, and explain how much I have always loved him, why I was unable to show it on that last day, and why I cannot go on living without his forgiveness. I would find a way to make him understand how grateful I am to have discovered that he loves me as much as I have always loved him.

But now, today, these are things I cannot do. I am bathed in sweat, each breath a challenge. In the months after Anthony's death I had similar attacks; I still have the bottle of pills I was given to get through them. I take one. I could ring my doctor but today is Sunday, and he'll tell me to go to the emergency room. At the end of August they will be understaffed. I cannot see the point of spending the day in chairs only to inform some dull-eyed resident that the source of my panic is that I betrayed my lover on the day he died.

It is still very early for a Sunday morning but for lack of a better course of action I call Miranda in New York. I have not spoken to Anthony's sister in a couple of months. I must hear the closest thing to his voice that will ever greet my ears in this lifetime.

"Hello. You have reached the residence of Miranda Payton and Ed Rosen." Goddammit. Ed's voice, not Miranda's. "We are unable to answer your call at this time, but if you'd like to leave a message, please do so after the beep."

"Hi, Miranda, it's Reb. Sunday morning, August 29th, and I'm not—"

Click.

"Reb. How lovely to hear from you. Sorry about the machine, but—"

"It's fine, it's fine. Thank God you're there."

"Is something wrong?"

"Panic attacks. They're back. Worse than ever."

"You poor dear—you sound dreadful. What brought them on?"

"I don't think I can talk about it on the phone. It has to do with Anthony."

"Anthony?"

"He really loved me."

Silence, and then, "Of course he really loved you, darling. What in the world are you talking about?"

"No, I mean right from the start. He was frightened I would leave him. I never believed it, and I did." All I can think of is his sweet, defence-less face that last minute, when he didn't want to let me go. "Miranda, please come to Madison. I can't be alone right now. I don't know how to go on without him."

"Reb, you must try—"

"No more pep talks, please. I appreciate it, really I do. I've done what you said. I've tried not to blame myself. I've done what everyone's said. I've kept busy. I can't do it anymore."

Another silence, much longer this time, quite reassuring: if she stops and thinks about it, she'll have to come. Do I hear voices in the back-ground? Perhaps she's discussing it with Ed. She knows Anthony would want her to come in his place. If she says no, I'll bring that up, guilt-trip her into changing her mind. I'll resort to anything.

"Reb, listen to me. Have you got that medication the doctor gave you?"

"Yes. I've taken one."

"Good. Have you rung the doctor?"

"It's Sunday and he'll send me to the emergency room. I can't go back to that place anymore, that hospital. Not one more time."

I can hear Miranda taking a deep breath. "Reb, I want you to come to New York. You can stay with us as long as you'd like. I would come to Madison, honestly I would, but I simply can't. Antonia's got a bad sore throat. Ed's in California and I can't leave her with . . . without finding some—"

"How can I come to New York? You know I can't get on a plane. I would flip."

"You must. You can do it, Reb. You may not believe you can, but I am certain of it. Do you understand? I want you to hang up the telephone and book the next flight. If you're short on money—"

"No, no, that's not the—"

"Then just do it. Don't think about it. If Anthony were here, he would say the same thing."

"If Anthony were here, I wouldn't need to go anywhere."

"You know what I mean."

I do what she says. I manage to get a late-morning flight to O'Hare with a connection to Newark at the height of the vacation season the LaGuardia and JFK flights are completely booked up. The short lead time leaves me only an hour or so to throw some things into a bag, pay a few bills, and arrange for a neighbour to take in the post; it is unclear how long I will be away. I down another pill and call for a taxi.

The last time I've sweated as much as I do at the Madison airport was when I ran a marathon, a piece of cake compared with those forty-five minutes of torture at the gate. The flight from Madison to Chicago, on a tiny commuter plane, is touch-and-go from start to finish. The hardest moment comes at the beginning, when the stewardess announces that the hatch is being shut and I can no longer change my mind unless I'm up for some skydiving. Miranda told me on the phone that writing is a good way to make it through a claustrophobia attack, so I scribble indiscriminate word associations on a yellow legal pad, a technique which, judging from their results, is also apparently favored by my students when they are composing their term papers. In my case it is more effective, distracting me from the narrow aisle, the low, low ceiling, and the tall heavyset man sitting next to me who keeps stretching out his legs and hogging the armrest. The second plane, from O'Hare to Newark, is bigger, and I have the first flight under my belt; with the help of an additional pill, I am able to doze. Soon I hear a flight attendant announcing that we are starting our descent.

Miranda will meet me at the airport. I wonder what it will be like to see her again for the first time in more than two years, since Anthony's funeral. I heave a sigh of relief that for now my ordeal is at an end.

My trial by fire is about to begin.

I have a feeling of elation when I spot Miranda striding up to greet me as I enter the waiting area at Newark Airport. My relief is mixed with astonishment when a few steps behind her, fidgeting with a strand of limp grey hair and staring blankly into the middle distance, I glimpse a shrivelled old lady it takes me a good ten seconds to recognise as Julia.

I have not seen Julia since a month after Anthony's death; she and Gerald stayed on in Madison for several weeks after the funeral to keep me company and help me get his affairs in order. Gerald died four months ago, of liver cancer. Miranda reported to me that his illness, detected not very long after they returned to England, was treated aggressively, prolonging his utterly pointless suffering, for it was clear to her even before his diagnosis that he wished only to die. Julia is a shock to behold. Two years ago she had the face and bearing of a woman in her early fifties. Today, at seventy-two, she could easily be on the wrong side of eighty. She still holds herself as rigidly as an icicle, but her upper body now tilts forwards twenty degrees, and several inches of her have melted away; she is shorter than Gerald was in his prime. Her hair, ash-coloured without the tiniest reminiscence of blond, flops over her skull with disinterest. Her legs are inverted antennae, her face a soufflé that, once splendid and impressive, has deflated at room temperature.

Miranda approaches wearing a broad smile. She gives me a long, tight hug.

"Reb. I'm so glad you've made it. I knew you could do it!"

She is as lovely as ever. Motherhood has filled out her figure in a way most becoming to a woman of her height. Her hair, worn long again but now in a single braid, has taken on a few natural swirls of grey as tasteful as the décor of her sitting room.

"Miranda, it's good to see you. Hello, Julia. What a surprise." No point overstating my case with her. "Miranda didn't mention you were in New York."

"How was your flight, Reb?" Julia asks quietly in an old lady's voice.

"Not too bad. It turned out OK."

Miranda squeezes my shoulder. "That's marvellous! Now you'll be able to visit often and go all sorts of other places as well. Make up for lost time, as they say."

The phrase, however anodyne, saddens me.

"Miranda, why didn't you tell me Julia is here? Couldn't she have looked after Antonia?"

Julia fusses with something in her handbag. Miranda says, "Mummy doesn't like to be left alone with her. We got a sitter for the afternoon so we could come meet you." Julia continues to stare down at her purse.

The traffic on the New Jersey Turnpike is heavy, not unusual for a late Sunday in August when folks are returning to the city after their summer holidays or weekend getaways, but it moves along at a decent clip. I shut my eyes and lean back, grateful to breathe an air other than that of the place where Anthony breathed his last. I visited New York with him many times but, unlike Madison, the city is not, in my mind, completely synonymous with him, for I have taken other pleasures here as well, with Anne, with Willis and Molly, alone and with other friends. I inhale a lungful of New York air with its peculiar sweet-and-sour bouquet, and for the first time in as long as I can recall, the images conjured up in my brain by my surroundings are not of sickness, separation, and loss, but of fun and enjoyment, as if remnants of life's pleasures have escaped being sucked into the black hole I now inhabit.

I hear Miranda downshifting and feel the car slowing down. I stretch my legs in contentment; Julia, who is sitting behind me, has insisted I put my seat back as far as it will go. Without opening my eyes I ask:

"Where are we? Are we in the city yet?"

Miranda replies, "Not quite. Coming up to the Holland Tunnel. It's nearly always backed up on a Sunday."

I open my eyes and glimpse a vision of hell.

"Reb, are you . . . ? Oh, dear. The tunnel. I hadn't thought."

"I can't do it. I'm really sorry, we'll have to turn around."

Other cars, millions and millions of them, cover every inch of the New Jersey Turnpike all the way back to the Pennsylvania state line. We have passed the last exit. There is nowhere to go but into the tunnel.

Miranda's voice remains calm. "Have you got your pills on you?"

"Yes."

"Take one."

I do, but it will not start kicking in for at least five or ten minutes. Perhaps if the traffic jam continues, the sedative will have taken effect by the time we have reached the mouth of the tunnel.

Out of nowhere the congestion ahead of us suddenly eases. We roll forwards next to the toll booth.

I pull up the button and reach for the door handle. "I'm going to get out."

"Reb, you can't. Don't be silly. Where are you going to go?"

"Nowhere. I can wait in the toll booth."

"Darling, you can't."

"Anywhere. Just not in the tunnel."

Miranda turns to face me. Behind her I hear the irate voice of the toll-booth man.

"C'mon, lady, make it snappy. I ain't got all day."

Miranda reaches for my hand.

"Listen to me. We are going through the tunnel. The three of us, together. If you don't do it now, it will be harder the next time."

I am about to open the door, take to my heels. Cars are everywhere, ants swarming over spilt sugar. But where can I go? Back to Madison, to Anthony's house? The house I left behind when he needed me the most, the place now empty of everything but his absence—and my unpardonable sin of omission? I can never return to the drought of days that has been my existence for as long as I care to remember, for remembering further back is remembering in the desert the cool waters of the last oasis.

We are in the tunnel. The walls are everywhere. Not Miranda, not Julia, but they are my travelling companions. There is nothing but them. They come at me from left and right. From above and below. From behind.

Worst of all, from ahead. I am being hurled forwards against my will towards a vanishing point that will release me nevermore.

I close my eyes, concentrate on the movement of the air. Is the pill working? Surely we'll soon be through. If I open my eyes, perhaps I'll see the light; the light at the end of the tunnel.

I do not. We come to a halt. Eerily glowing worm eyes, segment after segment of unnatural light. Cars full of bodies and souls not my lover's. I must seek him elsewhere. If I slashed the worm-belly open from inside, I could hold my breath and swim for the safety of the waters above before its mucous cocooned me away from the river's cleansing.

The traffic is stopped, and stopped, and stopped. Not the smooth continuation of a stable state but each moment a renewal of torment. A victim of torture feels not the ongoing pressure of a thumb on his eyeball, but with each passing instant the thumb's refusal to let up, a refusal that will last forever.

I close my eyes again. We are still not moving in space. My brain must free me from these walls, so it whisks me back in time. Back to the time of the crime. To the time and the scene of the crime.

It is the morning of 1 February 1991. Gerald and Julia arrive at the house around six to spell me after my night-watch. I must keep an eye on Anthony, who sometimes pulls his oxygen tube out in his sleep, I arise at ten to find him having tea with Julia. He looks alert and cheerful, better than he has in days. He says:

"Mummy, I want to sit with Reb now. Just the two of us."

Julia nods, walks wordlessly from the room, and returns shortly carrying a cup of fresh coffee with exactly the right amount of sugar. She wears an uncanny expression I have never seen.

It is a sunny day, cold pale light flooding the room. We watch an ice fisherman waiting for a bite, a little dark statue of human forbearance surrounded by miles of dismal whiteness. I have never had the patience of a fisherman, but sometimes in the past few weeks, basking in the receding dream of Anthony's presence, I have felt myself in a pure here and now, unsullied by worries about the past or concerns for the future; a transitory state of grace.

A few minutes before 11:11, like a man awakening in dread on a blizzardy morning shortly before the alarm, I force myself to stand.

"I'd better get going if I want to make it to the pool by eleven thirty. We'll sit in here later and watch the lake some more. A nice sunny day, isn't it? Not so bad for February."

In these last weeks of his life Anthony cries more easily than he used to, and he sniffles now.

"Darling, please don't go, not yet. Sit beside me, just a little longer. It's so lovely sitting next to you and looking out at the lake."

"Yes, it is. We can do it all afternoon if you'd like. I won't be away long." I am not teaching these days; I have taken a leave of absence to look after him.

"Can't you go later? I thought the pool was open till two. Go in an hour or so. By then I'll be ready for a nap."

I almost decide to revise my plan. If I get to the pool at twelve thirty, I will have enough time for my swim. But aside from the charge I get out of being the first one in the pool, it gets too crowded later on for me to swim at the quick pace that gives me the daily boost I need. If I knew this was to be Anthony's last day, leaving him even for a moment would be out of the question. But to my eyes he looks stronger than he has for quite some time. With greater presence of mind, I would remember that the gravely ill sometimes rally just before the end and then suddenly take a turn for the worse. But the siege of his illness has worn me down. For an hour or two I need to be in water, to inhabit a healing atmosphere in which I feel at home in the world, like a sea creature who by some accident of fate, evolution, or divine vengeance has been condemned to live life on land.

I know I should delay my departure and am about to do so when a wheedling voice, a virus of the spirit, draws close and whispers in my ear. Have I not rearranged my entire life to look after Anthony when he got AIDS from the man with whom he would have preferred to spend his life—if only that had been possible? What would Anthony have done if our places had been reversed, if he, a runner-up in the contest for my heart as I have always been an also-ran in the competition for his, had been called upon to care for me? Would he have looked after me with such devotion? Would he have given up all that I have sacrificed—my freedom, my work, my mobility, my privacy—everything, in fact, except for my swimming? I think back to the night I learned of Anthony's illness and to my vow to devote myself to his care. He has needed me since that day, to be sure, and I have done my utmost to place his needs above my own. But has he not come to need me only in sickness and death? Has he ever needed me in life, as I have always needed him? What he needs is not I, but someone to look after him. For the next few hours, Julia and Gerald will do.

It is a small concession Anthony is asking of me, a momentous request I am about to refuse him. For not needing me enough, for denying me the intimacy he shared with his Rebecca, I cannot find it within me to give him the greatest gift I have to offer: my loving presence by his side until he is ready to close his eyes. Sitting, for the last time, inches away from the dying man I love more than life itself, I buckle under the strain and blame him in my heart for not loving me as much or as well as I think I have loved him. And at a single tragic moment of immeasurable sorrow, I punish him for it.

"No, I think it's better I go now. The pool's emptier when it opens. I promise we'll spend all afternoon watching the people out on the lake. Maybe there will be some skaters."

He lets me go. It is not his style to cajole or beg. When I have put on my coat and am about to leave, he says, "Reb, can you do something before you go?"

I am impatient to get out the door. "What?"

"Can you stroke me?"

This is our usual routine before I go out, because at this late stage of his illness he needs to be soothed before I depart. Normally I sit next to him and stroke his hair for a few minutes, but on this particular morning I am in a mighty rush.

"Sure, but a little later, OK? How about a pat on the head for now? Will that do?"

He spares me his fears. His hair has started to grow back since he has become too fragile to continue with chemo. He cocks his head like a fuzzy puppy and lovingly receives my flawed final touch like a blessing.

My eyes still shut, I feel the beginnings of movement. In fact it is the traffic jam in the tunnel, easing at last, but I am no longer in the tunnel. I am pedaling along the lake after leaving Anthony. I have forsaken my lover. I will not be given another chance. I have killed Anthony.

These, I suppose, are the words that I scream. When I will not stop, Miranda attempts to control me. My eyes have flown open, I see her take hold of my shoulder. I can feel her pinch, it is hard and unyielding, but I still go on.

I have never yet heard the wail of the banshees. It is lower in pitch than I would have expected. It comes from the back of our automobile. It has borrowed Julia's mouth.

"Reb! Stop it! You did not kill Anthony! Stop it at once!"

We are moving again. I can see it at last, the light at the end of the tunnel. My breathing has calmed to a canter. So Julia's powers are not to be scorned, however her frame has diminished. I make myself turn in my seat. How I hate to lose sight of the light, but I must tell her thank you.

"Thank you."

"Are you feeling all right?"

"We're almost out now."

"Yes. Before we are, I must tell you something. I must do it quickly, before we leave the tunnel."

Julia, too, looks quite demented. Her eyes shift side to side. A strand of hair bisects her face.

Miranda peers in the rearview mirror. "What is it, Mummy? What's the matter?"

"I'll tell you later, Miranda. I'm talking to Reb."

Her voice is deranged and punctilious, like that of an asylum inmate who fancies herself the headmistress of a posh girls' school. She turns back to me.

"Reb, you must understand this once and for all. You did not kill Anthony. Gerald and I did."

chapter 23

Julia refuses to utter another word; Miranda drives like a robot. At home she checks on Antonia and pays the sitter. Julia heads for her room straight-away and returns with a black leatherbound diary. She has collected herself to a certain degree. At least she has combed her hair.

She gives me the book. "Gerald kept this diary for the entire year we were in Madison. It was one of his mad ways of trying to save Anthony's life. He thought if he wrote down every change in his condition, he could keep it from getting worse. His usual superstitious nonsense, like lighting candles in church, as if that could heal anyone." Julia's face, on the brink of collapse, pulls back to the safety of her anesthetised state. "I read the diary after Gerald died; he would never let me. It's the last entry. It explains how we killed Anthony."

Prudent Miranda has carried her pain with a stiff upper lip so complete it has turned to a concrete that only my echoing shrieks in the tunnel could shatter. She addresses her mum in a voice that her mum doesn't know.

"Stop this bloody rubbish! You didn't kill Anthony, you just made things worse by blaming him for getting it." Miranda falls to the sofa, buries her face in her arms. Her language can barely be heard, but her words and her weeping are mine. "Why didn't you tell me the end was so close? Why didn't I come to show him the baby? He died more than a month after she was born. It would have been hard, but I could have managed it. I promised him. That's what killed him. He was waiting for us and we never came."

Miranda bolts from the room. Shall I follow her, serve up the usual plat-itudes? Pat her on the head and tell her it's not her fault? Or face a more daunting task?

Julia stares straight ahead, her features blank. I am uncertain of the meaning of her pronouncement; I don't know how to comfort her, but I must sit beside her. I fear touching her; it is something from which I cannot refrain. I do not know where to pose my hand, so I place it on the nape of her neck. And to my surprise, as her son used to do, she, too, leans into my shoulder and buries her face in my chest, her body wracked with sobs.

"Julia," I say, "Anthony wouldn't want you to blame yourself. None of us gave him everything he wanted. I suppose that in that sense we all feel as if we killed Anthony."

Julia weeps for a good long while, then pulls away, takes a hanky from her handbag, and dabs at her eyes.

"I am going to my room to rest," she says. "It was kind of you to sit with me. I don't believe I ever thanked you properly for looking after Anthony so splendidly. Would you mind if I gave you a hug?"

She does so, lightly, and shuffles off. I listen at Miranda's bedroom door. Silence. Back in the sitting room I pick up Gerald's diary. I lock myself into the office, the very room I shared with Anthony on a tumultuous late-December night of passion and misapprehension many lifetimes ago. It is time to mourn, at long last, for my Anthony.

✳

I open the little book. Not since Gerald's Christmas cards of years past have I had occasion to see his careful script. There is something hypnotic about the pages and pages of even, beautiful writing describing the prolonged nightmare of Anthony's final months.

Julia said to skip to the end, 2 February 1991. A few hours after Anthony's death.

Anthony's house, 2 February 1991, 3 a.m.

Our Anthony is gone. Four hours ago, 1 February 1991, 11:11 p.m. So much to live for, so many gifts, and yet for a reason I shall never comprehend, God called him home in his thirty-third year of life. If only I could have taken his place.

The men from the funeral parlour have removed his earthly remains. We must endeavour to make it through the night somehow. We've rung Miranda. She took it calmly, or would have us so believe, but Antonia screamed and wailed in the background. The poor little lass knew she would never meet her godfather.

In the morning we shall see to the arrangements. Anthony would not begrudge his old dad the comfort of a Catholic funeral. Julia knows what I think but she'll win out, so I shan't say a word. It would look bad if it was not C of E, and so it shall be. Julia has never believed in any of it, but it's how she was reared. Perhaps it gives her the strength I lack.

But it was a shock, as they were tending to his poor body, to hear her speak of cremation, though I can see her reasoning. I can't bear the thought that they will put my poor boy into a fire. Still, I shan't make a fuss. My job is over. I've done what I could to spare his pain. May I soon stand before God and discover I was right. Whatever He says, I shall harbour no regrets.

Last night, after we returned to our little flat, I told Julia I could no longer bear to watch him suffer. She stood before the mirror removing pins from her hair and said nothing. I thought I'd have another go after a night's rest but when she'd finished, she said why didn't we have a cup of tea. I thought she would repeat, yet again, that we must soldier on. My reply was prepared. We may be soldiers, but our boy is not. I'll not have him fighting for nothing. But for once her line of thinking was quite the same as mine.

She mentioned the morphia straightaway. Dr. Hertz prescribed it a month ago, and Anthony has needed it but once or twice. She said he wouldn't suffer, just close his eyes and fall asleep.

I waited for her to say if it was the right thing to do but she spoke as a nurse, not a mother. I blurted out, "But have we the right to take our son's life?"

She let a moment pass. "We shan't be taking his life," she said. "He took it himself by getting this thing."

In all the time since Anthony told us he was ill Julia had never spoken such words, but I wasn't surprised. I've suspected all along that she blames him. I blame only myself. I have been unable to protect my child from the most grievous harm imaginable. God knows I have achieved nothing else of worth in this life. Now I have failed in this as well.

"What can it matter how he fell ill?" I said. "He's our son, and he's dying. Hasn't he suffered enough? Is that what you think I'm asking? Whether we should punish him more than he has already been punished?"

Julia wept. In all our years together, with the rows and the misery we've caused each other, I've never seen her sob so.

When she had calmed herself, she said, "I've been wrong to blame him. None of that matters. Only helping him."

We would administer the drug while Reb was away. He would never have the strength to consent. He is devoted to our boy and has tended to him commendably. But romantic love is selfish. He could never love Anthony as we do.

We would wait until Reb left for his swim. Julia said Anthony would not suspect a thing if we mixed it with some juice. Her idea was to give it to him immediately. I said it would be kinder if we did it just before Reb was due to return. He could sit by Anthony's side as he drifted into his final repose.

The timing went awry. Reb usually returns at two, but today it was closer to three. He'd had a spill and it slowed him down. He'd have rung to say he'd be late but feared he might disturb Anthony's rest. We administered the morphia at a quarter till two. Anthony asked again and again when Reb would be home, fighting to stay alert, but by the time he arrived, Reb was unable to awaken him.

We rang the nurse and she came straightaway. She spoke with Dr. Hertz: nothing more to be done. It was decided not to intervene. Reb agreed when the nurse said Anthony would otherwise die in hospital.

When it came to it, Julia could not give Anthony the morphia. I did. He'd been in good spirits today and seemed to have gained a bit of strength. Immediately Reb left for his swim, Anthony made a phone call, then dozed. At half past one he surprised us by saying he would join us for lunch if we would help him into his wheelchair. So we brought him to the table and he took some soup. Julia had mixed up the potion with cranberry juice. I gave it to Anthony and he drank it right down. Then, at around two, he brightened, as he always does when Reb is about to return.

I wheeled him back to the sofa and settled him in. He needed more oxygen than usual after his exertions. I raised the level until he felt comfortable. It was a sunny afternoon. Skaters and ice fishermen were out on the lake. Julia sat in the rocker knitting. She'd been making Anthony a woolly cardigan, royal blue, his favourite colour. She knew he'd not live to wear it. It was to give him hope he'd go out of doors again and breathe the fresh air.

He asked for music. I put on one of the Brandenburgs, which he loves. He smiled to signify he was pleased but looked so very tired. Every few minutes he asked what time it was. He was trying to stay awake until Reb arrived home but was having trouble. He nodded off. At ten to three he awoke and said he'd had a dream.

"Have you, darling?" said Julia.

She managed to control her voice. We'd agreed we mustn't let our boy see fear or sadness. He would be surrounded by peace and tranquillity to the end, protected by our love.

"Yes, Mummy. A lovely one."

Julia could add nothing more without breaking down. I said, "Would you tell it to us?"

He did. I memorised every word. I shall never again hear my boy's voice in this life.

When Reb got home he could not wake Anthony but his face was peaceful. I took a sheet of paper and wrote down his dream. I shall end my diary by copying it out. I pray to God that one day I might hear my son tell his dream again in a better place.

Anthony's Dream

"It was a sunny day," said Anthony. "I was lying on a mat and dozing. A guard came in and told me the end of days was approaching. The sun would be robbed, the world put asunder and plunged into darkness. I said, 'No matter, we'll make our own!'"

I asked Anthony, "Your own what?"

"Light."

"And did you?"

He nodded.

"Who's 'we'?"

He thought for a few seconds, smiled, then shut his eyes.

There is no light under Miranda's bedroom door, but she must not be asleep, because she hears my footsteps and before I have a chance to knock tells me to come in. She switches on the night-light. I am shocked by her face contorted with remorse. Her eyes are swollen, the floor littered with tissues.

"I'm sorry to disturb you," I said. "This won't take long. May I have a word?"

She nods and sits up.

I edge onto the bed, stroke her hair, kiss her on both sides of the forehead as I used to do with her brother. She says nothing but seems to take a small measure of comfort from these simple ministrations.

I set Gerald's diary down on the bedcovers.

"I've just read the final entry in your father's journal," I begin, "the one that Julia suggested. Miranda, have you read it?"

She shakes her head.

"You must." I choose my words with care. "You didn't kill Anthony. Your parents, that is, Gerald and Julia . . ."

I can't bring myself to spell it out. I have no doubt that theirs was an act of loving mercy, but it is better that Miranda read Gerald's own words and judge for herself.

"Please don't blame them," I go on. "It was a terrible thing for us, for you and me, not to have the chance to say good-bye to Anthony. But the way things turned out in the end, it was better for him."

I expect Miranda to question me, but she nods gravely and reaches for the diary.

"I promise," she says. She kisses me on the cheek and turns her attention to the little book.

Out in the hallway I see that Julia's room is illuminated. I tap lightly.

"Come in."

She is sitting at the desk in a white nightgown, writing.

"Sorry to bother you," I say. "May I speak to you?"

"Of course. Do sit down."

Her face is calm. In the past hour she has shed a decade of age.

I take a chair.

"It's my turn to thank you for looking after Anthony. You and Gerald both. You cared for him far better than I did." I hesitate and gather my courage. "I would have said something sooner if I had known. But now, today, I want to say thank you from both of us. That's what Anthony would want me to tell you."

Julia's eyes, a soul ascending from Purgatory.

chapter 24

In spite of several serious flight delays that would have had me flailing in the aisles if they had occurred on my way to New York, the return trip to Madison two days later, on 31 August, is a breeze; I have plenty to think about to keep me occupied.

Even though I know in my heart that what the Paytons did for their son was right, Gerald was not mistaken when he wrote that if I had been approached ahead of time, I never could have consented to it. It was magnanimous of him to speak in generalities; if romantic love does indeed tend to be selfish, he could not have realised the extent to which that truism is epitomised by my own particular case. So desperately did I need to be reassured about my worthiness and Anthony's devotion that I never understood how much he needed me—not for a similar form of reassurance, for he was comfortable in his own skin and knew and accepted that I loved him, but rather because just as people turn to those they love in times of great happiness, they also do so in times of duress, when they are feeling especially susceptible—which is also, in fact, when they are most lovable. In the end, I loved Anthony more because of my own vulnerabilities, which he understood as well as I did, than because of his, which he was disinclined to reveal and which it never occurred to me to seek to discover.

I have found out a great deal about my relationship with Anthony in the past month, but the mystery of his 11:11 message persists, my attempt at unearthing the truth behind those numbers an utter failure. Events seem to confirm that my mother is actually right in her conviction that one tends to find the things one is not looking for. It might be time for me to drop my initial quest and be content with those aspects of my love story with Anthony that I believed I already understood but the deeper truth of which I have come to recognise along the way.

The most important mystery that remains, then, is Eric. The way I look at the world has been fundamentally changed by what he has revealed about himself, Anthony, and me. But about his shocking disclosures it now appears I have nothing but questions.

✳

I assume Eric is still at work when I get home from the airport at 5:30 p.m., so I go for a swim in Lake Monona. On the last day of August the water will not long be warm enough for such activities. To my surprise I find myself feeling nostalgic about the events of the first evening I spent with Eric, one month ago. I am astonished at his composure as he gazed at Anthony's portrait on the sitting-room wall and divulged nothing of the turbulent emotions he must have been experiencing. And after our swim, how did he find it in himself to express his condolences over Anthony's loss and then patiently watch over me, his nemesis, as I slept through the night?

At the end of my swim I pull myself back up onto the pier, take a cold shower, and decide to dude myself up, at least by the standards of my usual summer attire. I don my best khaki shorts, the beige Ralph Lauren polo shirt that Anne Younger gave me for my twentieth birthday back when we were still together and that I save for special occasions, and my one pair of fancy shoes: expensive brown moccasins. I seem to recall having squirreled away a partially used decanter of English Leather from Anthony's store of toiletries and find it with surprising ease. I splash some on my face; it is a novel sensation being reminded of Anthony by my own scent. On the spur of the moment I open the box in which Anthony kept his small store of jewelry, mostly tie tacks and cufflinks, and find the star-sapphire ring his parents gave him for his thirtieth birthday. I have never tried it on. It fits perfectly on the ring finger of my right hand.

I pedal over to Eric's place, dismounting as the sun dips beneath the horizon.

It is obvious when he answers the door that he has just arrived home: his navy corduroys are unfastened at the belt but not unzipped, the matching tie loosened. His pearl-grey oxford shirt is wide open, and over his right shoulder he has slung a charcoal-coloured sport jacket. He has removed his shoes and socks and I observe with dreamlike detachment that his feet are indeed clodhoppers, as was pointed out at the Halloween party where we first intersected, if only glancingly, nearly thirteen years ago.

"Reb, come in. I've been hoping you'd stop by one of these days."

He seems pleased to see me but hesitant. As we move through his flat, he sheds his jacket and tie and does his fly up properly, but his shirt still flaps in the breeze and I am amused to catch a whiff of English Leather on him as well. I wonder if he copied Anthony's tastes or if Anthony copied his.

"What'll you drink?" he asks.

"Got the makings of a seven-and-seven?"

"Sure thing. Nice summer drink—I'll have one, too."

After a minute or two he brings out two glasses on a tray and shows me to the screened porch, where there stands one of those old-fashioned swinging loveseats that only in backwaters like Wisconsin still seem destined to be used for their original purpose rather than being postmodern ironic quotations of an innocent past. We sit close—the loveseat is not designed for two large men. Lake Monona murmurs in the background. The sky is overcast and I regret that the moon, which I know would be full, is not visible.

"Eric, do you mind if I ask you about a few things?"

He chuckles in a way that makes it clear that he doesn't find the question amusing.

"How about a jump start? I am HIV-positive, but I don't have AIDS."

I already knew he was positive, of course, but have been wondering about the other. I am relieved he is not ill and say so.

"Are you taking anything?" I add.

"Yeah, AZT and another drug, can't remember the name. It might just be a placebo at this point. I'm getting it through a clinical trial."

"I hope it works out for you."

"Thanks."

I reach over slowly and take his hand. He seems surprised but doesn't resist.

"Eric, when I first bumped into you on the bike path, how did you realise I was Anthony's lover?"

He looks away. "I didn't—not right away. But after you fell off your bike and I was helping you, you took off that hat with the face mask. I got a good look at your face and that was when I knew."

"But how did you recognise me? At the Halloween party we were both wearing masks."

"You had yours off after you won that stupid prize."

"Yeah, for all of twenty seconds—Anthony made me put it back on as soon as the two of you came back into the room. Why remember my face for thirteen years?"

A pause. "I can explain that if you like," Eric says in a curt voice, "but just you think about it. I'll bet that if you try real hard, you could figure it out all by yourself."

"I don't know," I say. "Why?"

Eric pulls his hand away before responding.

"As I said the other day, Anthony had told me about you but claimed it was nothing serious. At the Halloween party I dragged him into the kitchen and challenged him. He tried to make light of it, but I wasn't convinced. When we got back to the living room and I saw you had removed your mask, I came over to take a closer look. It was only for a few seconds, but yours was not a face I was about to forget."

"So when Anthony ended it with you two months later . . . You've remembered my face all this time because you disliked me, is that it?"

"I wouldn't put it that way."

"How would you put it?"

A pause. Eric is obviously preparing one of those polite midwestern euphemisms—"I don't care for him," "she's not my favourite," and the like—designed to avoid expressing strong negative emotions.

"How I would put it is that I remembered your face not because I disliked you, but because I wanted to rip your heart out."

Eric falls silent. Eventually I have to say something.

"Do you still hate me?"

His features soften. "I guess not." A crooked smile. "What about you? I don't know how much Anthony told you about me, but do you hate me?"

"He didn't say much, but that didn't stop me from hating you—that's another story. But no, I don't hate you. Not now. I still don't see why you don't hate me. What's changed?"

"It's a pretty long story, and I don't want to upset you. Sure you want to hear it?"

"Not sure, but I think so."

"I'll take that for a yes."

Eric remains seated on the swing but positions himself farther away from me than before.

"When Anthony left me," he begins, "I really thought, I won't make it through. They might as well bury me now. I never considered suicide, but at some level I wasn't ready to go on living."

Exactly how it's been with me.

"I honestly don't know how I survived the next few years. I dropped out of law school at the end of my first semester and left New Haven. I couldn't tell my parents the whole story, so I said I missed the Midwest and needed to rethink things, take some time off. I came back home and worked on the farm until harvest time. I felt like I was just running on automatic pilot, but I guess those sixteen-hour days helped me get through the worst of it.

"In the fall of 1981 I transferred to law school here. I worked my butt off. I had no personal life, didn't want one. Eventually I started going to the bars and I did have a few flings, but nothing that stuck. Once I made it to a one-month anniversary with a nice medical student who was from Britain and looked a little bit like Anthony. He wanted to get serious and I wasn't up for it. We parted friends, but there are a certain number of guys around here who probably wouldn't mind ripping my heart out either, because I never could find a reasonable explanation for why things couldn't continue.

"And I have to admit, Anthony was not the only one I was obsessed with during those years. I couldn't get you out of my mind—you'd ruined my life, and I despised you. I went into therapy, got a punching bag. If I'd had a photo of you, I'd have pasted it up and used it for target practice. I had nightmares about you where I pushed you off a cliff or ran you over with a motorcycle. It was unbearable. I talked to a minister, tried meditation, yoga. Nothing helped.

"Then, in 1988 I found out I was positive. It was a total shock. I had not done anything risky since Anthony and I broke up, so I knew he must have infected me rather than the other way around."

My shock reaches 9.9 on the Richter scale: Rebecca did not transmit HIV to Anthony, but the reverse. It is all I can manage not to disrupt Eric's sad tale.

"I knew I'd have to contact Molly as well as Anthony," Eric continues, "but I didn't know how. So I called the History Department at Yale and was told Molly was teaching at Stanford and Anthony had taken a job right here in Madison.

"That was a shock of a different nature. My first impulse was to think Anthony and I might have a chance to start over—I didn't know if you two were still together. It was exciting to think I might bump into him by accident anywhere—at the grocery store, the farmer's market, even Union Terrace.

"When I plucked up my courage and called him to give him the news, he was upset, of course, about me as well as himself. He said that you two were still together and very happy but that it was good to hear my voice. We talked for a while to catch up. I asked him to let me know your test results once you both got them."

"Did you ever see each other in Madison?" I ask dully, dreading the reply.

"No, that is . . . The truth is I did look up your address in the phone book. One weekday afternoon I drove to your house and parked in front. Just once. I figured no one was home, but I almost rang the doorbell, knowing he might be so close. I would have given anything just to lay eyes on him. I sat there in my car, staring at the house and the life I might have had."

Agony pulses across Eric's features, and I am surprised that what I feel for him is not jealousy but sadness.

"It must have been excruciating," I say.

He takes a gulp of his drink and continues.

"After an hour of sitting in the car I came to my senses. I was reliving an old dream and it was a slippery path to somewhere I didn't want to go. I decided then and there I would never try to see Anthony again. To be honest, if he had asked me to get together, I probably wouldn't have been able to resist. But wouldn't you know, that never happened—probably didn't even occur to him." Eric lets out a self-deprecating snicker.

"And when we got our test results?"

"He did call me then, just that once, to say he was positive and you were negative. For a short while I fantasised you might leave him for that reason and maybe I could catch him on the rebound. It sounds awful when I say it out loud, but it's true." He blushes. "I put an end to that line of reasoning just in time to preserve my last shred of self-respect."

"How did you find out he died?"

"Saw his obituary in the paper. A few days after the incident with your bike. I knew it was coming so I looked for it." Eric's face barely holds steady. "It was the worst day of my life."

It is too much, this story of loss and self-denial. The only thing I can do for him now is to complete the dreadful tale myself, tell him that I understand and that I forgive him.

"So when we bumped into each other at the farmer's market," I begin, "you couldn't take it anymore, right? You wanted to get back at me, get me to fall for you."

He nods.

There's no point pussyfooting around.

"Did you want to give it to me?"

Eric looks me straight in the eye.

"I'm not going to lie. I had been angry for so long. The idea did occur to me, but I would never have gone through with it. It was just a sick fantasy. Then once I got to know you, I couldn't hate you anymore."

We sit in silence for a long while. Finally I work up the courage to ask, "What now?"

"I don't know."

"I'm glad you don't hate me. But are you still angry? If you are, I can take it. Just tell me the truth."

Eric finishes his drink.

"I don't think I realised it until now," he says, "but I'm not really angry at you anymore. In fact . . ."

Beneath an emergent moon, the low profile of a train rumbling across the causeway.

"Reb, I know it sounds crazy, but I've grown fond of you. When you left my place the other night, I was beside myself."

At the time I had no way of guessing what was going on in Eric's head, of course, but his revelation does not take me entirely by surprise. Although I haven't quite admitted it to myself, in my mind he is no longer Rebecca, an object of resentment and loathing. That we both loved Anthony made us enemies. That we both lost him has brought us together.

He has been watching me, on his guard. Once again I take his hand.

"Eric, this probably sounds crazy, but I'm starting to fall in love with you."

The tension around his eyes eases. A miniscule area of his upper lip seems to be trying to express happiness.

"Would you like to stay over?"

The question hangs in the air. Tempting as the offer is, I'm not quite ready to accept. They say you can't make it through mourning by yourself; I've never really understood that until now. To me the pain of loss seems as nontransferable as bodily suffering, but as I gaze at the sombre smile overspreading Eric's face, it occurs to me that mourning is about forgiveness as much as suffering. No one besides myself can suffer my pain and allow me to see my way clear to go on living. And yet I am not, on my own, in a position to forgive myself—not only for surviving but also for what, in the course of my heartfelt but imperfect ministrations, I neglected to do for the person I have survived. My only hope of salvation is to confide the truth of it all to another and to await his honest assessment with a humble heart.

"I'd like to stay," I say, "but I don't know if I can. At least, not until I tell you about something. About what I did and didn't do the day Anthony died, and why."

chapter 25

Eric nods. He is a lawyer, not a priest, I a lapsed Catholic, but this is as much a confession as a law trial. I must find the words to inform another of the most unforgivable actions I have committed in my life and accept his judgement.

I cross over to a chair facing the loveseat to collect my thoughts and give some breathing room to my jury of one.

I relive with Eric the uncertainty of those first difficult months with Anthony and our subsequent years together, tainted by my lingering belief that he had loved another man in a way he could never love me. I tell him of Anthony's reserved demeanour in moments of intimacy and what it meant to me; that his heart would remain forever inaccessible. I speak of the shock of his HIV status and my vow to forget the other man who had been in his life and devote myself to him heart and soul. Finally, I explain that on that last morning, a metastasis of my long-dormant obsession prevented me from understanding that the end was near and Anthony needed me by his side, and I left him to die without me.

I await my fate. It is two chance encounters that have thrown Eric and me together and made him my judge. And yet I accept this wisdom of the universe. If anyone in this world is my peer, it is Eric.

He thinks for a long while before speaking.

"It boils down to this," he finally says. "Anthony was really happy with you. You have nothing to blame yourself for. You didn't kill him. He just got sick and died."

"But if he was happy with me, why did he remain so reserved?"

A pause.

"I don't know if I should . . . Anthony and I . . . we talked about this," he begins haltingly. "After your test results—both of you. I pointed out how weird it was that you were negative after so many years, and . . ."

Silence.

"Just tell me."

"OK, your call," says Eric quietly. He ponders for a few moments, gathering his memories.

"Anthony was traumatised by our breakup," he begins, "even though it was his decision. He saw how much I was suffering. He knew that he would never leave you, but as I told you a few days ago, he thought there was a real possibility that you might leave him, and that really frightened him. He needed to keep a lid on things to protect himself until he felt certain you would stay.

"When he was finally starting to trust that you were in it for the long haul, he was afraid of making you sick. He had been somewhat promiscuous at Oxford, although not nearly as much as plenty of his friends. He had had no clear symptoms of AIDS but knew he might be carrying the virus. He also realised you had had much less experience with men than he had and were almost certainly negative. He couldn't face getting tested but had to find a way to protect you.

"He was happy with you, Reb," Eric goes on. "He said things were great. He just needed to avoid becoming too vulnerable at the beginning, and later on to prevent you from catching something from him. He hoped that one day I would meet someone who loved me as much as he loved you."

It is too much, this might-have-been head-over-heels love affair with Marc Anthony Payton that I was dreaming of at the same time as I was squandering it away.

As I begin to weep Eric pulls me close. In a trance I breathe in his scent, Anthony's scent. I don't know how long we remain like this, but finally Eric sits up straight and looks at his watch.

"It's getting late and I've had a long day. If you'd like to stay over, you're welcome to, but it's fine if you'd rather go home." The apprehension in his voice belies the breeziness of his words.

I open my mouth to say that I will stay over. I am grateful beyond measure that Eric has done what he could to exonerate me, but suddenly Anthony's pleading face appears again before my eyes. How can I forgive myself if he is not here to forgive me?

"What is it?" Eric says.

"I'm sorry to sound like a broken record. But that last day, to leave him that way . . . I can't thank you enough for telling me I don't need forgiveness. But how can I ever live with myself without knowing that Anthony felt the same way?"

"Stop crucifying yourself," Eric says. "He was happy with you, even that last day. I promise you, he did forgive you for leaving him."

"You can't know that."

"Actually, I can."

"How?"

"Because I talked to him right after you left him on the day he died."

❋

So that's why Anthony's address book was open to S.

I nod and await Eric's explanation.

"I had taken the day off," he begins, pacing around the room. "The phone rang a few minutes before eleven fifteen. It was Anthony."

I try to picture it, Anthony ringing Eric just after I left him to go swimming. I do my best to will myself back into that instant in time and space, to relive those final moments when I still could have changed the course of my life by making the right decision and staying with Anthony until the very end. I have revisited this memory more times than I can count and tried to free myself from the life sentence of that decision, to no avail. Even knowing what I now know, and with Eric here to support me, what he has to tell me may change nothing, or even make things worse. But it's worth a try.

I lean back and close my eyes, reinsert myself into that point in time, pedaling along John Nolen Drive, haunted by Anthony's face beseeching me to stay. I feel the February cold gripping me, the wooliness of my face mask, the urgency of being immersed as soon as possible in the healing waters of the pool before hurrying back to my lover's side.

"I picked up the phone," continues Eric. "I recognised Anthony's voice immediately." He pauses. "At first I was ecstatic; he asked me about my health, and I told him I was fine. But then he said that he was very ill. That the end was near but he was ready. That you had had to go out and he didn't know if you would return in time to say good-bye, but his parents were there with him. Perhaps, he said, it was better that way, for you would be spared the pain of seeing him leave."

He is ready. Probably he would have died that day even without Gerald and Julia's assistance. Be that as it may, they will give him what I have not been able to provide; unlike me, they will think only of their son. Gerald will be willing to face eternal damnation, Julia to live the rest of her life with remorse to spare their boy a day of suffering and ensure that he dies in peace.

"Anthony said that he hoped he hadn't upset me by phoning. I told him how much it meant to me that we could talk one last time. He said that he too needed to speak to me, to say good-bye."

He is reaching out to the man who has always shown him his love with every fibre of his being. I, too, have always felt that kind of love for Anthony, but I was not able to let him see it when he needed it most.

"I told him that I was very grateful to be able to say good-bye and he said that he was, too."

Because I did not give Anthony that opportunity. Because as the end approached I told him nothing he wanted to hear. Understood nothing he tried to say. Helped him with nothing he needed me to give him.

"And he also wanted to tell me how sorry he was that he had hurt me."

Which I will never get the chance to tell Anthony, by my own fault. Or rather as he will never hear—when I return home in a few hours I will say it to him again and again as he lies on his deathbed, how sorry I am to have left him. But it will be too late for me to wake him, to make him understand.

"I told him that I forgave him for hurting me. That I was glad he had found happiness. That I had always loved him and would always love him."

At least he is hearing it one last time from Eric. He has not heard it today from me.

"And he told me he loved me, too."

So Eric, not I, is hearing Anthony's final message of love. A nanosecond's pulse of spite flashes through my mind before dissipating in the realisation that I am not jealous, that neither I nor anyone else in the world has a greater right to hear Anthony's last expression of love than Eric.

"Just before he hung up, he repeated what he had told me all those years back in my room. You were the love of his life, that was just the way it was and would always be."

I have not heard it from Anthony's lips, but I have heard it the only way I could, from Eric's. In the end I left Anthony, as he always feared I would. And yet he has told Eric that I remain the love of his life.

He has forgiven me.

"The last thing Anthony said was that he hoped one day the two of you would be together again."

I come out of my trance, open my eyes.

"Anthony said he hoped we'd be together again? That's strange. I was never under the impression he was a believer."

"It surprised me, too," said Eric, "but those were his very last words."

Eric stands, walks to the window, and gazes out over the night.

"After we hung up I had to get out," he says, his voice breaking. He takes a deep breath. "I grabbed my bike, didn't even dress properly for the cold, and went downstairs and started pedaling. I didn't know where I was going. It really didn't matter. I just had to get outside of myself, be where there were other people around me. That's why I started talking to you at the stoplight. I had to say something to somebody, to try to convince myself I was still alive and in the world and could have some sort of connection to other people. I had to feel that not all of me would be buried with him." He pauses. "The more I think about it, the more amazing it seems that I bumped into you right then. You and Anthony had lived in Madison for over two years, yet that was the first day I crossed paths with either of you. And then again with you at the farmer's market a few weeks ago. I imagine you may not be a believer either, but the way I see it there has to be a reason for both of those meetings."

He blushes, as midwesterners sometimes do when they've said something that they fear might sound grandiose, pretentious, or self-important, and looks down at his feet as if in penance.

I take him in from head to foot and from foot to head, in all of his splendour. Although in some ways I hardly know the man, in others I know him better than I ever knew Anthony, for he has shown me the fallible depths of his heart, and of Anthony's, and is privy to mine as well. And all at once I feel my own flawed heart flooded with love for this unassuming, timid, and magnanimous giant. I grasp his hand.

He leads me into his bedroom.

I have so much to think about that I sleep no more than a few hours that night by Eric's side. One of the things he reported that Anthony said to him on that last day keeps running through my mind: "He hoped one day you would be together again." It doesn't fit with the Anthony I knew, but if there's one thing I've learned in the past month, it's that there was an awful lot about that boy I didn't know. What could he have meant by those words?

The 11:11 message: Friday, 11/11/33, 11:11 p.m. He wasn't referring to 1933 but to 2033. Televisions and VCRs don't programme for the past. Once you've missed the show and failed to record it, all you can do is hope for a rerun, which may or may not be available.

I wonder whether, for me, one may be in the works.

The moment of my death: 11 November 2033, 11:11 p.m. Our reunion. Anthony is telling me that he will choose me in death, just as, thanks to Eric, I have finally come to understand that he chose me in life.

I arise from Eric's side at dawn, make coffee, and sit on the porch overlooking the lake. It is September 1st, a new month; August certainly has been a humdinger. Eric's apartment faces east, and even in these final weeks of summer, the morning light seems as strong as ever. In its glare I wonder if my interpretation of the events of the past moon has not been sheer lunacy. Has my search for the meaning of Anthony's message—if it is a message at all—not been grasping at straws? If I've been trying to heal from my grief by resorting to dubious means—sleight of mind and number magic—is it not simply because I have found no other way to do so?

If that is true, so be it. And if the way I have made my peace with the world appears foolish when viewed in a certain light, perhaps it wouldn't if viewed in a different one.

When Eric joins me for coffee on the porch I thank him for everything he has done for me. He nods gravely when I explain that I must spend the next month or so writing down the story of what I have discovered; I assure him that I will ring periodically to check on his health and find out how he's doing. I will be available if he needs me, but I won't otherwise see him until I'm done with my story.

Eric nods again, asks no questions. He walks me to the door, folds me in his arms, and says he will wait for me.

❋

My prediction of how long it will take to complete my story turns out to be reasonably accurate. I have finished writing it today, 7 October 1993, which, if Anthony's message about the date of our reunion in the Great Beyond is correct, is the precise midpoint of my life. If my memory of the Western Civ course I took in college serves, Dante opens his *Divine Comedy* by observing that in the middle of his life the straight way was lost. I guess for me that happened quite a bit earlier, but what I did lose in the middle of my life was something much, much more important than the straight way or any other: Anthony, a human being measurable, like all humans, not only by straight lines but also by whirls and whorls; memorable, like all humans, for the fragile, powerful light he cast upon the world. Dante finds salvation in paradise, but for the moment at least, my ambitions are humbler: to make it through my life without Anthony by viewing myself through his loving eyes.

In another forty years and change, I hope to hear from his own lips, for the first time, how completely he has loved me from the very start. It sounds like a long time to wait, but when I think back on the first half of my life, especially my glory years with him, it seems to have gone by in a heartbeat. Paradise may or may not be in the works for me, but if I am allowed to see Anthony again, I feel certain that the first thing he'll ask me is to what earthly use I've put his love in the second half of my life, so I haven't got a moment to lose. It is time to call Eric, to ask him to spend the night and, if he wishes, a lot longer.

On the phone I invite him over but say nothing about the future, preferring to discuss the matter when we are together. Since setting out on my quest to interpret Anthony's message I have grown somewhat accustomed to long-distance communications about love, but I don't plan on spending my next forty years discussing matters of the heart remotely. Over the telephone it is enough to hear that Eric is doing well, that he sounds happy to receive my invitation, and that he will be here as soon as he can.

In anticipation of his arrival I make my way upstairs. Anthony's moon has sat patiently on the shelf for over two months; it is time to lift it up once again to its rightful position in his little heaven. I don't remember exactly where it was before it fell; it doesn't seem to matter all that much. My tube of Elmer's glue in hand, I give the little crescent pride of place directly above our bed.

When Eric arrives we have a beer and catch up. Soon I am leading him upstairs. The first words he says to me when we are lying side by side beneath Anthony's moon are precisely the last ones that Anthony uttered on the day I left him: "Can you stroke me?"

Anthony's final question to me, now transformed into an invitation to make love, gives me pause. Is Anthony's spirit warning me that unless I change my ways, I am again at risk of running away, leaving Eric stranded as well in his time of need? And yet it will be difficult to give to Eric now the very thing that I refused to give to Anthony. Would I not be committing an act of betrayal?

It comes to me not as a clap of thunder but as a flap of wings. A butterfly's flight plan, quietly shifted, has altered my destiny. I never told Eric of Anthony's last words to me, his final request, which I denied. Anthony has dictated the words to Eric; my rerun may begin sooner than I thought. They have decided, together, to give me a second chance.

As I look at Eric through the eyes of Anthony's love, I vow that if the time ever comes when he needs me as Anthony did, I will not leave him. If Eric had not carried Anthony's message of love to me across the thin bridge of the years, it would not have saved me, as it now has, from myself. Anthony's love would have waited silently inside of me until the day of my death without my knowing it was still there, or that it ever really had been, or that I could pass it along to others as Anthony did me the honour of bestowing it upon me.

So when Eric asks me to stroke him, the least I can do is return the favour. I can't imagine a better way to try to make it up to Anthony for not stroking him when he asked me to at 11:11 on the day he died.

Acknowledgments

I am deeply grateful for the support and advice I have received during the long process of writing this book. At the University of Wisconsin Press, heartfelt thanks go to Dennis Lloyd and Jackie Teoh for their support and invaluable suggestions; to Ken Harvey and Lori Soderlind, who each read the manuscript with extraordinary care and generosity and made many invaluable suggestions; and to Porter Shreve for extremely useful comments that were of great value to me as I made the final revisions. Special thanks go to the late Carolyn Fireside, a colleague and very dear friend with whom I worked on revisions to the novel at an early stage.

Many friends and colleagues have read the manuscript in part or in whole over the years, and I would like to thank them all—any oversights in this list are purely a function of the limitations of my memory. Sincere gratitude go to, in alphabetical order: Meredith Alexander, Sonia Baku, Annette Becker, Susan Bernstein, Germaine Brée, Bill Contardi, Ross Chambers, Martine Debaisieux, Ben Gilbert, Pupa Gilbert, Elgy Gillespie, Mandel Goodkin, David Harrison, Kate Jensen, Anna Leach, Sonia Leach, Valerie Long, Lizzie MacArthur, Elaine Marks, Kim Marra, Anne Menke, Michael Metteer, Judith Miller, Claudia Mills, Chris Plum, Charles A. Porter, Cathy Potter, Arlyne Rothberg, Elisabeth Sifton, Harriet Stone, Andréc Valley, Jayapriya Vasudevan, Natasha Ventsel, Maura Whelan, and Georgia Wiley.

Finally, gratitude beyond words to Patrick and Charlie, who never met face-to-face but only in my heart.